Readers love AMY LANE

A Salt Bitter Sea

"I can almost picture Spinner's Drift in my head and I think I would love to visit a place where magic is alive."

—Love Bytes

Under Cover

"Congratulations, Ms. Lane, you truly have learned your craft!"

—Paranormal Romance Guild

Sean's Sunshine

"Thank you, Amy, again for a lovely romance. A special thank you for the extras at the end that had me screaming in laughter and caused my own critters to zoom."

—Rainbow Book Reviews

Published by DREAMSPINNER PRESS
www.dreamspinnerpress.com

Published by Dreamspinner Press
www.dreamspinnerpress.com

By Amy Lane (cont)

TALKER
Talker • Talker's Redemption
Talker's Graduation
The Talker Collection
Anthology

WINTER BALL
Winter Ball • Summer
Lessons
Fall Through Spring

*Published by DSP
Publications*

ALL THAT HEAVEN WILL
ALLOW
All the Rules of Heaven

GREEN'S HILL
The Green's Hill Novellas

LITTLE GODDESS
Vulnerable
Wounded, Vol. 1
Wounded, Vol. 2
Bound, Vol. 1 • Bound, Vol. 2
Rampant, Vol. 1
Rampant, Vol. 2
Quickening, Vol. 1
Quickening, Vol. 2
Green's Hill Werewolves, Vol.
1
Green's Hill Werewolves, Vol.
2

*Published by Harmony Ink
Press*

BITTER MOON SAGA
Triane's Son Rising • Triane's
Son Learning
Triane's Son Fighting •
Triane's Son Reigning

Published by DREAMSPINNER PRESS
www.dreamspinnerpress.com

WEDDINGS, CHRISTMAS, AND SUCH

AMY LANE

DREAMSPINNER PRESS

Published by

DREAMSPINNER PRESS

5032 Capital Circle SW, Suite 2, PMB# 279, Tallahassee, FL 32305-7886 USA
www.dreamspinnerpress.com

Weddings, Christmas, and Such
© 2023 Amy Lane

Cover Art
© 2023 L.C. Chase
http://www.lcchase.com
Cover content is for illustrative purposes only and any person depicted on the cover is a model.

Trade Paperback ISBN: 978-1-64108-703-2
Digital ISBN: 978-1-64108-702-5
Trade Paperback published December 2023
v. 1.0

Printed in the United States of America
∞
This paper meets the requirements of
ANSI/NISO Z39.48-1992 (Permanence of Paper).

TABLE OF CONTENTS

I wrote this a few years after the last Granby book. I was posting on a birthday blog for a friend, and my readers asked for Jeremy and Aiden. It occurred to me that Jeremy probably didn't have a birthday then—and why birthdays, whether celebrated with gifts or just a picnic in the park, or even a hug and a "happy birthday", seem so important to us. It's important to know the world is better with us in it. Jeremy deserved some celebrating, right?

THE GIFT OF A BIRTHDAY

JEREMY KNEW when Aiden's birthday was—the beginning of the fall. The first year Jeremy had come to Granby, Aiden was already eighteen, but as Jeremy's stay had grown beyond those first few months, when he lived in Craw's tack room, and into the years in his own apartment, he'd become part of the family unit that celebrated each birthday as it arrived. Aiden's in August, Ariadne's in September, and Craw's in November. For him, as he learned to knit—and mastered his craft—it was like he worked all year for those three months, and then the big payoff in December.

And because he'd been just the help—and because Aiden had been a callow boy who had grown into a strong and able man—it had not occurred to any of the people who loved him most that Jeremy didn't have a birthday.

Until Aiden turned twenty-four.

Craw and Ben showed up at their house first, since Jeremy had elected to host. Summer was holding onto its heat a little, and he'd had to open all the windows in the snug little two-story, letting the flowing curtains blow in and out as the wind swept the bowl valley of Granby. Aiden's mother brought the cake, of course, and Aiden's brothers and sisters showed up too. Aiden's father took the littlest ones out to go pet the bunnies and chinchillas and such in the outside pen, and Jeremy knew by now that they were gentle with the more tender of the critters.

Rory, Ariadne, and Persephone were almost late for dinner, but then Ariadne had still, after a year and a half, not gotten the hang of packing the baby bag, her purse, and the yarn bag all together. She'd told Jeremy once that Rory had gotten the hang of packing the baby's bag and putting it on a chest by the door, so all Ari had to do was grab her keys, wallet-phone, and yarn bag, but still. That baby was toddling around and making all sorts of problems, and that was just going to be Ariadne for a bit.

So there they were, all the people Aiden loved best—even Johnny and Stanley, who had taken the drive out before the roads got icy in September—and Aiden wasn't there.

"You don't know where he is?" Ariadne laughed, bringing the milk to the table with one hand while balancing the baby on her hip. Jeremy grinned at Persephone, who chewed on her teether toy in response. Her lip had been stitched up, but she would still need some surgeries to take the tubes out of her ears and make sure the inside was all matched up to the outside when she was grown enough.

Jeremy didn't care. She was his shining star right there, and his mother didn't mind that he called her Persy, even a little.

"I didn't realize he'd taken the car," Jeremy said, puzzled. "And Craw's not here either. I mean, it's my boy's birthday—you think he'd be here!"

Jeremy had knitted him boot socks, the kind that came all the way up to his knees and then folded over. They were thick socks with fine yarn, and handsome clocks ran down the sides. Jeremy had wanted to buy him something—maybe a new television or a gaming system, even though they didn't have much money. He'd thought that maybe Aiden would have grown tired of knitwear after nearly five years, but no, Aiden said he wanted Jeremy's work and Jeremy wasn't going to gainsay him.

But Aiden had said nothing about hauling off into the wild blue yonder with Craw as his copilot.

"Ben?" Ariadne called. Ben was sitting in the front room, playing chess with Johnny and losing. It bothered Ben a *lot* because he was supposed the be the smart engineering guy, but Jeremy could have told him that the organized crime guys could gut you at any game that involved killing time. He should have been relieved at the distraction—or at least amused by Stanley wandering over the house and fawning at all the hand-knit items that occupied space. Ariadne's lace valances, Craw's knitted throws—even the gloves or mittens that could be found pretty much on every flat surface of the house seemed to intrigue him.

Johnny could be heard frequently rumbling things like, "Sure, cupcake, I think you could make that—that's really pretty knitting there," with absolute patience.

But Ben did *not* look relieved. In fact, he looked a little guilty.

"What?" he asked, focusing on the dog who lay at his feet. "Jeremy, have you brushed Bluebell recently? She is positively shiny!"

Ariadne and Jeremy met eyes, and Ariadne crossed her thin arms and cocked her hips. "What do you know?" she asked, growling a little.

"Nothing," Ben said with a winning smile.

"You are so lying." Johnny laughed. "It's a good thing you've been straight your whole life, because you wouldn't have lasted past puberty in the mob."

Ben gave him a befuddled look. "I've been gay my whole life, and probably not."

Ariadne started tapping her foot. "Cute, guys. Really cute. Where the hell did Aiden and Craw go—"

4

"Is dinner ready yet?" Craw demanded, striding in through the door like they hadn't just been MIA.

"Aiden?" Jeremy said, trying not to be hurt. He was wearing an apron wrapped around his waist and oven mitts on his hands, and he was not so free and easy with this whole family thing that he appreciated being all alone there with the entire free world rambling about his house when Aiden was supposed to be the guest of honor.

Aiden walked straight to him and dropped a kiss on his forehead, then took the oven mitts and took over the food prep, ordering everyone into the kitchen to grab a plate and make an assembly line and then go about their business and eat.

Well, everyone was hungry, so it worked.

Food, cake, fun, and then Aiden's family left and everybody breathed a sigh of relief. Stanley and Johnny were getting ready to go too, but Aiden called them back into the kitchen. His gifts still sat on the table—Jeremy's boot socks in the place of honor, and the basic sweater Craw had knitted out of sturdy yarn, so Aiden could wear it any time and not feel bad if it got dirty. Ariadne had been experimenting with felting, and she'd made him a small area rug for the bedroom, which Jeremy admitted privately was maybe the best thing in the collection—but he wasn't looking at his gifts now.

"Here," Aiden said, pulling the chair back for Jeremy and then sitting down himself. "Okay—my family had to go because they do not know all the details of Jeremy and I didn't want him to be uncomfortable, but everybody here does, and I'll bet, if you think really carefully, you can figure out what this is about."

Ben looked at Jeremy with apology in his eyes, and for a moment, Jeremy panicked. "Boy?"

Aiden's hand on his shoulder settled him down. "Don't worry, Jer. This is all good."

"I'm at a loss," Ariadne said. Persephone had pitched a giant tantrum over her small slice of cake and then fallen promptly asleep on her mother's shoulder in a mess of chocolate cake and snot. Ariadne claimed her baby daughter was glued to her shirt, but Jeremy was pretty sure she just liked to hold the baby when she finally went still.

"I have no idea," Stanley said promptly, propping his chin on his hands. "But this is looking like a murder mystery or something and I love those—do go on."

Jeremy grinned at him, because he was cute with his little round face and big blue eyes—even cuter now that his hair plugs had totally taken and he had a thick growth of what he called vampire-white hair.

"It is shaping up mysterious," he said, beaming, and a little more at ease. "Why are we here, boy?"

"To celebrate a birthday," Aiden said softly.

"We just did that," Jeremy replied, puzzled and tired. Family gatherings were a lot of effort—he loved them, but he was glad this one was only once a year.

"Not his birthday, love," Ariadne said, looking suddenly like she got it.

Jeremy looked behind him and Aiden had the balls to *wink* at her, like she was now in on the secret.

"Well then, whose?" he asked, feeling bad tempered. "Aiden's August, you're September, Craw's November, Ben's September too, Rory's March, like Persephone, Stanley and Johnny are both in February which is just *scary*—whose birthday are we missing?"

He looked around him and realized that all the members of his family were staring at him in surprise.

"Oh my God," Johnny said, like something had just occurred to him too. "Jeremy. Do you even *know* when your birthday is?"

Oh. Jeremy shrugged and pulled out a rusty con man's grin. "Well, I'm sure it's on my driver's license," he said, all his nicely repaired teeth flashing. "I mean, it's no big—"

"The one on your driver's license was a lie," Aiden said, sitting down in the chair next to him. "You told me that yourself."

Jeremy could feel the heat rising to his face. Everybody in this room knew he was a con man's son. They all knew he'd been born and raised on the grift and had gone to prison for it.

They all knew he'd come out and had dedicated his life to two things. One was Aiden, and the other was being honest.

They even knew that much of his personal information had been a lie. He'd kept the name Jeremy Stillson because Jeremy was the only name he remembered, and Stillson had been his identity when he'd gone to prison, so he had a social security number in that name. It was the name that let him get a bank account and earn credit and help Aiden to buy his little house.

But until this moment, he'd thought he'd manage to escape the embarrassment of having them know that he'd never had a birthday party in his life.

"I...." He looked around uncomfortably. "You know, I don't want to be a bother—"

"Jeremy, you've made us gifts for every birthday celebration we've ever had. Did you hate doing that?"

Jeremy smiled into Aiden's green eyes, thinking as he always did that Aiden was just so beautiful—even when he was being cranky grumpy and irritated, he was beautiful.

And now he was looking at Jeremy with one of those gentle sorts of expressions that told Jeremy he was about to be introduced to a new facet of an honest man's life.

"I loved doing that," he said, remembering how he'd had to work on the boot socks in secret, and how he'd chosen the

7

clocking pattern because it made the socks not boring as shit to knit.

"Well, you're being selfish," Craw said, scratching restlessly at his beard. "Selfish, that's what it is. Not letting us knit for your birthday."

Jeremy glared at Aiden. "You gave me mittens on my fake birthday for years," he complained.

"Yeah, but you wouldn't let us celebrate with the family, because you said it wasn't honest."

Jeremy squirmed in his seat. "Well, yeah—"

"So," Craw said, "that's what we were doing. We wanted it today, so you could have some time to prepare."

"I don't understand," Jeremy muttered. "Time to prepare for—"

"For your birthday, dumbass," Aiden muttered back. "See, remember Rich from the marshal's office?"

The man had helped out while Jeremy had been laid up three years ago. "Yeah, sure—how's he doing?"

"Married Mrs. Fullmer's daughter—they just had a baby. Anyway, he still keeps in touch, and we had him do us a favor."

Jeremy blinked at him, suddenly unsure if he was going to like this or not. "What… I mean, them's federal people, Aiden, what sort of—"

Aiden pulled the chair out next to him and sat down, taking both his hands. "Jeremy No-Last-Name," he said softly, "don't you want to know when you were born?"

Jeremy caught his breath. He'd never known—it hadn't mattered. His birthday had been whenever Oscar had found it convenient. Did he need to be fifteen in December? December 12th was his birthday. Did he need to be twelve in March? March the 3rd it was. There had been no parties because there were no friends because you didn't *get* friends when you were grifting on the road.

And maybe because he'd never mentioned it—because it had never really occurred to him—he hadn't had a birthday. He was pretty sure of the year—wasn't he? The ID he'd had when he'd been arrested and imprisoned said he was twenty-four at the time, which made him thirty-one now… *right?*

"Sure," he said, feeling confused. "Uh, I'm thirty-one, right?"

"Nope," Aiden said dryly. "Yeah, chew on *that,* Jeremy." He laughed evilly and Jeremy scowled at him. The beginning days of their relationship had, perhaps, been put off a little longer than Aiden might have wished, because Jeremy had been *convinced* that he was too old for such a bright and shining boy.

"Stop torturing him," Craw ordered. "You tell him or I will."

Aiden scowled back at Craw. "No, I'm sorry. Three years we've been together, and it comes up at least once a month. 'I'm too old for you, Aiden. Nine years between us—you should have someone your own age.'"

"I do not sound like that!" Jeremy protested, because Aiden was *whining* and Jeremy never whined.

"Oh bullshit you don't," Aiden shot back. "And it's been bothering you since we met. And now it's going to bother you a little less, and I'm *fine* with that, but I just want you to see that it never should have bothered you at all."

Jeremy raised an eyebrow. "But… I was twenty-four," he said, because this he knew to be true. "When I went to prison I was—"

"Twenty-two," Aiden said, and now his voice was grim. "You were *twenty-two* when you went to prison, and twenty-four when you got out, which means you turn *thirty* on October 4th, so *there.*" Aiden pulled a brown envelope out of his pocket then, and pulled a piece of paper out of it. What he spread before Jeremy was a birth certificate, and while Jeremy didn't care

9

about the name because the last name was probably from a con anyway, it was the birthday that got his attention.

He gaped at the piece of paper.

"I'm not even *thirty* yet?" It was like his entire brain had gone exploded in sunshine and chicken feathers. How could that be?

"Nope." Aiden grinned, evil as sin, the darkness that once only Jeremy knew there on display for all to see. "And it's not *nine* years between us, it's less than *six* , and you know what? For all you know it could have been *five.* Or nothing. So could you leave it alone now?"

"I'm not even *thirty*?" Jeremy's voice pitched, and he felt a little bit of panic seep in. His boy knew him, though—his high-triumph faded, and he stroked the side of Jeremy's face.

"Nope," he said kindly. "Is *that* going to be a problem?"

Jeremy just shook his head, still flummoxed. "It's just...." He thought of it all. The being a con man, the going to prison, the getting out and going straight. Coming to Craw's place, and meeting Aiden. The three years of getting to know himself, getting to be an honest man, and then getting beaten to a pulp to save Stanley—and the recovery that healed them all. "It's just...." his voice quavered. "It's been a lot of living in thirty years."

Aiden's thumb wiped moisture from his cheek, and Aiden's lips followed. "Yeah," he said softly. "A lot of living, Jer. So, in October, let's say we celebrate that, you think?"

"A party?" Stanley chirped, unmindful of the tenderness between them. "Yes—absolutely. My treat. A party. Johnny and I will plan it, is that okay, Johnny?" Stanley paused. "Johnny?"

Johnny was looking decidedly uncomfortable. "Uh, yeah, sure, Stanley. We can definitely help plan Jeremy's birthday party. That will be awesome." He smiled greenly at Jeremy. "I'd like that."

And then Jeremy remembered. Johnny and he—before the arrest, and prison, and Craw's, and Aiden—they'd had a blowjob and a kiss.

And Johnny had been well into his thirties.

For no reason at all, Jeremy started laughing.

The rest of the family hugged him and made promises of plans later, and Jeremy spent much of the time pondering, a little stunned.

Aiden saw their guests out—with help from Bluebell, who was the size of a human and probably looked like Aiden's significant other in the lowering summer twilight—and then came to pour him a cup of coffee and sit in the yellow light of the kitchen.

"Still poleaxed?" he asked, amused.

Jeremy glared at him. "What in the hell made you decide to—"

Aiden's amusement faded. "I wanted to celebrate you," he said. "And I felt foolish—it wasn't until you started planning this shindig here that it really hit me. We never knew. Even Craw felt bad when I brought it up. You never said, 'Today's my birthday'—it's such a simple part of us, and you never had that."

"It was always a lie," Jeremy said, surprised. He'd never even thought to bring it up.

"It's not anymore." Aiden's eyes—mysterious green and oh-so pretty—rested on Jeremy's face, and when he looked like that, Jeremy forgot about the scars from the beating and about the fact that he was older. Aiden *loved* him, and he'd be young and beautiful forever.

He smiled back, shyly. "Nope."

Aiden squeezed his knee and whispered in his ear. "Want to celebrate a little early?"

Oh yeah.

They were on their way up the stairs to the bedroom, Aiden's hands relentless in the quest for more of Jeremy's skin, when Aiden brought it up.

"So—what was Johnny's problem? He looked *really* put out when he found out how old you were."

Jeremy couldn't stop a chortle. "Well, you know how me and Johnny—"

"A blowjob," Aiden said dryly, because yes, this was well covered territory. "A blowjob and a kiss."

"It was the blowjob and the kiss that saved my life, so don't discount it," Jeremy said tartly. "But yes. Anyway… see… Johnny's turning forty this year and—"

Aiden started chuckling. "And oh my God."

Jeremy had to smile. "Yup."

"*Jeremy*—you were the younger man!"

The thought made him giggle—right up until they got to the bedroom and Aiden's mouth and his hands got serious.

Yeah, it was going to be a bit of a stretch, wrapping his brain around having a birthday like a real person. Especially when he was finally coming to understand that age was just a state of mind.

I wrote this story for just a slice of Jeremy and Aiden's life—and, of course, in making Persephone three-and-a-half, it begged the question: Why weren't they married yet? Obviously because life got in the way—but because Jeremy is Jeremy, there had to be a lesson in there for both of them.

BUNNIES

"AND HERE'S her pull-ups, and here's her little potty, and here's her best blanket. Her clothes are in the bag with the pull-ups and—"

"Ari, honey," Rory said gently, "it's time to go."

Ariadne's eyes filled with tears. "But we're going to be gone for five days," she said, lower lip wobbly. "I hate to leave her—"

"We'll take care of her, Miss Ariadne," Jeremy reassured. He tried to keep his voice even and happy and upbeat, even though his heart was beating super-fast like a terrified bird.

"We'll be fine," Aiden said, sounding much more confident. "Ari, go. Rory's going to crap his pants, and you have to get over the mountain and through Denver traffic. We'll be fine. See you in five days. Remember, we've got Craw and Ben, and Ben seems mostly civilized. If all else fails, we've got my mom, and she hasn't lost a kid yet."

Ariadne gave him a flat-eyed stare, and her sharp featured face made that "mom" look a thing of deadly beauty. "You are not funny, Aiden Rhodes," she said.

"I am a goddamned delight," Aiden replied, deadpan. "And you be nice to me, or I'm going to leave your adorable daughter out with the rabbits at night."

"He will not!" Jeremy's voice cracked in panic, and he shielded Persephone from the idea even in jest. He was pretty

14

sure it was in jest. Jeremy's boy had a streak of hard in him, but mean and cruel were not in his makeup.

"Oh, I know he won't," Ariadne snapped. "He's just trying to piss me off so I'll leave."

"Is it working?" Ari's giant blond husband asked plaintively. "We don't have so many chances to go on vacation, Ari!"

And that seemed to work. Rory had been making good commissions lately—tourists were coming to Granby to buy his paintings and, oddly enough, Craw's yarn. It had been Craw who'd told Ariadne she was bitchy as hell and needed five days with just her husband to chill her out, and he hadn't been far wrong—Ariadne was worried.

Persephone had been born with a cleft palate, and that was a lot of operations between birth and three-and-a-half years old. Her little ears had tubes in them, and the tubes had gotten infected more times than anybody could count. Jeremy and Aiden, Craw and Ben—even Johnny and Stanley in Boulder—all knew the drill. Warm oil, compresses, and only call the doctor when her fever spiked over 100. Hurting ears were rough on a toddler, and hence rough on everybody around the toddler, and Ariadne and Rory were ragged. The little girl had another surgery in a month, and if Ariadne wanted to keep her sanity for another trip to the hospital with her little one, she needed a break now.

But of course Jeremy and Aiden were happy to do it.

Aiden had been raised around children—he was a natural at them—but Persephone was Jeremy's only experience with a small person who kept growing, and Persy was his world.

The two of them had watched the little girl a lot in the past three-and-a-half years, from days when Ariadne was in the yarn shop doing books and Jeremy took her to feed stock with him, or the occasional evening when Ariadne and Rory had a rare date. She'd stayed in their guest bedroom before in her little porta-crib, and they had a routine with her.

"Okay," Ariadne said finally. "Bye, baby—you be good."

"Bye, mama," Persephone said tranquilly from Jeremy's arms. "Thee you wader!"

Her lisp would be worked with after her final surgery—but Jeremy could see how now, the imperfect words were probably ripping Ariadne's heart right out of her chest.

"Bye, sweetheart," Rory said, dropping a kiss on his daughter's forehead. "Guys, call us if you need anything." He said the words out loud, but they both saw him shake his head forebodingly, and they got it. If Ariadne didn't have a little bit of space, she was going to crack—this trip was for everybody.

Finally they were gone, their little Hyundai jouncing down the road, and Persephone struggled in Jeremy's arms.

"Bunnies!" she pleaded, and he set her down and let her go. Aiden had put in paving stones near the beginning of spring, leading from the driveway to the entrance of the house, and from the house to the back, where the critter cages were. Jeremy and Aiden kept an increasing number of rabbits and chinchillas bred for their fur, and feeding, watering, and brushing the gentle creatures took Jeremy about an hour a day. On this day, he was going to get some help.

He sang softly as he brushed out his second favorite critter—a chinchilla that Stanley and Johnny had bought him three-and-a-half years ago, when Jeremy had still been in the hospital from saving Stanley's life. Ariadne had been there too, on bedrest, and the hospital had let them room together, because Jeremy had been a mess and they'd both been lonely. Persephone stood on tiptoe and studied one of the older bunnies through his enclosure. This one was sort of a badass bunny, but he regarded her curiously, munching through a carrot Jeremy had given him as a bribe to be nice.

"Jemy?" Persephone turned to him and put her finger delicately on her upper lip. "Wook." She wrinkled her lips and her nose, and Jeremy smiled as he realized she was doing a bunny wiggle.

"Yeah, princess—is that what bunnies do?"

"Am I a bunny?"

Jeremy frowned. "No, you're an angel."

She tapped her scarred upper lip again, and Jeremy had an epiphany. A cleft palate used to be called a "hare lip" for just that reason. Because it split the upper lip like... well, a bunny.

"Yeah, princess. You've got that split in your lip for now. It'll get closed up as you get older."

She looked sad then, and Jeremy put the chinchilla back in its cage before picking her up.

"What's wrong, princess?"

"Wan look like bunny!" she protested, and Jeremy laughed softly.

"Well, you will look like Persephone even after it gets fi... uh, changed," he said. "It will help you talk, and you'll still have a little scar there, so you can remember when you were a bunny."

She brightened and brushed Jeremy's face gently with her fingertips. "Thcarth?"

It took Jeremy a minute, and then he remembered—he had scars too. "Yeah, but your scars will make you pretty," he said. His scars sort of made him the opposite of that. The beating he'd taken keeping his friend's whereabouts from a rabid mobster had taken away the con man's prettiness he'd relied on his entire life. He'd been devastated at first, but Aiden kept looking at him like he was pretty, and he'd just... forgotten, over the last few years. Sometimes he mourned his perfect nose and the dimples in smooth cheeks, but most days, he worked too hard by Aiden's side to think too much on what he'd lost.

He had his boy, he had his family with Ari and Craw and Ben—and even Johnny and Stanley. He had his bunnies and his chinchillas, and the sheep and alpacas at Craw's farm.

He had his work and his dog, Bluebell. And he had Persephone, who made his days brighter with just a smile.

"Your thcarth make oo pretty," she said carefully, and Jeremy grinned at her.

"You think so? I'll have to tell Aiden that."

She gave an exaggerated scowl then. "Aithen wook wike mean!"

Jeremy laughed. "That's just for show. He's got a heart softer than bunny fur. You know that!"

That night, Jeremy cooked chicken pot pies for them, a new recipe that Aiden liked and that Persephone could eat easily, because chewing was difficult sometimes. They sang songs and then sat in the quiet while she played with the toys her mother had brought, and finally, she fell asleep on Aiden's lap as he read to her from a magazine about tending stock.

"That about put me to sleep too," Jeremy admitted softly after Aiden laid her down.

"Well, next time we'll try one of those action books of yours," Aiden muttered. "Bluebell, down."

Bluebell, their Volkswagen-sized dog, knew exactly what that meant as they entered their room—and so did Jeremy.

"Bluebell down?" Jeremy said, and Bluebell—who was stretched across the felted rug Ariadne had given them for Aiden's birthday two years before—gave him a puzzled look. She *was* down, right?

"Yes, Jeremy. You heard what I said." Aiden was stripping off his clothes and heading for the shower, and he looked behind him impatiently. "Coming?"

Jeremy stripped off his clothes too, feeling a little naughty. They usually didn't do things like shower together when Persephone was staying with them. "I… I uh… you know."

Aiden caught his hand as he came into the bathroom to put his clothes in the hamper. "I did not agree to go without sex for a week, Jeremy. You need to put that out of your head."

Jeremy felt his smile blossom from somewhere around his toes. In the past three-and-a-half years, his body had gotten stronger. He'd still have frailties—his arm had been badly broken, and his hip would always pain him in the cold. But he'd been active and happy most every day.

He wasn't embarrassed to be naked in front of Aiden anymore. Aiden hadn't let him be.

The shower was short, but Aiden was ruthless about letting Jeremy know what would be expected of him when they got out. By the time Aiden backed him up to the bed and possessed Jeremy's body expertly, with the ease of a lot of practice, Jeremy would have died if he'd been denied any of those expectations.

Their sex was hard and fast—and quiet, because neither of them were in the mood to put clothes on and run into the other room to quiet down their houseguest. Jeremy's climax same so quick, so gracefully, he tilted his head back with a little cry and was transported to the clouds while his body did all the heavy lifting downstairs.

Aiden's climax was a little harder, and as he thrust in a final time, he took Jeremy's mouth, his groan reverberating down to Jeremy's toes. He collapsed on top of Jeremy, and Jeremy smiled dreamily as the kiss faded. Aiden rolled to the side and covered them both with the blanket because even in the summer, Granby got a little chilly after dark.

"God," Aiden said, rubbing his fingertips along Jeremy's lips. "You are so pretty."

Jeremy rolled his eyes. "Am not."

"Don't be an ass, Jeremy. You are too."

19

And Jeremy felt the wounding to his heart. "You know very well I haven't been pretty since... since, you know. Since my face got busted up."

Aiden sat up in bed and scowled. "I know that's bullshit, and I didn't know you still thought that."

Jeremy swallowed, hard, rolling to his side. "Look, just drop it, okay?"

"No."

Jeremy scowled at him. "What are you going to do? Compliment me to death?"

"No—I just want you to admit you're still a fine-looking man, Jeremy No-Last-Name."

Jeremy raised a corner of his mouth, a long buried hurt surfacing. Aiden had brought it up three years ago—but their lives had been so busy then. They'd been good lives—better than Jeremy had ever imagined having—but they'd been busy, and it had been forgotten between them.

"I must not be that good looking," Jeremy retorted, "Or I'd have a last name, wouldn't I?"

Aiden sucked in a breath, and let it out on an "Aha... "

"What?" Jeremy didn't look at him.

"God, I'm dumb."

"You are not." Jeremy hated it when Aiden said things like that. Aiden was perfect—Jeremy knew it in his bones.

"I must be if I haven't married you yet."

Jeremy peeked at him. "You *did* say something about it once," he mumbled, remembering that night before the benefit they'd thrown to help Ariadne and Rory with Persephone's medical expenses. It had been a beautiful, fairy-tale sunset, and Aiden had put it out there, and Jeremy had hoped.

"Can I help it if I'm so happy I feel married already?" Aiden asked mildly, kissing his shoulder. "Would you let me call you pretty if you wore my ring and had my last name?"

"It would be a lie," Jeremy said sullenly.

"It would not." Aiden tugged gently on his shoulder until Jeremy sighed and turned around and into him. "I would be proud to have such a man with my name."

Jeremy couldn't help it. He smiled into Aiden's chest. "Persephone said my scars were pretty," he said, remembering the stupid pride he'd felt at that.

"That's because she loves you best," Aiden told him, his big hand stroking Jeremy's hair. "But not more than I do, Jeremy. Marry me. Then you'll know I think you're the prettiest one."

Jeremy kissed him. "Sure. And everyone will know I'm your man."

And Aiden's clear-eyed expression lapsed into his habitual scowl. "And you can finally stop calling me *boy*."

Jeremy grinned. "Nope. Not even when we're a hundred."

Aiden's throaty laughter rang in his ears.

The next morning, when Ariadne called, sounding sleepy and happy and so much more relaxed, Jeremy told her he and Aiden were getting married sometime in the fall.

"It's about fucking time," she murmured. "Now tell me what Craw says after you go to the store."

Craw said exactly the same thing. It was like they were best friends or something. It was Ben who called Stanley and started the planning.

And Aiden who shopped for the rings.

Jeremy was too busy chasing his princess around the store and the stables, keeping her out of trouble. He told her that was the price you paid when you were beautiful—other people just fell over themselves trying to be nice to you.

She giggled like she understood the joke, and he giggled because he knew it was one.

He was pretty sure that other people fell over themselves trying to be nice to Jeremy for the same reason Jeremy's entire life stopped so he could take care of his princess angel bunny. Of all the changes in his life since he'd first come to Granby, the biggest, most important one of all was that he knew for a fact that he was very very well loved.

Except, they didn't get married that fall—a teeny tiny virus got in the way. Yes, I know I could make that time do whatever I wanted (I am a mighty and powerful goddess in my domain, after all) but that was before a bunch of things happened that made the following Thanksgiving story a necessary part of Jeremy and Aiden's canon.

During the pandemic times, I was surfing knitting and crochet patterns and I stumbled upon Ravin Sekai, a designer whose work I loved. Simple lines, some inner complexity for interest, practical to the bone, Rachel's designs were everything I loved about the craft. I bought a design from her and she took one look at my name and e-mailed me back. Apparently, the Granby knitting books were the reason she started yarncraft in the first place.

Yeah—I cried. I'll be proud of that until I die.

In the meantime, I was writing "Stand by Me" ficlets. I know that the debate as to whether the pandemic should be included in genre fiction still rages on, and most of us voted "No!" People were scared. Reading took them to a place where they were not scared, and how dare we yank that away. But the one thing I noticed was that, on the Patreon, where I was writing shorts about beloved characters who had already found their happy endings, people wanted to see those people getting through the dark times. Bad stuff could happen, as long as their people were okay in the end. That's what the "Stand by Me" ficlets were about. Inspired by the John Legend/Sam Smith version of the song, they were about our favorite people getting through the scary times.

When I realized that some of the scary times had actually touched Granby, the little valley that I'd come to love and make other people love with Craw, Ben, Jeremy, Aiden, Stanley, and Johnny, I felt like we needed to see that our people were okay.

AND THE MOUNTAINS SHALL CRUMBLE

A Stand by Me Fic

THE EAST Troublesome fire grew overnight, taking 100,000 acres between darkness and dawn, and people were lucky to escape with their lives.

Ariadne and Rory and little Persephone had been helicoptered to the evac site on the lake while their home for nearly ten years and Rory's studio with all his supplies and months' worth of canvasses and commissions went up in flames.

She'd been on the phone with Craw as they'd left, the noise of the rotors beating out everything but the fact that they were alive and they were going somewhere safe, and then Craw had hung up and he and Aiden had manned the pump and sprayed down the barn and the mill in a constant stream of water.

Until that night, as Jeremy and Ben hurriedly moved the alpaca and sheep to the small pond on the edge of the property by the road, the better to keep them cool and hydrated and surrounded by the road as a firebreak, it had never, not once, occurred to any of them that the farm was surrounded by road, with a stream on one side and the pond on the other. Since Craw had just given the grasses their last cut for hay, the odds of the place catching fire were considerably lessened—but not impossible.

Jeremy and Aiden worked feverishly at Craw's, but the whole time they were keeping worried eyes on Ben's old house, and the little outbuilding behind it filled with rabbit and chinchilla cages.

The mill was their livelihood—*all* of their livelihoods, and Craw had guest rooms to keep his family together if his house made it. Obviously his place took priority, but... but....

The air was thick with smoke—all of them wore cloth masks, constantly rinsed in water to clear the soot. Of course everybody had masks around now. The guys didn't use them unless somebody was going to town to get supplies, or dealing with outsiders. Rory, Ariadne, and Persephone were part of their little pod as well, all of them taking crap from the mostly rural population of Granby and Grand for worrying about "the flu" enough to put masks on.

It didn't matter—not to any of them. Aiden, Jeremy, Ben and Craw were all gay men in a world that was not always friendly. They could take a little ribbing from their fellow townspeople. The important thing was that Persephone, with her vulnerable ears and sinuses, was absolutely never, *never*, to be exposed to the damned virus when she was around them.

It was a solemn promise they'd all made, to Ariadne and to each other, and given that they were Ariadne and Rory's family, it had gotten them through a long, dry, summer and a sad, lonely spring.

And the masks right now were saving them again, keeping enough of the smoke out of their lungs for them to keep working to save their home.

Minute by minute they worked, Jeremy and Aiden's attention straying from their tasks every so often to look at Ben's little house and the rabbit pens and hope.

Not pray.

They saved their prayers for Ariadne, Rory, and Persephone, hoping they made it to safety—and for Bluebell, who was helping them round up herd animals but growing increasingly frightened.

At the worst moment, as snow and ice drifted through the smoke, and the field across from them blazed strong, Jeremy took the dog and waded into the middle of the pond with the alpacas and sheep, standing waist deep in the cold, murky water, as he held the animal's leads in one hand and carried their eighty pound dog like a frightened child with the other.

Aiden came running toward him right then, screaming, "Jeremy! Come up toward the house! There's the bare spot under the mountain Craw thinks'll be safe!"

But Jeremy could no more let go of those animals than he could let go of Bluebell. He stood there, holding the damned dog until Aiden waded out with him, wrapping one arm around Jeremy's shoulder and using the other one to help prop up the dog.

The fire roared by like a dragon, its hot breath stinging their skin and singeing their eyebrows and hair. The dog whimpered in Jeremy's arms and the critters all squealed and Jeremy had a moment to think, "Oh no. This is it. My boy's here and he could have been safe and I'm just so glad he's here!"

And a giant gust of frigid wind blew in the opposite direction, blasting across the road and pushing the dragon back on the fuel it had already burned, leaving it to peter out, only a few patches of embers left.

Jeremy's heart stopped as he surveyed the damage, and through the gusting wind, the beginning snow, he saw the first, faintest whispers of gray light.

The night, the terrible night was over, and they had made it to the dawn.

Gently, Aiden peeled the dog from his arms and set the poor thing in the cold pond, where she whimpered and swam and shook her head before making her way to shore.

And Jeremy and Aiden stood where they were and held each other.

And cried.

Over their shoulder, down the hill, their little house stood, the roof smoking a little but otherwise undamaged. Behind it, the bunny hutch sat completely undisturbed.

They didn't say much as the untethered the critters, leaving them by the muddy pond. Together they trudged, shivering, up the hill toward the big house, looking around with wonder and sadness at their mostly undisturbed home.

As they were watching they saw Craw, cell phone in hand, running for Ben's little car.

"Craw?" Aiden called, his teeth trying not to chatter over the word.

"Ariadne and Rory are safe!" he called. "They're at the shelter, and there's sick people there, and I'm gonna—"

The rest of his words were lost as he slid into the car, adjusted the seat, and slammed the door.

He didn't need to explain.

He was going to bring the rest of their family home.

"Our house or theirs?" Aiden asked, his voice leaden and quiet.

"Theirs is a little bigger," Jeremy said. "But we've got that upstairs room with the turret window. Rory might need a studio for a while."

Aiden made a sound and Jeremy glanced up at him.

"What?"

"You… you just stood there. And for a moment I was so mad. I thought… thought you were just frozen, and not trying to live at all."

27

"But Aiden—"

Aiden shook his head. "But you were the smartest one of us. You knew you couldn't make it up to the top of the hill by the cliff. You're always the smartest one of us, Jeremy. Just as long as you keep living to knit another day, I'm good with that."

Eight years. That December, Jeremy would have lived at Craw's alpaca ranch and fiber mill for eight years. And when he first arrived there, he'd done everything in his power to not let Aiden see the real him. He thought the real him was just too damned damaged, too scarred, a pig in a poke, he'd called himself.

But he and Aiden had fallen in love, they'd lived together. They'd survived some things that would have broken up most people.

And now, he could speak honestly, and he could cry.

"I was just so scared," he rasped, sobs threatening to take over. "I'm still so scared."

Aiden stopped and turned and pulled him tight—this time without the damned dog. "Me too," he whispered.

Another minute. Another two. They were dead on their feet and there were still their own critters to feed and water, and Ariadne and Rory to settle in.

But for just a moment, Jeremy and Aiden held each other and remembered how to hope.

One Month Later

THE VIRUS still raged.

Over three hundred homes had been lost in Grand and Granby—one of them Ariadne and Rory's, and another one Aiden's parents.

Aiden had gone to help his father—with the caveat that everybody mask up—as they worked on rebuilding the house while his mother tried to rein in her brood while they lived in a portable single-wide trailer. It was a good thing Aiden's sister Elaine had gone to live with her boyfriend in Boulder, or they might have split the trailer at the seams.

Rory filled in for Aiden, and while he wasn't the boy Jeremy loved, he was like a brother, and he was quiet to Jeremy's noise, and together they seemed to get along.

Ben worked inside the house—he had to. Most of Craw's business was from website sales, and while Ariadne could take care of the business end of that, boxing up yarns, taking them to the post office to be shipped, updating the website, etc., the loss of actual customers was such that finances were… thin. Ben was working double-time, taking extra commissions, and one day Craw told Jeremy to go inside while he and Rory ran the machinery.

Jeremy ended up in the office with Ben, doing basic secretary things. Stapling, mailing, sitting at a computer and filling in spreadsheets. Ben called it "data entry" and said that people got paid for it, but Jeremy called it damned boring.

It didn't matter. Ariadne was running the store and taking care of her little girl. Rory was working in the mill during the day and filling out commissions—and there weren't nearly as many of them with the crash—in Jeremy and Aiden's spare room at night.

And Craw was doing everything from selling stock and remortgaging his soul to keep them all afloat.

When Thanksgiving came, they were all so tired Jeremy almost forgot it was a holiday until Craw hit every last one of them up for their favorite dish.

Jeremy had said stuffing, because wasn't that everybody's? And then Aiden had asked him when they should start cooking, but Craw just shook his head, his mouth—which had been compressed into a permanent scowl over the last year—actually lightening up a little.

Wasn't quite a smile, but it wasn't bad, either.

Thanksgiving morning, he told everybody to sleep in. Of course, they all had to wake up early to feed and water the critters, but they went back to bed after that.

Jeremy woke up at nearly nine o'clock to find Aiden, face lit by the sun coming through their window, as he smiled softly at Jeremy.

Aiden wasn't his boy anymore, Jeremy thought in wonder, running his fingertips along the fine lines that could fan out in the corner of someone's eyes if they spent their day squinting into the sun—even at twenty-six going on twenty-seven.

Aiden captured his hand and kissed his palm, neither of them saying anything, and his mouth on Jeremy was healing.

No time, this month, for lovemaking. No energy for more than a mild grope before they fell asleep. But in that beautiful sunlit moment, they were naked, skin to skin, and for a blissful time, penetration and stimulation weren't the endgame.

Touching—that's all—just slow, languorous, *luminous* touching. They were *touching,* and Jeremy could have done it forever and ever and ever and—and suddenly he couldn't. Suddenly everything was urgent, until he was crying out, demanding Aiden thrust inside his body, begging for release.

Oh, they made a lot of noise, and it was glorious, this once, being the only two people in the house.

Ariadne, Rory, and Persephone stayed at Craw's, yes, but because Rory was there working, Ariadne and the baby were often at Jeremy and Aiden's place in the evening, watching TV with them until he finished. Jeremy had lost track of the number of nights he'd fallen asleep with Persephone on his lap. Most of the time he treasured it—the little girl had been a little bewildered at the loss of her home, of her possessions, but being surrounded by her uncles had eased up her misery a bit.

In the few moments of time they all had *to* knit, everybody was making her things from cotton dresses to knitted stuffed animals to try to replace some of the things she'd lost.

But they weren't there *now*. And Aiden and Jeremy got to remember what it felt like to be Aiden and Jeremy again, and it was gorgeous, it was beautiful, it was *oh God, Aiden, harder!* Until Jeremy cried out and came.

Aiden came soon after, exhausting his climax inside Jeremy, and both of them panted, staring into each other's eyes, insufferably pleased with each other.

"Us, together," Aiden said gruffly.

"All we need," Jeremy said.

And then Aiden's phone buzzed, and they realized they should shower and get their asses over to Craw's house.

To their surprise, Stanley and Johnny were there, sitting at the picnic table Craw kept on his porch so they could eat or do business outside.

They had their masks on and were bundled against the cold, but Craw had brought out a propane heater he kept out in the barn for the coldest days in February.

There was no handshaking or hugging, but as Aiden and Jeremy approached, they could see Stanley and Johnny's smiles under their masks, and Craw said, "You all talk. I'm going in to help fix the feast."

"What feast?" Aiden asked, still surprised. "He wouldn't let us cook."

"We brought a feast," Stanly gushed. "And clothes and toys for the princess, and even some extra sheets and clothes for Ariadne and Rory. I didn't think Craw was going to let us for a moment—you know that man and his stiff-necked pride, but...." Stanley shrugged.

"But Stanley!" Jeremy said, touched and shocked. "Don't you have people you eat Thanksgiving with? Your boss lady, her family?"

Stanley's face went grave. "Family stayed in New York," he said softly. "We're flying back in two hours to stay with boss lady this evening—but she had her affair catered. It's just...." Stanley's gloved hands went flying and Johnny captured one and pulled it to his lips.

"You're our family too," he said gruffly. "You invite us to all your things. You gossip with us on the phone. I know we don't do the animals and things, but...." Over his mask his big Italian eyes were wide and hurt, and Jeremy's heart twisted.

"Damned straight we're family," he said. His eyes stung and he thought of how tired everybody had been, how sad and exhausting this dinner had seemed. "You really brought dinner? 'Cause... I gotta tell you. We're about done in, you know?"

They both nodded. "We know," Stanley said softly. "We've been hearing it. That's why Johnny came up with the idea." Jeremy didn't have to see his little tush wiggle to know he was giving one of those smiles that made his eyes almost disappear into the eye-crinkles he probably loathed, but that Jeremy thought were his best feature. "Just call us Stanley Claus!" he quipped, and they all laughed.

They stayed for another hour, kept warm under alpaca blankets, and fed on Craw's giant morning frittata which was something he did on holidays before the main meal. He'd asked them if they'd wanted the family to eat turkey early, but Johnny had shaken his head.

"No—we're having turkey with Stanley's boss lady tonight. This is perfect—and wonderful."

When they left—after bumping elbows in lieu of hugs—Aiden and Jeremy went inside, taking their place by the fire while Ariadne and Ben moved in the kitchen to set the table.

The smell of the turkey and fixings, warming on the stove, permeated the house, but as grateful as Jeremy was for the food, that wasn't what made his eyes water.

It wasn't until Aiden put an arm over his shoulders that he realized he wasn't the only one.

"What?" Ariadne asked, coming into the living room and realizing that everybody—Craw, Rory, even baby Persephone were all staring into the fireplace, uncharacteristically quiet.

"Just being grateful," Jeremy said. "Sometimes, I can't believe all the good things I've got."

Ariadne burst into tears then, and Rory brought her to sit in his lap, and Ben walked over to Craw's recliner and bent over his shoulders, kissing his cheek.

They would eat later, Jeremy knew. And Persephone would not always be the quiet angel she was, playing with a newly knitted doll, at the moment.

But this moment, in his life was the first time he truly knew why they would call it Thanksgiving.

And... the wedding.

People are funny. They like to hear about a happy ever after, and most readers respect the hell out of the perfect curtain down moment... but there's just something about seeing a wedding. The planning, the excitement, the pretty details.

Somebody—I forget who—asked about ficlets for Jeremy and Aiden, and I pulled out the Stand by Me ficlet, and then I realized that, after all the delays, Jeremy and Aiden really did need that wedding. The ficlet grew into an actual short story, and I realized that all the conflict here was going to be in Jeremy himself. Jeremy, who doesn't like to make a big deal out of himself, is going to have to be the star of the show.

And all of his friends are going to make sure he takes front and center if it kills them.

It was nice to write something happy—but that didn't mean I didn't shed a few tears as it went down. There really is something special about weddings.

WEDDINGS AND SUCH

IT WAS a perfect spring day. The wind blew—well, it was Granby and the wind was always blowing—but this was a light breeze, cool, of course, but with overtones of summer. Grass and young trees had begun the long, slow process of reclaiming the bowl valley from the horrific fire three years before, and the new animals—the sheep, the alpacas, the goats and bunnies—were fluffy, with big eyes and adorable little sproinging dances, and were, as always, unfairly cute.

The small bit of pasture rising up into the border of the valley had been leveled as soon as the snows had cleared, and seeded with grass. Craw hadn't told anybody why he was doing that, nor why, suddenly, none of the critters were allowed past a makeshift fence he'd strung to protect the new meadow grass, but when Aiden had asked him, quietly, if they could have an event—a small one, he said—somewhere on the property, Craw had pointed to the newly seeded, newly leveled pasture.

"But," Aiden had said, baffled, "we were thinking the front yard of Ben's cottage—"

"There's rocks," Craw told him gruffly.

"But we'd be able to clean it up the next day—"

"You'll never know where your dog'll shit," Craw said.

"And I thought you were doing something with the animals up there," Aiden finished, almost desperately because Jeremy had insisted they not put anybody out.

Craw stared at him. "I am," Craw said. "You two farm animals in particular. You're almost domesticated. Don't stop on my account."

"Fine," Aiden had shot back, irritated because Craw was not allowing him to be grateful. "If that's where you want us to have the wedding, that's where we'll have the wedding!"

"You're welcome," Craw said, but not like he was mad—more like he was pleased Aiden saw things his way.

"Thanks, Craw," Aiden said on a sigh. "It'll look real good for my boy."

Craw reached out a massive paw and cuffed Aiden gently on the side of the head before pulling him in for a brief, fatherly hug. "Bout time you two assholes did the right thing."

Aiden scowled at him when it was done. "Should I mention—"

"No, you shouldn't," Craw said, looking smug. "'Cause we're getting married this weekend."

"I thought you were going to Boulder this weekend!" Aiden said, jerking away from Craw in surprise—and more than a little hurt.

"Yup," Craw said. "Civil service. Ariadne, Rory, you and Jeremy in attendance. Leaving Persy with your mother, and your brothers are taking care of the stock and the shop. If either of you wears a suit I'll kill you. Sport coats are allowed."

And with that, Craw stalked off, leaving Aiden with his mouth open, staring after him.

"We leave at eight in the morning!" Craw called over his shoulder. "Don't let Jeremy linger with the critters, and for fuck's sake, leave the dog at home! Your brothers'll be there before you go."

"Hotel?" Aiden asked to himself, figuring he'd ask Ben in a minute, when he'd recovered from the shock.

But Craw, who spent his days in a tiny factory with plugs in his ears, when he wasn't out in the windy, silent pastures with the farm animals, apparently had not lost a single stitch where his hearing was concerned.

"Got it covered!" he called, and then he disappeared down the rise of the hill into the lower pasture and that was that.

Aiden was so poleaxed, he almost forgot that he had his own wedding to plan, and he didn't remember until he went inside the store to find Ariadne and maybe boggle a little with her before he broke the news to Jeremy, who was mucking out the stalls.

"Did you know—"

"Craw and Ben are getting married?" Ariadne said, her hands flying as she knit a sample shawl on their new bamboo/alpaca yarn. They'd had to order the bamboo top special to spin in with the alpaca with a little bit of wool for stretch, and the result was a sort of amazing, lightweight, drapey fabric that Aiden couldn't stop petting.

"Yes, that," Aiden said shortly, looking at the deep azure of the shawl. "That's real pretty, Ariadne—you do that yarn proud."

She grinned at him. "I'm stealing the sample for your wedding, you know—this is one of your best colors yet."

"Wait," he said, surprised. "How did you know *I* was getting married?"

She stared at him blankly. "What in the hell did you think he was doing with that bit of pastureland on the rise above the farm?"

"I don't know—special grass to make softer wool?" Aiden burst out. "Seriously, Ari—how did you all know we were planning on getting married this June?"

Ariadne's eyes softened. "Because you were all set to do it before COVID, and then shit got weird. But you wouldn't let Jeremy stay unattached for long."

"He's been attached since he got here," Aiden grumbled. "He's been attached to *me*."

Ari didn't argue that Aiden was barely eighteen at the time, or that it took Jeremy three years to be ready for that relationship—that Aiden and Jeremy were attached in some way, *every* way, was something nobody at Craw's would argue.

"So yes—Craw's been planning that since before the snows started to melt. Any other questions?"

"What do we get them for a present this weekend?"

Ariadne's eyes opened. "We doing that?" she asked, mostly to make sure.

"My mother would never forgive me if we didn't," Aiden muttered.

"Maybe you should ask Ben about it. He's inside doing...." She made vague hand gestures which was what they all did when it came to Ben's amorphous software consulting job that seemed to pay him a lot for... well, whatever he was doing in the house.

"Yeah, okay," Aiden told her, knowing what she meant. "Let me ask him before I tell Jeremy we're going somewhere this weekend."

"What about *your* wedding?" Ariadne asked him.

"He knows when we're having our wedding," Aiden replied, his grumpiness not going away. "I was asking Craw if he could help us have it in front of the house and he hit me with 'wildflower pasture' God save us all. We got the date set and everything—we just need to tell my folks and, you know, Stanley and Johnny and I think that'll be it."

Ariadne sent him a look that was damned unfriendly. "If you don't send out invitations, like an *honest* couple, I will sneak into your house, pet your stupid happy dog, and beat you to death with a spinning wheel."

Aiden's lips parted in surprise. "Wait a second," he muttered. "Craw gets to just sneak out of town and barely tell us we're coming and we've got to—"

She scowled. "Are you or are you not making an honest man out of that boy."

Aiden groaned. Jeremy's whole life had been on the down-low. He didn't even have a real last name. This wedding was the most legal thing Jeremy had ever had the opportunity to do, and Aiden was damned if his boy would think he wasn't worthy of the whole shebang.

"Aw crap. It's going to have to be the whole thing, isn't it?"

She looked at him without pity. "How long you two been together?" she asked.

Aiden frowned. Persy had just turned five, so…. "Five and a half years," he said.

"Now I get things got hairy there for a bit," she conceded. "Jeremy had to get better, and then Persy was born, then there was the pandemic and the fire and everything growing back." Ariadne and Rory had only just gotten their own home again, six months before. All of Ariadne and Ben's plans for the wedding had gone up in smoke two years ago, which was why Aiden and Jeremy had decided that *small* and *unpretentious* was the way to go.

"We just didn't want to put anybody out," Aiden mumbled, suddenly feeling like he'd let Jeremy down.

Ariadne shrugged. "I mean, doesn't he *deserve* his fancy invitations and his cake and his good suit and half the town hugging him when Craw pronounces you guys husband and husband?"

"Can Craw do that?" Aiden asked, stunned.

"I hope so," she said soberly. "He's been studying on the internet, and he's already paid a fee."

Aiden rubbed his eyes, absurdly touched. "Man," he muttered. "Can that man *not* gut punch me three days out of the week?"

"So," Ariadne asked, "what are you going to do?"

"Well, for starters I'm going to ask Ben what they want for a wedding present!" Aiden exclaimed and stalked away without another word.

BEN WAS no help at all.

"You're coming, right?" he asked expectantly. "I mean, a couple of my old friends from the city might make it, but seriously—you guys and Ari and Rory were the only people we wanted."

Aiden's eyes burned and he hated that, but Ben was just so sweet! Aiden couldn't even be *grumpy* at him.

"Well, of course we'll be there," Aiden said. "I just... I mean, Craw didn't give us much notice. What do you guys want as a gift?"

Ben blinked at him. "For you guys to be there."

Aiden was wearing a watch cap Ben himself had knitted for him after the last one Jeremy had made had gotten singed during the fire, and it was all Aiden could do not to rip that thing off his head and throw it at the slight, happy, unassuming man sitting at Craw's kitchen table and working assiduously to keep his business and his boyfriend's—*fiancé's*—business afloat.

"That man has *literally* replanted the north pasture with wildflowers so Jeremy and I can invite... I dunno, *everybody* to our wedding, and you give us four days' notice before going to yours? Ben, you're a sweet guy and all, but can you *see* how this is making me a little crazy?"

41

To his surprise, Ben didn't chuckle. Instead, he regarded Jeremy soberly and looked around, as if to make sure nobody was going to come in when he said this.

"Remember the fire?" he asked, which was a stupid question because Aiden *and* Jeremy sometimes woke up gasping for breath, imagining that the dragon that had almost blown across the road had consumed them.

"Of course we do," Aiden muttered.

"You guys didn't go down to protect your own house, or your own stuff. You climbed into the pond with the sheep and the alpaca and the goddamned dog and held on for dear life."

Aiden shuddered. "You don't gotta tell me that, Ben, I was there."

Ben nodded. "Yeah. And you were there through the months afterwards, splitting your time between rebuilding your parents' house and working on the mill."

Aiden nodded. "It was sort of a blur," he confessed. "We… we didn't get much sleep that year."

"And you stayed," Ben said, with a quiet little smile. "You stayed."

Aiden scowled. "Well, you're family," he said. Not "like" family, because that was just stupid talk right there.

Ben nodded. "Yeah, well, my mom and my Aunt Gertie are the only family I would have wanted at my wedding besides you guys, and sadly, they're both passed. Same with Craw. And we knew you'd come. Be there. Come to dinner with us afterwards—it'll be a steakhouse because I know you all love your red meat, and that's all we want. Sleep in the hotel, have brunch with us before we drive home. Be our family." Ben gave a small, almost sad smile. "The last five years, Aiden, haven't we learned what's really important? You can knit us a bedspread for Christmas. I mean, Jeremy's getting pretty good at crochet—I love granny squares. Between your color choices and his skill,

42

I know it will be beautiful. But we wouldn't care if it was crap. Just… just be with us on our day and let us plan yours. I lived in the city, Aiden—everything was performative. 'Did you go to the benefit? Are you supporting the right politician? Oh God, don't follow that entertainer, he's *bad.*' And it wasn't about being there for each other, it was about *looking* like you were. You and Jeremy are *there* for us. And we want to be *there* for you. I don't want a performative wedding—but Jeremy? He *deserves* for everything to look right, to be beautiful, to be done for him. He deserves a new suit and new shoes and pictures to put in a memory book, so he can show it to Persy again and again, and you deserve that sort of pride, that you gave him that."

"But you and Craw—" Aiden waved his arms, trying to encompass *everything* they deserved.

Ben looked around Craw's farmhouse, at the equipment on the kitchen table, at the rustic living room with all the hand-hooked rugs and hand-knitted throws and the DVD's he'd managed to sneak into Craw's life.

"Do you know how much that man loves me?" Ben asked, closing his eyes, a beatific smile on his face.

"More'n all of this," Aiden said, knowing that for sure.

Ben nodded. "Knowing that's how somebody loves me—that's all I've wanted in my life."

Aiden's breath caught in his chest and he found himself letting it out. "So," he said, his throat tight and his ears aching with it. "You got ideas for my wedding?"

Ben nodded, a pleased smile on his face. "I'll send you some wedding invitation designs—remember, I know what wildflowers are going to bloom up there."

Aiden nodded, smiling a little at the thought of Jeremy and Bluebell and Persy and his entire family celebrating love in a field of flowers. "Ben?" he said, letting some of his vulnerability show.

"Yeah?"

"I just… I don't want Craw to ever think I take him—or you for that matter—for granted. Me and Jeremy—we know we got it good."

Ben's gentle smile showed under the perpetual scruff around his mouth and on his cheeks. "Never ever crossed our minds," he said.

Aiden nodded. "Don't let it," he said.

And with that, he ventured off to the barn.

JEREMY HAD spent all morning cleaning stalls and then moving the alpacas back indoors, because shearing day was coming soon and there were enough burrs out in the fields to not want them to get into the fleece.

He was giving all his favorite critters some carrots, rubbing their necks, nosing them gently—only the ones who wouldn't spit, of course, because those creatures were *vile*—but generally, Jeremy was kind to the gentle animals and they were kind back. He considered himself fortunate in that Craw had stopped shearing the critters himself and started hiring shearers—it was a specialized skill, but Jeremy didn't think he could bear it if, say, this lovely, smoke-colored female who liked to bump foreheads with Jeremy at least once a day, was suddenly afraid he'd jump on her and shave her bald. That was no way to build a relationship.

He felt rather than heard Aiden as he walked into the barn, but his boy's warmth along his back, his strong arms around Jeremy's shoulders and his breath in Jeremy's ear were all pure luxury, regardless of the lack of surprise.

"So what'd he say?" Jeremy asked, leaning back into Aiden's embrace and feeling safe as a puppy.

"Said he'd planted wildflowers in the north pasture just for you," Aiden told him, and Jeremy tried to struggle out of his arms in surprise.

"He did not!" The... the *audacity* and the *attention* of that statement were terrifying!

"He did," Aiden said. "Now stand still 'cause there's more, and I want you right here."

"What do you mean more?" Jeremy fought the temptation to wriggle around in Aiden's arms, mostly because they felt *so* good around his shoulders. His boy wasn't big on words, but he was pretty great at touching Jeremy as often as possible. Jeremy hadn't known it before Aiden had cornered him and kissed him in his old apartment, but being touched was a highly underrated and almost necessary thing.

"Well," Aiden said, drawing the word out in a way that meant *Brace yourself, this is gonna be a surprise!,* "Seems that Craw and Ben want us to go into Boulder with them this weekend. They're spotting the hotel for everybody—you and me, Ariadne and Rory—and my mom's on for babysitting duty, cause it's for a good reason."

Jeremy turned carefully in his arms, the prospect of going to the city—not a huge one but not small by any means—with the people he loved most stretching a smile across his face at the same time common sense told him there was a catch.

"Sounds great," he said. Then, "What about Bluebell?" He dropped his voice when he said her name because the dog was happily snoozing in a corner of the barn and he didn't want her natural exuberance to ruin this sweet moment.

"My brothers are on to tend her and the stock, but if you want, we'll drop her off at my parents so she can have a romp with their dogs."

Jeremy's smile went fond. "She does like playing with her mama," he said, and he knew something was up when Aiden didn't remind him that animals often lost that sort of attachment when their young were weaned.

"She does," he said instead.

Jeremy's eyes narrowed. "What's up? You usually tell me not to get all soft on her. What's wrong?"

Aiden swallowed. "You didn't even ask why we're going," he said.

Oh no. "What's wrong?" Jeremy's voice pitched so sharply that Bluebell gave a startled *whoof* from the corner of the barn.

"Nothing's wrong," Aiden said. "In fact, this is a right thing. A real right thing. It's just gonna be a bit of a surprise and you gotta admit, you're not great with surprises."

"What... what *kind* of surprises?" Jeremy asked, knowing he was starting to panic.

Aiden's smile was so bright and artificial that for a moment, Jeremy wondered if somebody was *dead* before his boy blurted out the truth. "Well, we're goin' to the Justice of the Peace in Boulder so they can get married. That's what we're going for. This is their wedding celebration before they help with ours in the north pasture."

Jeremy struggled with that, his mouth working, torn in a thousand different directions. Happiness for Ben and Craw—yes. Absolutely. Long time coming. They should've been married years ago. But... but... but....

"Why do *they* get to elope and we gotta stay here and do ours in front of God and everybody?" he asked on a wail. "Boy, I don't know nothin' about weddings—if all I get to go to is a Justice of the Peace, how'm I gonna know how to do ours right?"

"You didn't know anything about weddings before we decided to have ours in our front yard!" Aiden protested, but Jeremy was in a panic spiral and he couldn't seem to stop.

46

"But it's not gonna be *in* the front yard!" he protested. "It's gonna be in the north pasture, and there's gonna be wildflowers and… and boy, it's gonna be *big,* cause it's under God's sky right there and—"

Aiden shut him up with a kiss, the long, sloppy kind that made Jeremy stupid. Jeremy lost himself in it, hiding in Aiden's mouth on his own, on his hands roaming Jeremy's back, like he'd hide in their bedroom under their bed. He hid so long and so breathlessly that by the time he pulled back, Jeremy could barely remember what he'd been panicking about before the kiss started.

Aiden hadn't forgotten, though. "Don't you wanna marry me under God's sky, Jeremy Soon-to-be-Rhodes?"

"Yeah," Jeremy whispered, wanting to hide in more kisses but knowing they were in the middle of the barn with half a day's work waiting for them. "More than anything. But how're we gonna know how to do it right?"

Aiden's chuckle rumbled against Jeremy's chest, and Jeremy was reminded—yet again—that Aiden hadn't stopped growing until he was twenty-three years old, which meant he was bigger and broader now than he had been when Aiden had stopped friending him and started courting him.

"Jeremy," Aiden murmured, "you are not the usual person. You are not an everyday man. You are *special,* dammit, and our wedding is going to be right because it is *ours.* Now tell me you'll wear your sport coat and your jeans to Craw's wedding like he asked, and we'll have a real nice time this weekend, and then you and Ben and Ariadne can have a ball making invitations and planning flowers and such for *our* wedding, which we'll have in the last week of June."

"That's awful close," Jeremy murmured, because it was two and a half months away, but most of the fight was out of him and he said it against Aiden's shoulder.

"Yeah, if we were having it at a 'venue' it might be," Aiden conceded. "But apparently our venue was planted in March, and the only people who might have trouble with the date are Stanley and Johnny, but they'll change their plans for you." Stanley and Johnny liked to travel in the summer, but Aiden was right. They'd move heaven and earth to come to Aiden and Jeremy's wedding. "My folks know, 'cause we talked about it with them, which means my sister knows so she can come out and visit. And it means everybody in town knows, so they can start telling Ari if they'd like an invitation or not. In fact, by the time we pick the invites, I reckon we'll know who to send them to."

Jeremy frowned. "Is that how it usually works?"

Aiden scowled. "Hell if I know. I'm just saying—Craw offered his field, so we can fit as many people as we need to—"

"What about food?"

"Potluck."

"At a *wedding*?" Jeremy cried, and Aiden rolled his eyes.

"You try telling my mother she can't bake pies for our wedding. Go ahead. I dare you. Besides—can't you see? This is the stuff you and Ben and Ariadne can chew over until it's in all the digestible pieces. Me? I'm gonna take my man to our friend's wedding and then out to dinner afterwards and be proud of my family." He shrugged. "That's a perk of being your boy."

Jeremy scowled at him. "You don't like it when I call you 'boy'."

Aiden's expression softened. "It'll go down better when you call me your husband, gotta admit it."

And Jeremy couldn't help it. He melted in Aiden's arms, anxiety and all flowing out of him with the cross breeze from the open barn doors.

"We're gonna get married," he murmured. Then, oh my God! "Don't we have to get them a present?" he squawked.

Aiden chuckled and kissed him again and he went back to "We're gonna get married," and everything else seemed okay.

CRAW'S WEDDING was just as simple as he and Ben had promised—but for Jeremy, it seemed just as profound as weddings were supposed to be.

Aiden remembered to bring a handkerchief for the occasion.

When the brief ceremony was over, Craw and Ben each said a few words to each other—both of them characteristically brief, but, Aiden thought, also surprisingly profound.

Ben went first, winking at the rest of them before he spoke. "I know you all knew I'd go first, because you think Rance here doesn't talk emotion without a guide dog and a stick, but I need to assure you that's not the case. I knew Craw loved me from the very beginning. He saw a tenderfoot in Colorado before the snows, and he knit for me. He designed wool and a hat and a scarf and even mittens with me in mind. He fed me. He kept me warm. I knew everything I needed to then—and learning the rest, being a part of his family, it's as solid and real and important as his knitting. High ideas are fine, but real love is hard work. And it's loving the work as you do it. Craw, you taught me that. Please don't ever stop."

There was an electrified, sniffly pause then, and when Craw spoke, his voice graveled and rough, it felt inevitable, somehow, like mountains speaking, or the sky.

"I saw you, looking so vulnerable, bare in this rough world, and I knew you were worthy. You were precious. You should be protected at all cost, through the winters, through the snows, through fire and frost. You're stronger than you look, tough like cat tails or sawtooth grass, but you showed me kindness and I couldn't help it. I had to be the one to protect you. You let me. I'd move mountains for you, Ben, to keep the sun off your pink nose. I'd knit worlds for you, to make one worth your kindness. All I ask is to give you shelter, to be your harbor in the storm."

"Always," Ben promised, his own eyes misting. "Always, Craw. I promise."

Craw's embarrassed smile then was the all the answer he seemed to need.

Jeremy 'bout soaked through the sleeve of his best suit jacket, and Aiden's handkerchief was sopping.

Nobody talked much as they walked from the courthouse to their cars, but all of them—Aiden and Jeremy, Rory and Ari, Stanley and Johnny—were holding hands.

It seemed a tender sort of day.

It wasn't until they were all sitting in the restaurant, their plates cleared, everybody exhausted from eating things like twenty-two-ounce rib-eyes and loaded baked potatoes, that the world turned its attention to Jeremy and Aiden.

"So," Ben said slyly. "What'd you think, Jeremy. Is that what a wedding's supposed to be?"

Jeremy did his rabbit in the headlights thing for a second, and Aiden watched with amusement as color swept his face, blotching unevenly because of his scars.

"That was about the most perfect thing I ever saw," he told Ben solemnly. "It was simple—we're not complicated people. That's all Aiden and I need—"

"Bullshit," Craw grumbled. "Aiden, tell him."

Aiden sat up a little straighter in his chair. "Jeremy," he said softly, "Ben and Craw—they had birthdays their whole lives. They had Christmases and graduations. They had big landmark days to show the world their milestones. You—you get this wedding. This is our way of making sure the world sees *you*, and all the good *you* have accomplished. You get to be the person of the hour. Now I know that's a hardship for you." He grimaced. "Not always my favorite thing. But I'll do it, so you know what it feels like to have everyone you love look at you and say, 'I love that man so much. The world is better because I get to see him happy.'"

He paused, wondering if he'd have to talk any more, and was appalled when he heard Ariadne's sniffle in the silence.

And then Ben's.

And Jeremy's.

And then, to his horror, Stanley's and Johnny's.

"Shit," he muttered, looking at Craw in despair. "What'd I say?"

Craw grunted. "Damn, boy—that was pretty. You savin' anything for the wedding?"

Aiden rolled his eyes. "Just 'cause you don't have to talk again until Christmas doesn't mean I have to stop there."

Ben leaned his head against Craw's arm. "He'll talk again before Christmas," he said, his voice still a little choked from whatever that was. "He has to, remember? He's officiating your wedding! Now what do you want him to say?"

"Well, hopefully he'll say it's over now and everybody can go eat," Aiden said, and he was relieved when Jeremy slugged him gently in the arm because it meant the crying part might be over. Everybody laughed and ordered dessert, but that night, Jeremy brought the subject up again.

"You know," Jeremy said, resting his chin on Aiden's chest, "I never thought of weddings like that."

"Like what?" Aiden asked, feeling very man-on-a-mountain-ish. He and Jeremy had made loud, satisfying love when they got back to the hotel, and Jeremy's sweet body—lean, muscled, so responsive to everything he loved to do with it—had pretty much made Aiden as happy as a bunny in a carrot farm.

"Like a chance to celebrate the people getting married. I mean, I guess in the old days they were like, a transaction.

Like with dowries and such, and giving money for the person, and whatever. But now, we get to marry who we want, and you think, 'Well why's a wedding even necessary?' But today, we saw our friends together and we got to know they were happy."

Aiden smiled slightly and ran his hand down Jeremy's shoulders to the small of his back.

"That was nice, right?"

"Yeah," Jeremy sighed, and he rippled his body in a way that let Aiden know they might not have to be done yet.

"You gonna let us do that for you?"

"And you," Jeremy said hurriedly. "'Cause you're in the spotlight too."

"Sure," Aiden said, rolling over and covering Jeremy's body with his own. Jeremy spread his legs, sweet as could be, and wrapped them around Aiden's hips so Aiden could slide into him slick and easy. The way had been well stretched and lubricated by their earlier activities, and Jeremy's soft sigh let Aiden know that as long as he went easy, more of—ah, yes, *this*—would be welcome.

As he arched his back and thrust into Jeremy's yielding flesh, he held the truth to his heart and treasured it.

Jeremy was going to stand up in front of all his friends and neighbors, and he was going to be *seen*. He was going to have a day in his life that was, for once, all about Jeremy. Aiden too, to some extent, but Aiden was like Craw and Ben—he'd had days that were all for him before. This was Jeremy's big day. It was the gift he wanted to give his lover with all his heart. Jeremy was going to know that he wasn't an afterthought, a criminal who had to con his way through the world, a grifter who benefited from a very lucky break. He was *Aiden's* Jeremy—the man with the big heart and the kindness, who wasn't afraid to work hard for his friends and who deserved all that was good for himself.

Jeremy let out a soft cry beneath him, his body shuddering in climax, but Aiden kept powering through. *His* Jeremy. His heart. The man who let him be soft, who let him be kind, who reminded him, every day, that there was good in the world when Aiden could be as hard and thorny as mountain scrub.

As he let go and flooded the tightness of Jeremy's body, he pictured Jeremy in the sunlight, smiling and happy, the celebrated beloved of his friends and neighbors, the hero Aiden knew him to be.

Oolf! Persephone was getting a little big to be balanced on Jeremy's hip and carried around the barn, but Jeremy loved doing it so much he hated to put her down.

"An' apacath?" she asked.

"Alpacas," Jeremy repeated, and Persy gave him a chirpy smile.

"I' ged it righ' somedime," she said, her words impeded by her late-developed palate and the ear infections she suffered throughout much of her toddlerhood.

Jeremy grinned at her. "I know you will," he said. "You're my Persy and you can do anything."

She rolled her eyes. "Excep' cake fo' bweakfas."

Jeremy laughed. "Except that. I just mean, little Persy, you can fix your words and go to school and get good grades and go on to college and do anything. Be a doctor or an artist or a lawyer or a—"

"'nidde'," she said, and he blinked.

"A knitter?" he asked, surprised.

"Wike you an' mama."

Jeremy held her close and moved across the way to the other alpaca pen. "Well, you can do that *and* do all the other

53

things too. In fact, you can probably knit anytime you want to. You were a crack shot learning to tie your shoes."

Persy laughed. "I'm sma't."

"Yeah, you are. What do you think of this one? Isn't he pretty?" They'd gotten a new stud with a fur color of the palest gray. They were hoping he'd breed true because they could get a lot of money for that color, either spun up or passed on to progeny.

"Pu'ddy," she echoed, following Jeremy's example and patting him on the nose. In addition to being a pretty boy, this particular alpaca had the disposition of a cloud of marshmallow fluff—sweet, soft, and pretty harmless all in all. "Gonna wide 'im a' 'oow weddi'g!"

Jeremy gaped. "You're going to ride him at my wedding? Honey, I don't think so—"

"A' der will be odde' pacath wea'in' fwowes an' sickens an'…."

She went off into a ramble about how there would be an alpaca parade with flowers and she'd come in as her role of flower girl, riding the lead alpaca, holding the rings, with a crowd of chickens in attendance, and everybody would know Jeremy and Aiden were super special because the queen flower girl got off the alpaca because her big strong daddy helped her and she gave the rings to her two uncles.

Jeremy couldn't follow what she was saying—he was pretty adept at speaking Persephone, but he suspected many children had rambles like this that grownups were expected to neither follow nor retain.

What mattered was he got to show his favorite girl the animals during the evening feeding, and she was sleepy and ready for her bath and story by the time he gave her to her mama, who was on her way home.

But apparently the alpaca parade wasn't a new thing at all.

"She's still going on about that?" Ariadne laughed, fastening a drowsy Persy into her car seat. "That's amazing—she's been talking about the alpaca parade at your wedding since you told her she could be a flower girl—she's got the whole thing planned." Ariadne gave a private little snort. "Right down to the chickens."

Jeremy grimaced. "Oh, Lordy—I hate to disappoint her. I mean, alpacas with flower garlands and her on the back and her daddy lifting her up like a queen—that's not going to happen, right?"

Ariadne chuckled, the sound low and appealing. "I don't know, Jeremy—it's your wedding, and it's coming up fast."

Jeremy grunted, not sure what to say to that. Organizing the fundraiser for Ariadne and Persephone had given him some valuable wedding planning skills—he'd remembered to rent chairs and picnic tables and shade canopies, to account for generators to power the refrigerators for the food and a kid's table with activities because little kids weren't always excited about weddings. Craw was already officiating, they weren't having attendants because the people they loved best would all be in the front row anyway, and Persephone got to be flower girl, much to the relief of Aiden's little sisters. There would be live music provided by Aiden's old high school hookup (or friend, Jeremy decided charitably) and, as far as Jeremy was concerned, everything was set up for a potluck picnic for half the town, which it felt like they'd invited.

But then there were the things that made it special just to Jeremy and Aiden, and that had been... a problem.

"Jeremy," Ariadne had said patiently, the week after Craw and Ben's wedding, "What do you want to do for flowers."

Jeremy had frowned. "But aren't we going to be in a field of wildflowers?"

"Yes," she said, "but what about the flowers as centerpieces for the picnic tables, and the ones to decorate the rows of chairs, and the bower over your heads."

Jeremy executed a slow blink. "Ariadne," he said, "that's an awful lot of flowers. Do we *need* that many flowers?"

She'd stared at him. "For a wedding, Jeremy, it's not a question of need. It's a question of having so many flowers all over the damned place that it's criminal not to put a Sudafed station by the cake cutting one."

"But Ari, Craw already planted a whole field full of flowers—why will we need more!"

"Jeremy soon-to-be Rhodes, we will have an entire goddamned *wall* of flowers if I have to pick every last one of them myself!" she snapped. "Do you at least have a favorite to give me someplace to start?"

And Jeremy had been terrified. "Bluebells, daisies, snapdragons and red roses!" he'd squeaked before literally running out of the yarn store and across the way to the mill. He'd been so panicked, Aiden had needed to kiss him to calm him down because his boy had been afraid Jeremy would try to work the mill machines when his brain was all frazzled and that would send him to the hospital again.

Ariadne hadn't mentioned flowers again, but Jeremy knew she was dealing with orders and invoices and flower arrangements. Aiden had spoken to her after he'd calmed Jeremy down, and he'd come back saying, "Don't worry, Jer—Ari's got it handled," and Jeremy had taken him at his word.

The invitations had been just as rough.

"Jeremy," Ben had said, holding out a couple of samples on the kitchen table one day as Jeremy had gone through Craw's living room to get ice for the giant cooler they all drank from when they were running the mill. "Which one of these do you like?"

Jeremy had stared, delighted for a moment by the rich, creamy paper, the bright colors, and the fancy lettering. "I like this one," he'd said without hesitation, pointing to one that had tiny flecks of flower-colored paper speckling a creamy background. The lettering was a rich purple, and it looked like a field of flowers in a way, with a backdrop of snow.

"Excellent," Ben said. "Wait one moment—I need you to tell me what you want in the body. Do you want us to use Jeremy Stillson since that's what half the town knows you as, or do you just want us to put Jeremy and Aiden?"

Jeremy felt stupid. "Wait—you mean this is for our invitations?" he'd asked blankly. "But Ben, I thought we were just going to call people, like—a phone tree or something." His eyes picked out the price points on the table next to the invitation samples. "Oh my God, *Ben*—that's a lot of money for—"

Ben looked like he'd stubbed his toe. "Don't worry," he said, "Craw and I are handling the cost—we just need to know what's in the invitations."

"But...." Jeremy's mouth worked and no words came out. "But...."

Ben had taken a deep breath and put his hands on Jeremy's shoulders. "You're not going to run out on me like you did on Ari, are you?" he asked patiently.

The shame cut deep. "I just don't want all the—"

"The fuss is going to be given," Ben said. "We know which invitations you like—do you want your fake last name or just your first name?"

"Jeremy and Aiden will be fine," Jeremy said in a small voice. "Who are we mailing them out to?"

Ben smiled slightly. "Everybody. You'll see."

Jeremy nodded. "Don't forget Stanley and Johnny," he said. "And Stanley's boss and her daughter. And the bar people. And those nice Federal Marshals who helped us out after I got hurt."

Ben squeezed his eyes shut and laughed. "Absolutely everybody," he confirmed. "I promise."

"Thanks, Ben. Do you need me to help anymore?"

Ben shook his head. "Absolutely not," he said firmly. "Carry on."

"Okay."

He hadn't been panicked that time, but Aiden and Craw had figured out something was wrong as he hauled the giant thermos out to the mill anyway.

"What's with you?" Aiden asked, taking the thermos from him and swinging it easily over his shoulder.

"Nothing!" Jeremy defended, but then he shot a guilty look at Craw. "Just… you know. You all weren't kidding about making a big deal out of us for the wedding."

Craw's laugh was a little bit malevolent. "Just wait until we're picking out cakes," he said. "Now let's get working so we can pay for all this finery."

The cake part was actually fun. They had a tasting—but they made it a family event, with Persy there too as the final word. Everybody had a bunch of tiny pieces of cake in front of them and they had to taste the cake and rank it from their favorite to their least favorite. Jeremy wasn't sure who came up with that idea—he thought it might have been Aiden's mother—but whoever it had been was a *genius,* because anybody knew yellow cake with chocolate frosting was the best thing in the world and after that it didn't matter.

Of course Aiden thought chocolate cake with raspberry filling was good too, and Jeremy might have changed his answer but apparently they could have more than one kind of cake on a wedding cake, so that meant Ben's favorite of chocolate cake with lemon frosting and Ariadne's favorite of confetti cake would all get a tier. Persy thought they were all her favorite, so that was easy too.

In his entire life, Jeremy hadn't known how much fun it could be to compare food with other people, and when they came out with different kinds of decoration examples, he was in a good enough mood to just blurt out, "The white kind with all the frosting flowers spilling down the tiers."

Everybody had gasped and exclaimed then because it was a pretty cake and a good choice and, in Craw's words, "Thank fuck this one wasn't like pulling teeth."

And Stanley and Johnny had pretty much already picked out their suits and bought them as gifts. All Jeremy and Aiden had to do was trust that the other men had Jeremy and Aiden's best interests at heart and shut up as the tailors were poking them with pins.

So, with the wedding in a week, and all that fussing under their belt, Jeremy was ready to put dreams of an alpaca parade with flowers and Persy in her flower girl's dress to bed with Persy herself.

"You work on your vows," Ariadne said, a gleam of determination in her eye, "and let me work on Persy."

Jeremy gave her an unhappy look. "But Ariadne," he said, some of his anxiety showing. "How in the world am I going to come up with words to tell you all how I feel about my boy?"

Ariadne's smile was warm and glowing, and it gave her angular face a sort of radiance that people who didn't know her might not expect. "Just think about how you feel, honey. The word will come. You're an honest man now, remember? You're not trying to sell us on him—you're trying to tell him how you feel."

Jeremy pursed his lips, taking her words to heart, and nodded. "I... I feel like the only reason I'm worth it, for people to make this fuss over me, is because my boy loves me, and thinks the fuss is necessary. Is that a bad thing to say?"

She smiled softly. "No—but don't forget to include the things that make Aiden *Aiden.* Remember—he's getting fussed over too."

Jeremy's smile made him five pounds lighter. "Oh my goodness—that's a load off my mind. If I can praise my boy, *that* I can write about."

"I gotta get her home and into the bath before she falls asleep," Ariadne told him. "But don't hesitate to call me if you think about anything else, okay?"

"Okay," he said. As she drove away, he turned up toward the hill where the wildflowers were starting to bloom, the sun dropping behind the edge of the bowl valley as he watched. In his mind's eye, he saw himself and Aiden, hand in hand on the top of the hill, and it hit him.

They *would* be. Hand in hand. Not just in his mind, but in *reality.* And all the people he loved would be with him. And suddenly the flowers and the invitations and the suits and the cake—all of it meant that for that brief, shining moment, *they'd* be in the sun.

And all the fuss people were making over him fell into place. Because in his heart, it had always been him and his boy, silhouetted in the light. That's how bright and shining Aiden *was.*

Love was a funny thing, he realized—so close and painfully personal on the one hand, but cementing people together as a part of a community on the other.

It was like the sun, really—love moved through the sky, doing different things in different part of the day with different intensity—but it all served the purpose of giving people heat and light in their hearts, no matter what part of the day it was.

Bluebell ran up to him then, barking, and he dropped his hand to her head and whistled as he started walking down the hill and across the fields, toward his and Aiden's little house. They were going to get married, in front of everybody, and God the sun, and for a brief, shining moment, they would be the center.

It all made sense now. Even an alpaca parade with garlands of flowers would fit in there, because everybody got their place in the sun.

"YOU OKAY?" Aiden asked, straightening Jeremy's bowtie. Jeremy hadn't been aware he was the kind of man who *wore* bowties, but when he went to put his suit on, all showered and clean-shaven, with his new haircut that only needed a little product, he realized that the suave James Bond tie he'd sort of visualized hadn't come with his fancy gray suit. Instead, a lovely purple bowtie had been there, and Aiden had gotten the James Bond tie in the same color. They'd both put their suits on, one piece at a time after that, and Jeremy had marveled at how well Stanley and Johnny had chosen, while Aiden preened because he'd picked out his own suit and was damned proud of himself.

"I look surprisingly good," Jeremy said, eyeing the two of them critically in the full-length mirror on the back of the bathroom door.

"Good, yes," Aiden said proudly, setting his hands on Jeremy's shoulders, the better to drop a light kiss on Jeremy's temple. "But I'm not surprised."

Jeremy watched color hit his cheeks and he ducked his head, checking his breast pocket for the umpteenth time to make sure the carefully written vows were there.

Aiden heard the crackle and grimaced, putting his work-roughened hand on top of Jeremy's to calm him down. Jeremy looked at Aiden's fingers and realized he'd gotten a manicure from his little sister, who did nails professionally. Aiden had done Jeremy's the day before, and Jeremy kept looking twice at his own hands to make sure they were his. Aiden's hands looked like his own, though—cleaner, a little, but wide-palmed, with blunt fingers and lots of power, for all Aiden was barely older than twenty-six.

"It's okay even if you lose it," Aiden said, his words a gruff rumble. God, Jeremy's boy had gotten broader across the chest in these last four, five years. All that promise in the gangly eighteen year old who had so dazzled Jeremy at the beginning had been fulfilled, and Aiden looked like a man who could stride mountains and talk to wolves and put God's world to peace.

Then Jeremy realized what Aiden had said. "But Aiden!" he protested. "I worked for a week on these! I... how will I say it right if I lose what I wrote?"

Aiden shushed him. "Baby," he said softly. "Do you love me forever?"

Jeremy's eyes burned. "I love you forever," he whispered.

"I love you forever back." Aiden's lean lips twisted up, and while Aiden could look hard and determined a lot, this was a gentle smile, meant only for Jeremy, and Jeremy basked in its glow. "See?" he said, after the words had settled in. "Those are our vows. I know what's in your heart. If you lose that piece of paper, you'll remember what to say."

He kissed Jeremy then, a quiet, purposeful brush of the lips, and it was like all of Jeremy's flutters subsided, and he took another look at the two of them in the mirror.

"We do look handsome today," he conceded.

Aiden grinned. "We sure do. Let's go get married."

At that moment, they heard Ariadne's car beeping in the driveway, and the two of them rattled down the stairs, remembering Bluebell as they bundled into the minivan.

The dog was clean and brushed, trimmed and groomed, and looked ready to win a Westminster dog competition, which was hard to do when a dog was Bluebell and basically looked like a mix of every medium to large dog ever born—except for the brown curly hair. That was exceptional, and Aiden had once proclaimed their entire yard safe from cockleburs and foxtails because Bluebell's fur had sucked up every one for a mile around.

"Ooh," Jeremy breathed as he climbed into the back, next to the baby in her carrier, while Bluebell took the way back, the better to slobber alone. "Miss Ariadne, you are the prettiest woman in the whole state."

Ariadne knew these roads well enough to risk a glance in the rearview mirror, where he could see her blushing. "Jeremy, you almost have me believing that. You are so sweet. You and Aiden are handsome enough to be on a magazine—you'll make the world's best grooms."

Jeremy felt his cheeks heat again and wondered if that would be happening all day. When Ariadne had offered to get them and drive them up to the top of Craw's property, one of the few vehicles allowed on the little service track that made it up there, Jeremy had been tempted to say no, but then he'd remembered that he and Aiden would be wearing the best suits they'd ever owned, and everybody else they loved would also be in *their* finery. No, it would be best to concede to being the people this whole wedding was about, and to allow himself to be bused to the wedding location.

Craw had made concessions for parking up there, and as Ariadne pulled along the track, they could see a line of cars, one on either side of the track, parked in the mown hay-lawn. The cars stopped abruptly where the planting of wildflowers started, and Ariadne parked her vehicle between Craw's truck and her husband, Rory's, little compact. On the other side of the compact, Jeremy saw Stanley and Johnny's black SUV, because they were family too, and not just the connected kind, which Johnny still sort of was in his heart.

Once there, they hopped out, and Rory rushed out to get Persy, who had awakened from her nap as they'd jounced along the dirt road, while Ariadne fussed over the guys in their suits, making sure they hadn't rumpled a thing in the ten minutes driving around the two properties to the top of the hill overlooking Craw's farm.

"Come along, baby," Rory clucked. "You've got things to do!"

"Thickenth?" she asked, popping awake almost immediately. "'pacath? We doin' i' *today,* Daddy?"

Rory chuckled then, the sound deep and absolutely evil, and Aiden and Jeremy looked at each other in a little bit of alarm.

"Uhm, Ari?" Aiden said. "You, uh, did not—"

Ariadne just gave them a cryptic smile, her glorious wildflower-strewn gown uncrumpling from her drive to show the goddess they both worshipped and loved.

"Remember," she said, nodding sagely. "You can't get mad when it's Persephone's idea."

And before they could answer, she herded them across the field of flowers to where the chairs were set up, an aisle opening between the two columns, each chair bedecked with more flowers.

"Ooh...." Jeremy breathed again. "Ariadne—snapdragons, bluebells, rose, baby's breath—these are the flowers I told you about!"

She laughed shortly. "Yeah, they are—Jeremy, did you think I wouldn't take your recommendation to heart?"

"But I didn't know you meant to do this to 'em," he murmured, looking at the bedecked chairs with stars in his eyes. And then his gaze traveled down the aisle and up to the arbor that stood as the focus of everybody's gaze. Two large bouquets of flowers were arranged up there, where Jeremy and Aiden would be standing, surrounded by dark purple satin bows at the bottom.

"That's real pretty," Aiden said. "Ariadne, you outdid yourself."

She failed to look modest. "Jeremy gave me a basic blueprint, and, well, Rory helped with the rest. He really does have an artist's eye," she said. "But yeah. It came out pretty. I hope the photographer got it—it's going to be my only chance to do this until Persy gets married!" One of Stanley's art friends was taking the pictures. It was Stanley and Johnny's other present to them in addition to the suits, Ben had said, and Jeremy was made to understand that he would be writing many thank-you notes when this was over. He didn't mind that—notes were fine. You didn't have to blush when you wrote a thank-you note.

"Hush your mouth," Jeremy told her now, horrified not by the idea of the photographer, but by that other thing she'd said. His Persy was going to be his baby *forever.*

Ariadne laughed softly and said, "Now you two go up to the altar. See Rance? All decked out in a tie and everything? He'll tell you what to do next."

Jeremy had asked about a rehearsal dinner, but the rest of them had flat out refused.

"Nope," Ben had said. "We've all rehearsed. We're fine."

"But aren't Aiden and me supposed to—" Jeremy started. He was beginning to feel bad about all that panic at the beginning of this endeavor.

"We've made the plans," Aiden told him. "Don't worry. You're standing up in front of people and reading your speech. But the rest of it is us, celebrating you and me. So you sit back and take it. It'll be fine."

So now, Jeremy had no choice, he realized. The meadow was full of people, listening to Eli's band playing an acoustic version of "Take Me to the Church", and he and Aiden got to go up in front of that great flower arbor and be… them. In front of the world.

"Hey, Craw," Jeremy said, fighting the nervousness of being in front of all those people.

"Hey, Jeremy," Craw said gruffly. "You're not gonna rabbit on us *now,* are you?"

Jeremy thought with shame to the times he might have rabbited, way back when he'd first arrived at Craw's ranch. But he'd proven, again and again since then, that he was an honest man, and he wasn't taking any steps that didn't lead to his boy— and to his people.

"Naw," he said, giving Craw a smile between equals. "Too old to rabbit now."

Craw grinned. "Good. We like you where you are."

Jeremy grinned, but then he noticed that Craw was looking at Aiden and nodding down the aisle. Aiden looked down too, and Jeremy noticed that all the folding chairs on the field were full, and the two picnic tables were as well—everybody they'd expected to come had arrived, along with their potluck dishes, and inched just close enough to the edge of the bowl valley to remind everybody that they had about three hours before the pleasant summer day grew chilly and everybody would want to mosey on to their own homes and remember other days when there'd been a celebration of two people in love.

"All right then," Aiden said, and he gave a nod to Rory, who was standing back behind all the folks in the chairs, just at the place where the field started to drop off a little. It wasn't steep, but it did create a sort of horizon for things to come over, and Jeremy had a sudden premonition that he was about to be surprised.

"Ready to roll?" Craw asked, and Aiden grinned.

He turned toward the guitarist, his old friend from high school, and held up a finger before turning to the folks in their seats. Craw handed him a little pin to put in his lapel, and Jeremy was stunned to see it was one of those portable microphones, and it was hooked up to a speaker hidden behind the flower arrangements.

Jeremy was so invested in *that* little surprise that he missed all the cues Aiden had given that he was about to speak.

"Thank you all for coming today," Aiden said, "as we celebrate me and Jeremy and how we managed not to run and not to kill each other, and how we hope to be here, together, under this sky, for as long as we both shall live. Now, some of you might recognize the tune to the song I'm about to sing, because it's beautiful, but the words were real sad, and I decided that if I was going to sing a wedding song to my boy, I was going to sing words that meant he'd be happy. So I meddled a little. Forgive me."

Eli and the Alpaca Hats Band played the first chords to the Foo Fighter's "Home", then, and Jeremy's throat swelled as Aiden began to sing.

Oh Lord, could his boy sing. Every note was pitched just right, and Jeremy recognized the words he'd changed because they were the words Jeremy changed in his heart when he heard the song. Just when Jeremy's eyes started to burn and he thought, "Oh Lord, I'm not gonna make it through my own damned wedding," he heard a muffled, affectionate laugh from the folks seated, and he turned to see what was coming over the crest of the hill.

Aiden was watching too, his eyes dancing, and for the rest of their days, Jeremy would wonder how his boy could continue to sing that beautiful, romantic song while the spectacle advancing on them with all decorum continued forward.

First came the chickens, dressed in hand-knitted tuxedos.

At first Jeremy thought the little open-sided sweaters with the bowties were part of the fever dream he'd been having about this wedding since Craw had told him that they were getting ready today, but nope. Some enterprising soul—or souls, Jeremy guessed—had created little chicken dickeys in the same colors as Jeremy and Aiden's suits, and the birds advanced in a puzzled formation, spurred on by whatever the hell was going on behind them.

Jeremy's jaw literally dropped when he realized it was a team of alpacas, decked with flower garlands, their placid expressions not changing an iota as they plodded forward, pulling a small cart, the kind that bicyclists attached to their vehicles to put children in them—boogers, Jeremy had heard them called, which was a funny word and almost did him in, but he couldn't… couldn't double over laughing because, oh my God, Persephone was in the back of the cart.

She was dressed in purple taffeta and tulle, with a little crown of flowers around her blond head, throwing flower petals along her path like an emperor in a chariot, throwing grace.

The wedding attendees were waving at her madly, their smiles luminous, to show her support. Rory was guiding the alpacas and as they drew up to the altar, he turned them, so they were pointed away from the band and back down the hill, and then proceeded to lift his daughter out of her harness so she could give Jeremy the ring pillow with their rings tied on with a satin ribbon.

Jeremy took them as the last strain of the lovely song faded over the heads of the wedding party, and he was torn between laughter and tears. There had never been a more perfect wedding train.

"Thee!" she said excitedly. "'pacath and thickenth and a *pawade*!"

Jeremy's nerves had melted away. "It's the best chicken alpaca Persephone wedding parade *ever*," he pronounced. He'd seen the photographer snapping pictures like mad, and he knew that one of those shots would be his and Aiden's pride and joy.

"Yeth!" she proclaimed, and then leaned forward to kiss Jeremy's cheek before saying, "Now 'oo ge' mawwied. Aw' wath."

"That's fine, you watch," Jeremy told her, and Rory set her in the seat next to Aiden's mother, Bluebell following her closely, probably to make sure Persephone did not get swept up by chickens or alpacas or any other nonsense going on this day. Aiden's mom was holding spots for Ariadne and Rory too, because they were probably going to take a moment to wrangle the animals into good hands before returning to their seats.

"We done?" Craw asked, but his normally gruff, scary voice was soft now, indulgent, and Jeremy knew he'd want one of those pictures of Lady Persephone and her team of wedding alpacas for his very own.

"Yup," Aiden said, sounding so smug Jeremy wanted to launch himself into his boy's arms.

"That was a pretty good start," Jeremy said, knowing his smile and shiny eyes were ruining his chance to blow smoke and not caring. "Let's see what you got next."

"My turn," Craw said, and then he spoke louder, his voice carried by the microphone. "So, folks," he said, smiling out at the crowd through his trimmed red beard, "back when Aiden here was about eleven years old, my father passed, and I came here to sell his ranch and get the hell out of this fleaspeck town."

There was a moment of shock, because Jeremy was pretty sure he wasn't the only one surprised by this intro, but Craw plowed on.

"And there I was, looking over the stock of yarn the old man had been spinning and thinking that he needed to change his wool source, and that there were some colorways there that showed a whole lot of promise but a lot of it was as fun as mud, when this tall, skinny kid wanders in and starts poking around. He sees the skeins I'm looking at and gives me this disgusted look. He says, 'See those three you set aside?' and I say, 'Yes.' And he says, 'I found the fleece for that wool and he let me pick the colorways.' They were the best in the batch, and I said, 'Did the old bastard pay you?' and he said, 'No—didn't even give me the damned yarn.'"

There was a chuckle from the audience and Jeremy smiled at Aiden, thinking that sounded very much like his boy.

"I was fresh out of art school with no talent and no fu—er, frickin' use for my degree, and I thought those were some of the most beautiful colorways I'd ever seen and they were designed by a scrawny kid because he felt like it. And there I was, planning to be rid of this place and out of this valley forever when I found myself saying, 'Stay here and help me and I'll let you design the yarn and I'll pay you.'" Craw shook his head. "Kid wasn't even twelve yet, and he knew what he wanted to do. We tried to talk him out of it. Tried to show him a bigger world. But I guess if we wanted him to leave, I shouldn't have brought Jeremy here after Aiden turned eighteen. It was damned near like hauling in a mail order bride. Aiden and Jeremy fought like cats and dogs for the next three years—but they were inseparable. If I'd known anything about courtship talk, I would have seen this day coming, but I gotta tell you, it surprised the hell out of me."

He turned his attention to Jeremy, his eyes… oh God. His eyes kind, in a way only a few people had seen them, and Jeremy was suddenly cognizant of how honored he was to be one of those people.

"And you," Craw said, his voice gruff. "You surprised me too." He looked up at the assembly, and his smile twisted and his eyes grew shiny. "You folks didn't see him that day. He hadn't

70

eaten in most of a week, and his feet left wet sock prints when he walked because his shoes were worn thin. Pretty kid—by God, he was pretty—but you could see the sun shining through his ribs. I fed him and spoke to him and you know what? All of that, and he was unbowed. He was going to talk himself to a better day if his voice went hoarse and all he had was a whisper and a dimple. Now Jeremy's life got plastered all over the newspapers a few years back, so you know more about the hard parts than he's probably comfortable with, but I'm not here to talk about that. I'm here to tell you that the kid who approached me, asking for five dollars so he could eat breakfast, had so much promise to be the man before you now. And never, not once, has he let me down. He worried about this day, I know. He had to make promises. Had to let us celebrate him. He is constantly worried that he will fail us, somehow, and not be worthy of our family. Not be worthy of our love."

Jeremy's face was wet, and he stared at Rance Crawford in absolute attention, waiting for the moment, the words, that he knew were coming, the ones that would set him free.

"Jeremy," Rance said, "you are more than worthy. You have made us—all of us—better. You've made me work to be more patient, made Ariadne relax to be a better mother, and Rory told me you made him proud to do the thing that makes him happy. Ben," and Craw's voice grew tender, as he looked at his own husband, sitting in the front row next to Stanley and Johnny, "Ben said that you made him feel welcome here, before he even knew he wanted to be a part of us. And Aiden—Aiden has his own words, but I tell you right now, Aiden was always going to grow up to be a good man, but he would not have been *this* good man without you. You've made him softer, probably, than he started out to be. And you made him stronger. You are as much a part of our hearts now as the sky and the earth and the wool with which we make our living. You are tangled into our lives and we

71

can't picture ourselves without your contribution. Don't worry anymore, Jeremy. You are more than worthy. You and Aiden are the best of us, and you make each other better."

Aw hell. Jeremy wasn't sure he could breathe, and he looked up and saw Aiden's eyes, red-rimmed and leaking, and thought that maybe it was okay. Maybe it was okay that he was tearing up. Maybe—oh God—this wonderful awful feeling of being loved in front of everybody you knew was the price of being celebrated, and he was ready to pay up.

Craw took a deep, shaking breath and looked out at the assembled friends. "How we doing? We need Kleenex yet?"

"It's in the flower arrangements, Craw," Ariadne called, and he repeated her for the microphone.

"Ari says tissues are in the flower arrangements—I'll give you a sec."

There was a moment of rustling and sniffling and some blown noses, and Jeremy's eyes widened as he realized he was not the only one who wasn't okay after Craw's words.

"Okay then," Craw went on. "Hope you all caught your breath, because Aiden's next. He wanted me to warn you that he put most of his thought into the song so don't expect much, but I suspect Jeremy's going to bring the house down, so that's fine."

Aiden rolled his eyes. "That there, folks," he said, "is the most I've heard Craw talk in fifteen years together. Hope you were listening."

There was some gentle laughter and Aiden went on. "We made sure I'd go first because you've all known me since I was in diapers and most of you knew I'd picked Jeremy for myself almost before he got out of Craw's truck that first day. Yeah, we fought. We both had some bad habits that we needed to take care of. I thought I was mostly right all the time—growing up gets rid of that notion damned quick. And Jeremy here…." His

72

face—rectangular and stoic and tender—almost crumpled then, like he couldn't bear the thing he was going to say. "Jeremy here thought he had to cover up all the holes in himself with words. Just this nonstop torrent of words like a river. We had to do a lot of yelling for him to realize his company was fine—he didn't need all them words. His heart—his heart was so pure all on its own, we didn't need the fancy talk to see it. And we sure didn't need to cover it up."

He bit his lip, almost like the boy he never was, and spoke directly to Jeremy then. "Jer, I wanted today for us, so you could see that you—you are my person. But not just mine. Everyone here loves you, and is so happy that you've found your home. Me. I'm your home. I will always be your home. I will always knit for you. I learned the hard way that I can't save you from everything, but I will always want to hold you, and your heart, at least, is always safe with me. I promised you we'd travel the world someday, but we'd always come back here. And just like you and me will always belong in Granby, doing the thing we love, you will always belong in my heart. *You* are my love. And now I've said it in front of the whole world—but mostly in front of you. I'm your home. You believe me now, right?"

For a moment Jeremy couldn't breathe. Couldn't *think*, couldn't talk, couldn't breathe. He stared at his boy, his magnificent, loving, amazing *man*, and had no words, just the swelling in his chest that stopped his breath.

After a moment he gulped in air, the oxygen so delicious it made his vision swimmy, and found that he could speak.

"My words aren't good enough," he said disconsolately, patting his pocket. "I'm sorry, boy. I did all that practicing and that writing, and there's nothing in there that's good enough. I never thought I'd have someone like you. I never thought I'd have—" he made a sweeping motion with his hand to indicate their family and friends, their place in the wildflowers, the transcendent sunshine in the glorious sky of their beloved bowl valley. "I never thought this would be my life," he said, the words so simple he didn't even have space to mourn their inadequacy. "You been showing me how to have a home since we met. You showed me how to trust that there'd be food. Trust that there'd be good times. Trust that there'd be—" His lips quirked. "—mittens."

Aiden's strangled laugh told him that yes, his boy remembered his old floor safe, all the things Jeremy had planned to pick up and carry with him should he ever have to flee Granby, flee this life he loved, the boy he'd come to cherish, all at the drop of a hat.

"And me showing up here, making promises in front of people we love—that's all trust. You know I love you," he said, hearing his voice breaking and not bothering to fix it. "You must—we're here. As long as you are offering me home—"

"Forever, Jer," Aiden prompted.

"Forever, then, boy," Jeremy acknowledged. "Then if you're offering me a home forever, then you are where I'll be."

There was a pause then, the only sounds the wind blowing through the wildflowers and the occasional sniffle from the assembly.

Craw cleared his throat and said, "The state of Colorado gives me the authority to pronounce these two men married, but I think you can all see that they've been married in their hearts for a lot of years now. Let's give 'em a cheer and celebrate true love. Guys, kiss or hug or something. We'll do the rest."

Aiden's arms wrapped around his shoulder and Jeremy raised his face for a kiss that seemed to go on and on and on, even when their family cheered around them, and then converged, hugging them and crying on them—Aiden's mother, Ariadne, even Stanley and Johnny—so many people wishing them well.

Jeremy had never known his heart could be that full.

They ate then, and visited with all their neighbors, although a special picnic table had been reserved for their family and friends. Stanley and Johnny got to sit at that table with them, and Jeremy grinned at Stanley, looking happy, with crinkles at his eyes that he didn't seem to mind and hair thinning from his hair plugs that he didn't seem to want to replace. Stanley, it seemed, had come to the realization that as long as Johnny's adoration remained undimmed—and it did— then he didn't need to obsess about his youth anymore. His heart would remain forever young.

Jeremy had nothing but praise for all the surprises of the day—the photographer and a videographer, whom he hadn't known about, and the flowers and the chickens in tuxedos, that Aiden's brothers' friends had returned to their proper pens, along with the baffled alpacas. He praised everybody's wedding finery and the variety of dishes that had appeared to feed them all, and had been genuinely flustered that there needed to be a separate table for gifts.

"But Aiden," he'd protested, "they brought food and they came! Look at your kinfolk and all our friends from town— they're having fun, they're dancing—why would they bring anything else?"

"Because they love us, Jeremy. Get used to it," Aiden had said, no bullshit in his voice, so Jeremy had to accept it. It was easier to accept knowing they'd be opening their gifts the next day, so he and Aiden could write thank-you notes that week, because it wasn't honest not saying thank you and Jeremy did not plan to do this wedding any way but honest.

Craw had laughed expansively, which had made him feel a little like Father Christmas and not Craw, but since Ben was the one talking to him quietly and making him laugh, it seemed that maybe Father Christmas was a role Craw had been longing to embrace his whole life, but he hadn't been able to until all his people were okay.

"And the song," Jeremy said out of nowhere, when people had just settled into their second plate of casseroles and salads. "The song was...." He couldn't finish that sentence. "You sang for me again," he managed happily, and Aiden wrapped his arm around Jeremy's shoulders and they were quiet for a moment in the middle of all the wedding chatter.

Aiden lowered his lips to Jeremy's ear and whispered, "I'll sing to you every day, Jeremy, if you'll believe I love you."

"I believe," Jeremy murmured back, his heart transcendent with the thrill of that promise, "but I still really love it when you sing."

Aiden chuckled softly, and Jeremy planned to hold him to it.

And that wasn't even the best moment.

The moment that Jeremy would always remember, the moment that marked their wedding day in his heart, was after the lunch, and after the cake had been cut and devoured and appreciated. After the ceremony, when everybody was eating, the Alpaca Hats Band had put on recorded music. Some folks danced when they were done, but mostly the wooden platform in front of the band stayed empty.

But after the cake, the band went back to their places and Aiden took that as a signal and stood, offering his hand to Jeremy.

Jeremy allowed himself to be led to the platform and pulled into Aiden's arms as the band did a lovely cover of Sam Smith's "Stay with Me" and Bluebell sat and watched them dance, bemused and impressed by her humans.

"Aiden," Jeremy said breathlessly. "This is our first dance *ever*!"

Aiden threw his head back and laughed, the sunlight cutting over the rim of the bowl valley behind him in a last glorious burst of gold and blue. The breeze had sprung up, making things a big cool, and Jeremy was grateful for the heat of his boy's body—his *husband's* body—keeping him warm.

"What's so funny?" he asked, but he wasn't feeling fractious in the least.

"Just… you know. We've got so many first things left to do, Jer. I can't wait."

Jeremy smiled then, quiet and full of joy in his heart, in his mind, in his body, and they moved to the beautiful song, the plea for a lover to stay.

Jeremy would stay. How could he go anywhere? This man here, his husband? This was his home. Aiden would be his home that evening, as they fell into bed, exhausted, to make giggly, sticky-sweet love, and he'd be Jeremy's home in the morning, as they opened gifts and marveled at things that were useful and beautiful and practical and chosen with love. He'd be Jeremy's home in the weeks to come as they got back to work, working the machines and feeding the animals and doing the knitting that they loved, and he'd be Jeremy's home in the coming year as they planned their first trip—this one to New York, first the city to see a play and then upstate, to see sheep and fiber festival. When they were on the trip, Jeremy would still be home, and when they returned to Granby, where their friends and their family—and their dog—remained, they would be home some more.

Home. It was all Jeremy had wanted and the one thing he'd never had, until he'd followed Craw to this little valley and met the man in his arms.

Home. It was the warmth in their chests when they held each other, and the fire in their words as they bickered, the love language that nobody else understood. It was Aiden's way of seeing rainbows in sheep fur and Jeremy's way of seeing friends in furry critters. It was their way of holding fast, through fire and flood, knowing that if only they came out at the end of the storm with their hands clasped, they would be okay.

Finally Jeremy understood what weddings were for. They were to tell all the people who loved you, and all those who worried, that you were okay, because you would always be home.

CROCHETING HAWKS AND KNITTING ANGELS

Ahem. I blame Elizabeth.

So, I finished the "wedding fic" as I called it, and the people on Patreon really loved it. I added all my tiny ficlets together, plus the wedding novella, and asked Elizabeth, "Hey, can I maybe put this out as a short collection? My Patreon people would buy it."

"Sure," she said. "But maybe add a short for Christmas. That way you can have a holiday collection."

Sure. A short. For a collection of shorts.

None of those ideas included this story, which grew to novel length very quickly, and not only revisits Granby, but revisits it through the eyes of another young couple, one that needs the love that Jeremy and Ben found, and some gentle words of encouragement.

And some forgiveness and atonement as well.

So this story—this novel-length story—is the heart of this collection, and it's never been published before. And still, it's a sort of a gift, for the people who have loved Jeremy and Aiden and Craw and Ben and Stanley and Johnny since the beginning.

Let's pick up our needles and hooks, people, and create things together, while I tell you a story....

SNOWMOBILES

THE HARD part about knitting for your significant others, Jeremy thought with a grumpy little scowl, was that if you were making them a Christmas surprise, you had precious little alone time to work on it.

Which was why he was currently *crocheting* his boy a wolf sweater in the rabbit and chinchilla hut he and Aiden kept on their property. Jeremy usually gave himself an hour to feed the critters, although it didn't take more than fifteen minutes. He found he liked their company, though, and while sometimes he spent the time handling them, making them tame, or brushing them for the fur he and Aiden would add to the specialty batches of wool yarn they made, enjoying the extra money they could charge for the luxury fiber, sometimes he just sat in the hutch and talked to them, telling them about his day or his plans or his latest knitting project or what awesome thing Persephone had done in preschool.

When half of Granby had burned down, Rory used one of their spare bedrooms for his studio, which put Ariadne and Persephone in their living room if not their other spare room more nights than not. During those times, that little hutch with the critters had become his sanctuary. He loved his people, and he sure did love talking, but sometimes that silent, unconditional company was just soothing on a body's nerves.

And that's when he'd realized that the time he spent in there, *pretending* to groom the animals for fur, could be better used to make surprise gifts for Aiden's birthday or Christmas.

Particularly when it was with a skill he wasn't great at yet, and he could do his swearing in front of the bunnies, who would never tell.

This year, he'd gone all out—as he should have, since it was their first year officially married and all—and paid Rory a commission to make him a pixel grid of a wolf. The sweater was done in two colors—Aiden's colors—of earthy brown as a main color and a dazzling azure sky to work as the wolf. And here Jeremy was, finishing the whole thing up—and it was a lot—two days after Thanksgiving. All the pieces were finished, and all it needed was to be sewn together.

Which Jeremy would have to do during his quiet time over the next two days—but for now, he folded the whole thing neatly, packed it in a plastic box to keep away spiders and vermin, complete with little sachets of lavender and eucalyptus oils to keep bugs away, and stored it on the shelves above the cages, where they kept the pet carriers in case any of the critters needed vet care, or there was a litter they could sell kits from, which happened a couple of times a year. As lovely as it would have been to build a bigger critter hutch, Jeremy knew that more critters meant more work, and at the moment, he and Aiden were pretty much tapped out for work. They had the perfect balance of critters and free time, and Jeremy was fine with keeping it that way.

He told the critters a gentle goodbye and left, making sure to pull the tarp away from the skylight so the rabbits had a good view, and to lock the door behind him. Not so much because the critters were that valuable—although they *were,* and they brought in a healthy dose of extra money—but because there were always dangers. Dog packs, foxes, hungry vagrants—

they lived in the country, and it was winter, and creatures got desperate when the ground was covered with snow.

And it was—about six inches worth, where folks weren't driving or animals weren't packing the snow down. Jeremy and Aiden's yard had a steady half foot, usually through February and into March, where it got really wet and deep. So did Craw's lower pasture. The areas near the farmhouse, the attached shop, and the mill were fairly packed down or melted now, the easier to park nearby.

Alpacas and sheep didn't really mind the cold, though. While they didn't mind heading up to the barn near feeding time, unless the snow was coming down thick and fast or the cold had hit close to zero, for the most part they enjoyed a day's ramble in the snow, down to the pond, and around the pasture. Since Aiden had left the house first to go let them out, Jeremy was not surprised to see them as he called Bluebell to his side and the two of them trekked across Ben's property and across Craw's pastureland to head for the mill.

As they were walking, Jeremy saw Ariadne's minivan putting down the road and up the hill toward the shop, and smiled when he realized it was Saturday, and he'd get to see his Persy. He knew the little girl was smart as a whip and enjoying her half-days in preschool *very* much, but oh, did he miss having her around!

He'd just stepped up his pace, the better to meet Ariadne and Persy as they unloaded the minivan, when he heard it. The unsubtle whining of two-stroke engines pushed beyond endurance. The actual hell?

He turned his attention toward the road and the property across the way. The place was owned by rich people who came to the valley for the skiing, and wasn't particularly maintained for anything during the summer months. Somebody came and mowed the hay before it could become a fire hazard, and every now and then somebody would come stay in the big house that was so far back from the road and behind trees that it could only be seen in glimpses. Through the skeletons of the burned trees that hadn't been cleared, even two years after the fire, he could see two snowmobiles pushing their way through the buildup of snow on the mostly unoccupied land.

As Jeremy stared, he realized two things.

One was that the land across from them wasn't fenced—it didn't have any critters, so why should it be? It wasn't like Craw infringed on it, and he was the closest neighbor.

The other was that, sometime in the night, the lower fence of Craw's property had blown down.

And the snowmobiles were heading right for it.

Jeremy would always describe what happened next as a horror movie in slow motion.

He saw what would happen before it happened, and he had to make a quick decision to keep things from getting bad real fast. He was midway between the stock and the house when the snowmobiles breached the hole in the fence and the young men on the back started to chase the critters, laughing and whooping as the alpacas and sheep took off in a panic.

Jeremy knew the animals would head straight for the barn, traveling through the flat area where Ariadne had just parked and was currently getting Persephone out from her car seat in the back of the minivan.

Jeremy was running as fast as he could toward the van, hoping to hurry Ari and the baby toward the house before the stock got there. He tried yelling, but between the snowmobiles and the stock, there was too much noise for them to hear him, and as his breath labored in his lungs, his worst nightmare came true.

Persephone, free from her car seat, saw Jeremy running toward her and started running toward him, mouth open in excitement as she squealed his name.

"Jewemy!"

Behind her, Ariadne turned and took in the scene, her face going white with fear as she called "Craw!" at the top of her lungs and took off running toward her baby.

Jeremy got there first.

He scooped her out of the snow, still running, and hauled ass toward the barn, which was closer, calling, "Get in the car, Ari!" before using all his breath for running for safety.

The lead alpaca hit him out of nowhere, and he had the presence of mind to curl his body around Persephone's as he went down, sheltering her from the sharp hooves of their entire herd as it ran him over.

AIDEN HEARD Ari's scream for Craw over the sound of the mill machinery and the plugs in his ears to soften the sound.

Craw hit the emergency shutoff for all the running machines and both of them went sprinting outside just in time for Aiden to watch Jeremy go down, facedown in the snow, hunched protectively over the child they all loved with everything in them.

"*Jeremy!*"

Aiden's bellow was enough to startle the stock, slow them down a little, calm them as they finished their final run toward the barn. Aiden knew stock well enough to know they'd calm down once they hit the warm interior, so he opened the doors to let them in and then turned toward the snowmobiles that were still frolicking in the pasture.

He'd felt this rage before, and a man had died, and he'd never regretted that, not once.

He reached Jeremy at the same time a weeping Ariadne did, and together they rolled him over gently. Persephone was sobbing in his arms, and Aiden picked her up gently, calming her down as much as he could before giving her to her mama to finish the job. And then he was down on his knees, his breath stopped in his chest, to see if his world had just ended.

Jeremy was still breathing, his chest fluttering like a bird's, and Aiden checked his back, moaning a little as he saw the blood and the tears in the jacket that the stock had left. There were hoofprints right over the back of his skull, and for a moment Aiden's vision blackened, but then Craw murmured, "Skull's intact," as he squatted down across Jeremy's still form. "He got bonked pretty hard—I'm betting he's got some cracked ribs, maybe a punctured lung." Craw took a deep breath and called, "Ari!"

"Here," she said, still cradling her whimpering daughter.

"Call the Medevac—he's going to need transport to Boulder. Call 'em now." Craw straightened, staring at the snowmobiles, still cavorting, his expression as murderous as he'd ever seen it. "Aiden, stay with him," he ordered, before striding toward the barn.

"Where are you going?" Aiden called, his hand trembling as he traced Jeremy's face, cold from the snow, bruised from the fall, still and white in spite of the blood feathering his lips as he breathed.

"*To get my fuckin' gun!*" Craw roared, his stride turning into a sprint.

Ariadne screamed, "*Ben, stop him!*" even as she held the phone to her ear.

BEN HEARD Jeremy's first scream to Persephone from way back in his office. Unlike Craw, who had to wade past the calming stock to get his rifle from the locked room in the barn, he grabbed the.45 they kept locked in the gun safe behind his desk and was able to jog at Craw's heels as they hauled ass through the trampled snow toward the two assholes who probably deserved killing.

"What're we gonna do when we get there?" he asked, wondering if law enforcement would let them have adjoining cells. When he worked in Sacramento and went to the theater once a month or talked politics until three a.m. because he wasn't bone tired from hard work, he never would have understood the loyalty it took to follow a lover across a snow-crusted field, both of them carrying firearms. But he'd seen Aiden and Ariadne, on their knees in the slush, tending to Jeremy, and while part of him wanted to be back there, making sure his friend, the darling of his family, was all right, the part of him who had fallen in love with Rance Crawford knew exactly where he belonged.

"Make those fuckers stop," Rance said, his voice uncompromising.

Ben might have asked more but at that moment, Craw got close enough to take aim at the guys on the snowmobiles. Ben's heart leaped to his throat for a moment, and he thought, "This is it. I finally get to find out what state prison is like. My mother would be so proud."

His relief when Craw pointed the shotgun in the air and fired stole all his bones. The effect was dramatic. The smaller and seemingly younger of the two men, dressed in an expensive white Tyvek suit that was complete overkill for Colorado in December, upended his snowmobile, getting dumped on his ass in the foot of snow and allowing the thing to take off until the engine failsafe killed the motor and drifted to a halt.

The other rider, older, it seemed, tougher, and dressed in a standard snowsuit, dark blue with orange reflector strips and a black helmet, ditched his machine in one smooth motion and pulled out a very large, very deadly looking gun.

Rance *and* Ben were both pointing their weapons at him before he could decide which one of them to shoot.

The sudden, wind-whispering silence was almost deafening.

The man in the blue snowsuit spoke first. "What are you doing on Madison property?"

Craw's growl actually shook Ben to the soles of his boots.

"This is *my* property, assholes! And you and this ball-less wonder there riled my stock and almost killed people! The actual *fuck* do you two fucking cockless flatworms think you're doing out here?"

There was another thudding silence, and then blue snowsuit allowed his gun to swivel downward by the trigger guard, and, holding out his other hand, indicated he was putting the gun away.

"Pippen," he said harshly, "Pippen, what were the boundaries your father's property manager set when you asked to go snowmobiling."

The younger man had sat, ass in the snow, hands up, as soon as the guns had come out. From behind the masklike snow-goggles, Ben could make out a delicate, Hummel doll face, with a little point of a chin and round cheeks, and wide eyes, with a soft little cupid's bow of a mouth.

"Gid?" the kid asked, his voice quaking. "Make them put away their guns."

"Peregrine," his—what? Guardian? Bodyguard?—enunciated, "tell me, exactly, what Giles Coulson said about boundaries."

"He said there was a fence that… that blocked off the other property," Pippen said. "I… I didn't see a fence, Gid. Did you?"

Surprisingly enough, it was Craw who spoke up. "Why in the *fuck* does a fence matter? Those animals were *happy* here. What kinds of assholes harass perfectly happy stock because they're too fucking bored and stupid to know better?"

Gideon moved first, pulling his goggles off so they could see his face. Lean, with pale brown skin and wide, dark eyes, he met Craw's eyes in something like shame.

"You're right, sir. Pippen here was blowing off steam and I... I thought they were wild stock. I didn't see—"

"Didn't want to see!" Craw shouted, his anger, his hurt in his voice. "Do you have any idea what you've done?"

A far away sound permeated the silence left in the echoes of his shout, and Ben glanced up to see the Medevac helicopter dip over the horizon of the bowl valley.

"That's for our friend they're coming for!" Craw snarled. "Do you hear that? Our *friend*—and we don't know if he's going to live or die, and he went down under all that stock keeping a *child* safe from your fucking carelessness. Go. Get off the property. Fucking learn to use your eyes or I will fucking rip them out of your head. If you set foot here again, I will shoot you. I *will* shoot you. I've lived in this valley most of my life, and my neighbors know me. We will bury you two cousin-fucking lunatics in the shitpile and not a soul will remember seeing your faces."

And with that he swiveled on his heel and stalked off to see if Jeremy was okay.

As Ben followed him, he heard the younger of the two men say, "Gid... Gideon—what did he mean?"

"I think he meant we fucked up, Pippen. We... we need to find out."

"But Gideon, he's got a gun!"

89

"Yeah, and apparently we almost killed people with our snowmobiles and stupidity!" Gideon snarled. "Let's go see if his friend is all right and we can decide what to do then!"

"You want to do something?" Ben said, looking over his shoulder. "Get your fucking noise machines out of here and fix the goddamned fence!"

As he and Craw rounded the plateau that housed the buildings, he heard Gideon mutter, "It's a start," and then, like Craw, he didn't have a fucking thing to say to either of them.

"HOW WE doing?"

Aiden glanced up at Craw as he crouched down to put his hand on Jeremy's forehead.

"Hey, Craw," Jeremy mumbled, his breath coming hard and fast. "I remember cracked ribs. I hate 'em. Can I not have cracked ribs anymore?"

"Sorry, brother," Craw rumbled. "I'm afraid you had another go of them. Good news is, your face is fine and you still got all your teeth."

"That's a plus," Jeremy murmured. "Boy, you hear that?"

"I heard," Aiden said gruffly, his heart likely to explode out his chest. "But we'd still love your face even if it got busted up again. You know that, right?"

"Yeah," Jeremy mumbled. He let out a little whimper of pain. "Persy okay?"

"Persy's fine," Ariadne said, bouncing the still trembling Persephone on her hip. The little girl was almost too big to do that, but today, when everything was the panicked shriek of their four-legged friends, was probably not the day to tell the little girl she had to stand on her own.

Bluebell whined and thrust her head under Jeremy's limp hand, and Aiden's heart almost started beating again as he saw

Jeremy scrunch his fingers in the dog's curly brown fur. Jer would be okay then, right? If he could pet the dog.

Aiden looked out across the field, noting the two figures doggedly walking the snowmobiles back across the downed fence as the Medevac helicopter made ready to land.

"They going back to hell?" he asked Craw gruffly.

"Dumb kids," Craw muttered. "Didn't know better. Don't care. Will gut 'em like fish if I see 'em again."

"Can't be mean to kids, Craw," Jeremy mumbled, and then he coughed and let out a wet howl.

"Craw?" Aiden's voice cracked and he tried not to cry. This was bad, but they'd seen worse, and if he cried, it would only freak Jeremy out more. He took a breath. "Can I ride in the Medevac to Boulder?"

"Probably not," Ben said softly, watching as the chopper approached the once-peaceful, snow-covered field. "But that's okay. I'll take you."

Craw made a noise then, a broken, angry noise, and he and Aiden met eyes, both of them anguished with the attempt to keep this practical, keep this low-key.

"Goddammit, Jeremy," Craw said at last. "Does it always gotta be you?"

"Next time," Jeremy wheezed, "let's let one of the cars take the hit."

Aiden squeezed his eyes shut then, feeling the mix of water behind them, and Craw said gruffly, "I'll take him, Ben. You stay with Ari and close up the shop and tend stock." He let out a breath then, not saying the thing Aiden was thinking. Once again their little shoestring operation was down a man— down more, in fact—because the whole world stopped when one of them got hurt.

At that moment the Medevac EMTs trotted up, a stretcher between them, and Aiden let out a little groan before placing a hard kiss on Jeremy's forehead.

"We'll be there soon," he said softly. "You don't need to call for me, like last time, okay? You're… you're conscious this time, you'll know I'm coming."

"Yeah, boy," Jeremy mumbled. "It'll be fine."

And then the Med-Techs went to work on him, and they were all shuttled to the side. Persephone whimpered about the cold, so Ariadne took her in, calling her husband on the way, and Craw and Ben went about closing down the mill and checking on the stock so Craw could leave the place for two days and the business would not come crashing down.

And Aiden, despite his resolve to be hard, to be practical, to remember that this time wasn't the last time, and that Jeremy was conscious and probably going to be fine, watched them load his husband on the tiny Medevac helicopter and cried.

Yarn and Regret

"Oh God, Gid. I'm so scared."

Gideon looked sideways to where his charge, Peregrine Madison, age twenty, sat in the passenger seat of the luxury SUV looking small and vulnerable, and determined and resolved not to turn the SUV around and protect them both.

He was twenty years old, for fuck's sake, and it was time he took some consequences for his actions, right?

But God, the kid's life was a lot more complicated than that. Gideon knew it—it was why he'd agreed to go snowmobiling in the first place, in spite of the fact that there'd been barely enough snow to not rip the machines to shreds.

"This was my bad call," Gideon said, hating himself. "I... I'm the idiot who didn't realize we'd crossed a road. I thought it was a tractor path or something. And the fence being down was bad luck."

What Gideon didn't know about rural living could fill a book—or get someone killed, apparently. They'd seen the sheep and alpacas, placidly drinking, and Gideon had given Pippen the okay to cut loose. Chase them a little. Let off some steam. God—after the things Pippen's old man had shouted in his son's face that morning, if Pippen Madison didn't scream and shout and get rid of some tension, his intestines would liquefy and explode. The kid already had an ulcer, anxiety, and symptoms of PTSD Gideon recognized in guys he'd served with, coming back from deployment. Living under Talbot Madison's thumb would do that to a kid—but that was no excuse.

Gideon's job as bodyguard extended to attending classes with him at the private university in New York and living with him in off-campus housing, a thing that had brought a new and exquisite hell to Gideon as Pippen explored his sexuality in the first taste of freedom he'd ever had.

Gideon remembered those days, waking up in brothels in other countries, pulling himself out of the body pile of an orgy, only to be waylaid by a *male* mouth on his cock that taught him whole new things about himself. Pippen wasn't nearly as debauched as Gideon had been, bringing home a couple of boys at most, one kid at a time. For the last two years, Gideon had been watching Pippen trying hard to spread his wings, to figure out life, and he'd very carefully kept Pippen's big gay secret from the man who signed his checks.

And then he'd drive Pippen home, first to the big mansion in Gotham City (as Pippen liked to call it) to tell Pippen what a failure he was in New York, and this year, for the Christmas holidays, he flew with him to this little resort town so Talbot Madison could emotionally and verbally abuse his son in Colorado.

Gideon suspected that when Pippen had been younger, there'd been blows involved, but since Gideon had taken over as his bodyguard, when Pippen was seventeen, he hadn't seen Talbot actually strike his son. Call him names, including *imbecile*, *faggot*, and *useless sack of shit*—yes, Talbot had done all that. But the one time he'd raised his hand, Gideon had stared at the man, his hand going toward his sidearm, and Talbot's hand had dropped. He'd sent Gideon a fulminating look but hadn't said anything.

And Pippen hadn't been struck since—but Gideon suspected it had happened before his arrival. Judging by Pippen's extreme skittishness, probably a lot.

"But the man was right," Pippen said now, his voice quiet. "I didn't think about it until he said it. The animals were just... just happy. Drinking from the pond. And... and I thought it would be fun to watch them scatter and... and it wasn't. It was mean. God, I'm stupid—"

"I let you," Gideon said—not for the first time.

"But I'm an adult!" Pippen protested bitterly. "I should know what mean is. I was just...." His voice broke a little and Gideon's heart ached. His latest dressing down from Talbot had been the worst. Pippen had gotten a B in economics. How fucking dare he. Gideon would forever see the awful, dead expression on Pippen's face as he simply stared ahead and took the old man's ranting. It was hard to find your soul when it had been bullied away from you. Gideon liked to think he'd made a difference in Pippen's life somehow, given him a foundation, a regularity. God knows, he wasn't keeping the job for the paycheck—not anymore.

Sure, that's what he'd taken the job for—he wasn't proud. Three years ago, fresh out of the service, private security had seemed like a cinch, a way to get back on his feet. Room, board, decent pay. Bodyguard—he could do it. Security had been his unit's specialty in the Corps—he was down for that.

The first time he'd seen Talbot Madison come unglued on his kid, he'd wanted to quit. He'd started poring over the internet for other security jobs, thinking, "I just need two months. Two months here, and I'll be back on my feet and I can go find something else."

And then there'd been that moment. Talbot had lifted his hand and Gideon had made eye contact, his own hand going for his weapon. And the look on Talbot's face indicating there would be retribution later, somehow, probably taken out on his own son.

Gideon had been trapped then. They'd both known it. He'd taken on the job to keep Pippen safe. That included from his own father.

Carefully, because Gideon was always careful, he turned down the driveway and onto the road to the little farm he and Pippen had violated. As he circled the Madison property from the west, he could see the definite outline of the fence that surrounded what looked to be two big properties between the narrow road and the wall of the valley. One property—the smallest—had a little house, a big yard, and two outbuildings, one of them probably a garage. The other one—the one he and Pippen had been on—had a barn and a farmhouse, another outbuilding and, attached to the farmhouse, what looked to be small shop, complete with a parking lot big enough for maybe five cars. The other vehicles—probably the home vehicles—were pulled around to the other side of the farmhouse under a carport. It was easier to see from the car, not on the ground with the roar of the snowmobile in his ears, but still, Gideon was nauseous from the realization of exactly what he and Pippen had violated.

"Oh God," he mumbled, and next to him, Pippen whispered, "Oh, Gid."

And in his head he heard Talbot Madison screaming, spit flecking his lips, as he called his child a cocksucking little faggot who would fucking marry a girl and give him an heir and then he could forget he even had a son.

"We'll make this right," Gideon murmured, but he and Pippen had looked up the hill at the people gathered around their friend, had seen their grave faces, seen the one man wiping his eyes repeatedly on his shoulder and the little girl burrowing her face into her mother's neck, and he knew the truth. He'd been to war. He knew what an irretrievable mistake looked like.

He swallowed and prayed for Pippen's sake they hadn't made one.

"What if we can't?" Pippen asked, proving for the umpteenth time that the boy wasn't stupid. Scared, maybe, and emotionally fragile—but there was a good heart pumping in that chest—Gideon had seen firsthand proof. He'd seen the boy volunteer his time—not for a photo op but just because. Because he'd seen the unhoused population near his campus and wanted to help. Because a friend needed tutoring in chemistry and he hated to see them struggle. Pippen had a lot of money—a generous allowance. His father yelled at him all the time for spending it, but Gideon knew the truth. Pippen had subsidized fellow students who otherwise might have needed to drop out.

He hadn't told his father because those were exactly the things that would get his allowance pulled.

Gideon's stomach clenched, hating the old man with so much of his heart he wasn't sure how he had enough heart to be worried for Pippen—but he did.

Pippen seemed to have carved out a bigger and bigger chunk of Gideon's entire soul over the last three years, and Gideon didn't want to think about what he'd do for the kid.

He glanced over at Pippen once more as he turned onto the long drive up the hill toward the farmhouse and the little shop. Pippen's eyes were wide, but his jaw was clenched, and Gideon could see a man's resolve tightening the muscles through the baby fat.

Man. Maybe Pip was becoming a man after all.

They parked and got out, fastening their jackets after they slammed the doors shut. Colorado had a dryer cold than New York, Gideon thought, shivering, but cold enough to snow was always cold enough to snow. He fished his hat from his jacket pocket and noticed that Pippen had apparently forgotten his.

"Here, Pip," Gideon muttered, handing the spare he'd found in his other pocket. He also pulled out a pair of cashmere gloves for the boy too.

Pippen took them without objecting that they were probably going inside to have this discussion anyway. There was a very real chance they wouldn't be allowed in.

However, as they neared the shop attached to the farmhouse, they saw that it was open, and the woman who had been clutching her child to her chest was sitting at the counter inside. They met eyes and Pippen went in first, looking young and scared—and resolved.

"Hello," Pip said, biting his lip. "Uhm...." He glanced around. "Is this all yarn?"

"It *is* a yarn store," the woman replied, her wide mouth twisting into a sardonic smile. "We grow it, we mill it, we spin it, dye it, and sell it." She was thin and sturdy, with hair once dyed optic red, probably, but it was half grown out and bleached. *A mommy,* Gideon thought, remembering her holding her daughter. *She probably has no time.* He remembered his own parents, always on the run with him and his sister, always taking them somewhere, school, activities, whatever, in between their jobs. His shame, which he thought couldn't cut any deeper, sawed through most of his bones.

"Oh." Pippen blinked. "Uhm, how do you grow it?"

The woman raised her eyebrows. "Well, aren't you just a sweet little summer child. Sheep and alpacas and the occasional rabbit or chinchilla. You shave or brush the critter, use the fur or the fleece, repeat. Do *you* want to learn how to knit?"

Pippen bit his lip in a way that told Gideon he was probably curious, but then he shook his head, violently, and stared at his hands. "Uhm, I—"

"We," Gideon prompted, because Pippen was not solely responsible for this.

"It was my fault," Pippen said, worrying his cuticles. He hadn't put his gloves on and he'd ripped them all bloody. "I... I wanted to let off some steam. I... I didn't realize they were stock, I just wanted to scream at something that couldn't scream back. I... I came to make amends." He looked up into the woman's face, and like Gideon, saw no mercy there. Her eyebrows were drawn down in fury and her sardonic smile was replaced with hot burning anger.

"Ben!" she called sharply. "Ben! Get in here!"

There was a clatter from somewhere in the farmhouse, probably, and then a door deep in the stockroom of the shop opened, and in a moment, the slighter man who'd held the pistol on them came hustling out of the bowels of the building. He had curly brown hair, placid blue eyes, and not quite enough beard growth to be an actual beard.

Those sweet blue eyes took in Pippen, young and miserable, and Gideon, older but still guilt-ridden, and they tried to harden.

Tried.

Gideon prayed for a little bit of mercy. "Sir," he said haltingly. "We... we wanted to... at least let us fix your fence."

Ben's eyebrows went up. "Is that all?"

"Anything," Pippen said hoarsely. He cleared his throat and met Gideon's eyes, and tried again. "Anything to help," he said, his voice firmer. "Fix the fence. A vet for the stock." He grimaced. "Hospital bills for your employee?"

"We have insurance," Ben said in a stony voice, and Pippen's teeth drew blood in his bottom lip. Ben let out a sigh. "But what we don't have—"

"Ben!" the woman snapped, and he held out his hand.

"We don't have workers to take Jeremy and Aiden's places," he told her bluntly. "Jeremy's out for a month, minimum—and he's going to need someone to take care of him for part of that time, no matter how much he says he won't."

99

Ariadne's razor gaze raked over Pippen before landing on Gideon. "That one," she said with a nod at Gideon, "can do a day's work. *That* one," she said, scrutinizing Pippen critically, "doesn't know how yet."

"We'll have to teach him," Ben said, the patience in his voice reassuring. "Look—they asked us what we need, and I say we let them give it to us." His voice dropped. "What can it hurt? I mean…." He grimaced. "Wouldn't Jeremy say they deserved a second chance?"

"Jeremy never hurt anybody," she snapped, but whatever Ben had meant by that, the barb had obviously gone deep. "He… and when he realized what he was doing, he stopped."

Ben gave the Gideon and Pippen an unreadable glance. "Ari, what do you think they're doing here?"

She scowled at the both of them through surprisingly strong brows. "Buying yarn," she said pointedly, staring at something in Pippen's hands.

Gideon glanced down to what she was looking at and saw a skein with a pale fawn color, with specks of wildflowers purple, gold, blue, and orange scattered across the strands.

"That too," Gideon said rashly. "Is there anyone here who can teach him how to knit?"

She let out a breath, and Pippen was so surprised he practically juggled the yarn.

"Jeremy can," she said harshly. "When your friend here sits with him. He's got some bruised organs, a bruised spine, some cracked ribs, a concussion, and a dislocated shoulder. He'll be home in five days, give or take, and in the meantime, your boy can help me in the store while I tend stock and you help Craw in the mill." She sighed and turned around to a large rack of what looked to be pattern books that sat behind the register. "And go find yourself a size H crochet hook over from that rack over there." She pointed to the wall on the other side of the hall back to the stock room, which held hooks and needles.

"You think?" Ben asked, and his eyes were alight.

"Have I ever been wrong?" she said, a seemingly reluctant warmth creeping into her voice.

"Nope."

"Wrong about what?" Gideon asked as Pippen went to the rack of hooks and needles.

"It's her superpower," Ben said proudly. "She can spot a crocheter from a knitter in a newbie. It's uncanny. Most people have to try both crafts, but she knows immediately."

Over at the racks they all heard Pippen say, "Oh—hello."

"Persy, don't talk to that ma—" Ariadne began.

"Hewwo," came a voice, young, and obviously hampered in some way with the pronunciation. "'Oo werning to cwochay?"

"Yeah." Pippen let out a breath. "Don't tell me you know already."

The little girl laughed. "No—bu' Jewemy gon' teash me."

Ariadne's expression crumpled a little. "Yeah, he will, baby," she said. "As soon as he's all better."

"Bad men," the little girl told Pippen soberly. "Dey scawed the cwidde's."

Gideon wasn't the only one in the store who could hear Pip swallow. "I'm sure they're sorry," he rasped. "For scaring the critters."

"Cwaw said der cousin—"

"That's all for now!" Ariadne intervened, rushing in to pick up the girl and drag her back behind the counter. "No more repeating what Craw says, okay?"

But Gideon grimaced. He could fill in the rest of that epithet himself, and he watched as Ben covered his mouth in an attempt not to laugh.

Ariadne scowled at him. "You laugh—but he's your husband. I thought after five years you would have taught him some manners."

Ben let his chuckle escape. "That way lies heartache and disappointment," he said, just as Pippen approached with another twist of the pretty yarn that had so captured him, as well as a hook, a pair of scissors, some yarn needles, and a little pouch to keep them in, as well as a canvas bag that would hold the whole works. There was a logo on the side, with a sheep and the store's name—CrawDaddy's Pacas and Yarn—on the side.

"Wow," Gideon said, eyebrows arching in surprise. "You... you, uhm, went to town there, Pip."

Pip gave him a smile—it was sad and strained, but it was still the closest thing to a real smile Gideon had seen since they'd left New York after finals, which Pip had taken early at his father's request. "Did you see the colors?" he asked, and the excitement in his voice may have been muffled by tears, and by shame, but it was still present. "They're...." He swallowed and looked nakedly up at Ariadne and Ben. "They're so beautiful."

Ben started to massage the back of his own neck. "Did you see the name of the colorway?" he asked, pointing to the label, which had the same grumpy sheep at a spinning wheel on it.

"Wedding Day," Pippen read, and looked up at Ben again. "Was this... you and your husband?" he asked hesitantly.

Ben shook his head. "Aiden designed that for his and Jeremy's wedding day. This summer."

Gideon wanted to groan. He wanted to throw himself between Pip and this emotional bomb, then grab the kid, pitch him in the SUV, and take off for New York, where nothing like this could hurt him again.

"They got married?" Pippen asked, and the expected guilt grenade wasn't there in his voice.

"Yeah," Ben said softly. "In the field up the hill. Craw planted it with wildflowers, just for them."

Pippen swallowed, and the look of wistfulness that crossed his face then stole what was left of Gideon's heart. "You and Craw, Jeremy and, uhm, Aiden—" He glanced at Ariadne. "You and your baby and...?"

"My husband, Rory," she said suspiciously, obviously as unsure as to where he was going with this as Gideon.

"You're family," Pippen said, his lips twisting a little. "You're family, and we hurt your family. You... you're not just down two men, you're worried about your business," he swept the shop respectfully with his eyes. "And your family."

"Yeah," Ariadne said softly.

"And we put them in danger," he said.

"Yeah," Ben confirmed. "You did."

"We'll do what we can to make it right." His voice was so level, so steady, that Gideon felt a shaft of pride where mostly pity had dwelled before. "We can't take it back, but... thank you. Thank you for giving us a chance to... to make what reparations we can. I... me and Gid appreciate that. Do you need us here tomorrow morning?"

Ben shook his head. "Craw's coming back tomorrow—be back the next day, seven a.m. sharp."

"Be back tomorrow," Ariadne contradicted. "Twelve-thirty." She raked Gideon with a flinty-eyed gaze. "I'll pick out the needles and ring them up with this."

"He's a knitter, you think?" Ben asked.

"Soldier," she said, those sharp eyes raking over Gideon. "They're always knitters."

"Hm," Ben said, nodding. "Fair. Why are you giving them your *valuable,*" he eyed Gideon and Pippen significantly, "class time to teach them yarn craft?"

"A hunch," she said, tilting her head.

"Wha' hunch, mama?" the little girl—Persy?—asked from her mother's arms, where she'd been watching the whole exchange with wide eyes. Gideon peered at her little face then, saw the scarring of the upper lip and the hearing aids and put that together with the speech impediment to arrive at a massive cleft palate when she was born.

"A hunch that these two cousin-fucking lunatics are worth it," Ariadne said bluntly, and then grimaced.

"Tha's *Cwa's* word, mama!" the little girl exclaimed, and Ben reached out his arms.

"Persy, how about you come with me and I'll give you some cookies."

"Why?"

"Because I want you to forget about Craw's word," he said bluntly.

"Okay." She reached out her arms, and Ariadne relinquished her hold on the child so she could ring up Pippen's purchases.

She eyeballed Gideon. "You—go get the yarn of your choice and I'll wind it for you. Make sure it's from there." She waved a hand, and Gideon got an impression of yet another rack of yarn—the store was packed with stands and shelves and even pegboards where the walls should have been, all of them stuffed with yarn in the same complicated looking twist.

"What's the dif—" he started.

"I'll tell you tomorrow," she snapped. "Now go so I can wind these."

He had no idea what winding was or why it needed to be done to yarn that looked pretty tightly wound, but he was still so astonished by what Pippen had done, had said, by the courage he'd shown in these few moments in this little shop, that he wasn't going to argue.

He was just going to pull out his own personal card, eschewing his work expense card, and pay for the items that had added up so quickly. Then he was going to sit at the table in the back of the store with Pippen for a minute, both of them looking over the instruction books they'd bought, and try to figure out how this day had gone so very wrong.

THE WRONG SORTS OF MEMORIES

"No," AIDEN hissed, conscious that Jeremy lay sedated on the other side of the hospital curtain. Oh God—he was having flashbacks to the last time, no matter how often he tried to tell himself that this wasn't remotely the same. Last time, Jeremy hadn't asked for help—he'd just hidden their friend and taken the near-fatal beating, hoping Aiden would forgive him if he didn't make it. This—this was different. Jeremy had been heroic—of course he had. He'd saved the little girl they'd *all* give their lives for. "Absolutely not."

"Aiden," Craw said, his voice ringing with an odd note, one that Aiden hadn't heard a lot in all their years of acquaintance. Was that... patience? Oh *hell* no!

"Don't 'Aiden' me—"

"Boy," Craw snapped, and that was more like it. "Boy—listen to me. The doc said he's going to be okay, if he takes the time to recover, which he will *not* and you well know it if we're a man down."

Aiden grunted and hoped it didn't sound like a whimper. His back.... Aiden had seen it as they'd laid painkilling patches along his cracked ribs. The swelling and lividity had been truly, truly horrific, and Aiden had to remind himself repeatedly that Jeremy's kidneys and spine had been *bruised,* not broken. His leg, though—that was going to take at least six weeks to get the cast off, but other than that? He was going to be okay after some time laying on his side, drugged loopy but not completely out of his mind. God—why Jeremy? But this time, at least, Aiden knew.

Jeremy had been closest, and he'd done what good men do. Protect the weaker, protect the people they loved.

"He's going to be okay," Aiden repeated shakily, scrubbing his face with a shaking hand.

"He is," Craw murmured. "And Ari called Stanley—you and me get his spare room tonight, which is right friendly of him. Do you...." Craw hesitated over this, and well he might. "Are you going to stay here for the week, or are you coming back with me?"

Oh, that was a terrible choice. This was their *season*. Yes, knitting—particularly in Colorado—seemed to be an all-weather sport, but like every other retail business, Christmas was when *everybody* was buying stock, and with knitting, people lost their minds in a way that kept food on the table for the next year. Aiden could never figure out how people thought they could knit a year's worth of yarn in a month, but by God, people did try. It was like Thanksgiving was a boxer's bell to a truly horrific melee and suddenly tiny grandmothers were elbowing grown men in the kidneys to fight their way to that one skein of yarn that was going to fix all their family problems for the next year.

And far be it for Aiden and Craw to tell them no, even if they knew it meant some of their gorgeous yarn was going to become "legacy stash" in somebody's cupboard.

While they spent much of summer and fall preparing the fleeces of the spring for use, that didn't mean that December wasn't fever pitch work time, either. If nothing else, they had to run at least one shipment a day to the post office to keep up with the website sales.

But Aiden wanted to be there for his husband, god*dammit*. That word still had some newlywed shine to it—Aiden didn't want to waste that shine pining for his man in a hospital, four hours away from home.

But the mill was their livelihood. *Their* livelihood. Throughout the good times—and there'd been some—and the bad times—some of those too, the mill had kept them fed and working. Even *if* one of these guys turned out to be a decent worker, he still wouldn't replace Jeremy, who had nearly nine years of experience under his belt.

But he'd still be better than no man at all—and someone to look after Jeremy would be a load off Aiden's mind, as well as a help to those in them mill trying to catch up. Aiden glanced toward the closed curtain and sighed. Jeremy was dozing, sedated, at the moment, but if Aiden woke him up and asked him if he wanted Aiden to stay, he'd be coherent enough to answer, and medicated enough to answer honestly.

Aiden had to respect that.

"Jer?" he said, opening the curtain and venturing in. To his surprise he saw Jeremy was awake, brown eyes wide open and calm as they sought out Aiden's.

"Hey, boy," he said softly. "How we doing?"

Aiden sat next to him and took his hand. "I would really rather not do this again," he said with a pained sigh.

"You are telling me," Jeremy agreed, sounding irritated.

Aiden smiled and kissed Jeremy's battered knuckles. "Craw just told me the damnedest thing."

"Yeah?"

"Those two yahoos who spooked the animals came into the store this afternoon and asked Ari how to make it up to us. Can you believe that?"

Jeremy hmmd. "That's… that's a good thing," he said after a moment. "What did they have in mind?"

"A good thing?" Aiden felt his anger all over again. "Jeremy, they could have killed you, and you think that's a good thing?"

Jeremy gave Aiden one of those smiles that reminded Aiden that he was, in fact, the older of the two of them. It didn't happen often—Aiden had learned to pay attention. "Boy, I live a good life. I am surrounded by people I love and I do a thing that fills my soul. I live in one of the prettiest places on earth, and I have a husband and a dog. I did not start out deserving this life. I hungered for it—but I did a lot of bad things before it hit me that I didn't want to hurt people just to survive. You can't say I'm worth all your love, worth all your forgiveness, and not give those boys a second chance." His eyes searched Aiden's face for understanding. "I don't get a free pass cause you love me, boy. It needs to be part of your soul."

Aiden's body, his face, his expression, escaped every roadblock he had in place to control them. His brows drew down and his mouth shook and the tightness in his throat absolutely would not let him speak for a moment, before the whole works collapsed and he sobbed into Jeremy's hand. "They hurt you," he gasped, and Jeremy pulled his hand away and used it to cup Aiden's cheek.

"But they didn't kill me. And even if they had, boy, they didn't mean to. I suspect, from what Craw told us, that bit of foolishness had everything to do with their own demons and not a thing to do with us. Let them make amends—for me?"

And Aiden couldn't do anything but nod for a moment, and let the sobs shake out of his chest, his relief and his anger and his worry so acute, they left no room for anything else.

By the time he'd calmed down, Jeremy's eyes were closed in sleep. Aiden felt Craw's hand on his shoulder and glanced up.

"What'd he say?" Craw asked.

"He said to let the boys work," Aiden said through a dry throat. "But I didn't get a chance to ask him about leaving tomorrow."

"Go," Jeremy mumbled. "Craw, make him go. Stanley and Johnny'll visit. If I learned anything since the last time, it's that I'm not gonna be alone."

Craw bent down then and kissed Jeremy's forehead, a gesture that surprised Aiden only a little. Craw hadn't just mellowed with the last eight years—he'd become more open. He'd stood before God and everyone and told the world that Jeremy and Aiden were his kin. He'd married Ben and told them all how much he loved his man. He'd faced the possibility of devastating loss and by God pulled his family through the hard times and into a hopeful tomorrow—he had nothing to prove to anybody by being an asshole when his people needed comfort.

"We would never leave you alone, Jeremy," Craw said softly.

"Not since my first trip here," Jeremy murmured, and Aiden was brought back to that moment, Jeremy almost exuberant, because once the painkillers had kicked in, having two friends in his hospital room with hamburgers was the closest thing to a birthday party he'd ever had in his life. They'd given him more since then—so much more—but his point had been made. Not even back then, when as far as they knew, his next step out of the little room in the back of the barn would be the one that had him rabbiting down the road, had they left him alone.

He had faith.

They'd have faith too.

"We'll be by in the morning," Aiden murmured, standing so he could lean down, feel his warmth, comfort him with his nearness. "If you're still feeling it, I'll go back with Craw and try to catch us up for Christmas."

110

Jeremy smiled a little and accepted Aiden's nuzzle of his temple. "Love you, boy," he said, falling into sleep again. "It'll be okay."

Aiden stood and squared his shoulders, moving aside as a nurse bustled in and started checking monitors and asking Jeremy questions. It was time to go.

"Why can't they just let them sleep?" Aiden muttered as they walked out. "I never got that. Last time, Jeremy would be in so much pain, and the minute the meds kicked in and he could just zone out, some damned busybody would come in and start checking vitals and asking him to pee in a cup—fucking infuriating."

"They're taking care of him," Craw said. "Annoyingly so, which has a lot in common with some people I know."

It took a moment for Aiden to realize Craw had actually said that. He turned his head slowly and scowled. "Here I was, just thinking you'd mellowed."

"Do you see me hauling ass to Granby with a shotgun to kill the two assholes who did this?" Craw asked.

Aiden had to chuckle because the thought occurred to him too. "No."

"Then that's both of us."

And it was.

New Skills

"HEY, PIP," Gideon murmured. "How's your, uh, thing with the yarn coming?"

Pippen sat crosslegged on his bed in his father's Colorado chalet and looked up from the yarn thing happening in his hands.

"It's...." He scowled. "It's supposed to square," he confessed, holding his yarn thing up in exasperation. The colors were still lovely—particularly in the oppressive furnishings of the chalet. Dark oak furniture, black tiled floors with dark brown throw rugs and black and brown bedding—he had to have three lamps on to see his own damned computer, not to mention the mangled thing he was creating in his lap. "It's more... trapezoidal. Come in, Gideon—have I ever not told you to come in?"

Gideon grunted, probably because he was trying to find professional reasons for them not to be friends. Pippen understood intellectually—Gideon was on the old man's payroll, right? He was supposed to answer to the old man, and that meant they shouldn't get too close, and Pippen shouldn't trust him too much, and Gideon should never, ever, ever keep a big flaming secret like Pippen's dating history for the past year from his employer, and he should definitely *never* look at Talbot Madison like he would decimate the old man at the knees if he ever raised a hand to Pippen again.

Pippen definitely trusted Gideon Haze with his life—and as for coming into his bedroom? Well, Pippen would trust him with a lot more than that, but first he had to, well, actually kiss a boy to figure out if that was really what he wanted. He'd kissed a few—a few had slept over and Pippen had suffered their hands on his skin but not much else. It wasn't that he didn't find *men* attractive—he really, really did. But the boys he'd taken back to the apartment he shared with Gideon were just that. Boys. He'd be deep in a kiss, and enjoying the simple luxury of human touch, and then, unbidden, would come the memory of Gideon, locking eyes with Pippen's father and Talbot Madison's hand stopping in midair.

Would *this* boy do that for him?

Probably not. They were all as callow and as scared as Pippen was.

But Gideon would. When Pippen felt like he was half the man Gideon was, maybe he'd have the courage to take Gideon to his room and do all those things he'd been dreaming about with those boys, but had never been able to follow through on.

But whether they ever did that or not, Gideon was *always* welcome in his room.

And in this case, he swung inside with his own bag of yarn, needles, and instruction book in his hand. He pulled the desk chair up to the side of Pippen's bed, and like they had in the yarn shop, took all the stuff out and laid it on the bed, where he stared at it in confusion.

"Oh my God," he said after a moment. "You've actually made a thing."

Pippen grimaced. He'd followed the directions—that was all. "It's a misshapen thing," he muttered. "I… I need to figure out why it's creeping. See?"

Gideon looked at the trapezoid forming under his fingers and nodded, then held up his two sticks and the string tangled between them. "Look—if you can help me cast on, I'll take a look at your not-square and see if I can spot the problem."

"But I'm supposed to learn one and you're supposed to—"

Gideon held up a hand. "Look, Pip—I don't know if you noticed, but we're both in the same shitpile here. We're going to have to help each other out."

Pip nodded, and filed the philosophy away for other things men should know but he didn't. Then he unraveled whatever the hell Gideon had been working on—knitting was *not* it—and stared at the how-to book.

"Hm...." He stared at the diagrams some more, and then picked up the needle and made the same slipknot he'd used to start the crocheting. Then he followed it up by moving the yarn... so. And doing the thing... so. And....oh. That was all?

He repeated until he had a series of secure loops on the needle, figuring thirty would do.

He held up the needle and said, "Okay, so I think you're making this too hard."

Gideon gave him a baleful look. "How in the hell did you do that?" He held up Pip's work. "I think you've got to do a chain-thingy at the end of each row to give yourself room to make the first stitch."

Pip brightened, feeling like the entire world had been suddenly gifted with sunshine, and exchanged projects with Gideon. "That's brilliant, Gid—thanks."

Gideon took his line of stitches and *hmm*ed, and then took the other knitting needle and studied the how-to book again. Pip went to work ripping out the mangled parts of his wannabe square and then starting to crochet again before he glanced up to see how Gideon was doing.

Gideon had put his knitting down and was staring at Pippen with troubled eyes.

"What?" Pippen asked.

"Why is this so important to us?"

Pippen swallowed. "Because I fucked up," he whispered.

"We fucked up," Gideon said automatically.

"No—this one's on me, Gid. I fucked up. I'm the one who said 'let's get out of here and raise some hell.' You… you came along for the ride."

Gideon blew out a breath. "You weren't the only one who needed to blow off steam," he muttered. "God, Pippen—I hope…." He shook his head, tightening his lips, and suddenly that wasn't enough.

"Hope what?" Pippen asked, feeling like he was begging.

"I… I hope every day you forget what your old man is screaming in your face," Gideon said after a moment. "I hope that you know, somehow, that you are more and better than the shit he says to you. I… I can't fucking stand it, watching him do that to you. I'd quit—"

"You can't!" Pippen begged, suddenly near tears. "Gideon, you can't quit!"

"No," Gideon said, meeting Pippen's eyes. He had the most amazing, soulful eyes, big and nearly black, with thick black lashes. Someone in Gideon's family line was Dominican—he'd said that once—and his eyes were that legacy.

"No?" Pip whispered.

"No, I can't quit," Gideon said, his lips twisting in a way that made the pronouncement personal. "I… not when he can get to you like that. But today—today he made me crazy. I let him get to me, and I nearly blew it for the both of us."

Pippen blew out a breath. "I need to stand up to him," he said after a moment. It was a lot easier to bully a bunch of farm animals around a pond with his snowmobile than stand up to his old man—but he'd learned that day that the cost was far too high.

"I'm not sure how," Gideon said. "He threatens you with everything from conversion therapy to destroying your trust—"

115

"He can't do either of those things," Pippen said, uncharacteristically confident. "I looked them both up. I contacted my bank and a lawyer *not* under my father's thumb. He can't do any of that shit to me. I… I sort of put stuff in place, so if he tries he'll get, you know, prosecuted for stealing."

Gideon chuckled, the sound mean and filthy and… *ooh.* Pippen's groin ached just hearing a laugh like that from the normally unflappable Gideon Haze. "Good on you, Pip. See? You can too stand up to him. You just do it smart."

Pip gave him a rather bashful smile. "I… I want my education. Is that so bad?"

Gideon shook his head. "No—"

"It is if it costs me my soul," Pippen said, answering it for himself. He could see Gideon would give him anything, even absolution he didn't deserve. If he was going to be a man—the kind of man who deserved Gideon—he had to not ask for it. He sighed. "I just need to put stuff in place so I can break away from him and live on my own." He swallowed. "And then… then you could be free. You wouldn't have to… to be my friend. If you didn't want to."

"I want to." The intensity in Gideon's voice made Pippen glance up. Those gorgeous, fathomless eyes were fixed on his face.

"I want you to," Pippen whispered. "I… I don't want to do anything that took you out of my life, Gideon."

Gideon nodded. "Then…then we won't. I'll work for the old man until you figure out a way, then… then we'll be in each other's lives just… just because."

Pippen managed a smile. "Because we want to," he said, knowing he was letting some of his longing slip through, and not caring.

"Because I want to," Gideon murmured, and Pippen stared at him, wondering if he could possibly mean what that sounded like it meant. But Gideon was suddenly busy with his needles and his yarn again, thrusting the needle into the loop and trying to wind another loop around it. Failing. "But that still doesn't explain why we're doing this because that angry crazy lady told us to."

Pippen sighed and picked up his own work. "Maybe because this is their lives," he said after a moment. "And she wants us to see just a little part of what we almost unraveled."

Gideon let out a sigh and gave up the stitch before trying again. "That's real poetic," he said.

"Thank you."

"Maybe she's hoping we give it up and skewer ourselves with the needles and she'll have her revenge."

Pippen chuckled like he was supposed to. "But she gave me a hook."

"Well, get going, boy, and hook yourself a noose. I'm not the only one dying for my penance."

Pippen laughed some more, and together they struggled with their sticks and their string and their self-imposed tasks of trying to make things make sense.

"OKAY, GOOD, Pippen," Ariadne said softly, looking over his shoulder. "And good with the sides—you've got a knack for this."

Pippen looked at her with glowing eyes. "Really? Do you think so?"

The woman's face was pointed and angular, right down to an almost masculine jaw. But the look she gave him was soft and kind, and he wanted to cry at her feet and, again, beg her forgiveness. "Yeah, I do," she said softly. Then she looked at Gideon's work and sighed. "You keep doing what you're doing, and me and Gideon are going to do some hands-on readjusting. You ready for that, Gideon?"

"Yes, Miss Ari," Gideon said dutifully, and Pippen glanced up to see if Ariadne caught the automatic respect he'd given her. She was a little harsher with Gideon than she was with Pippen—but maybe that's because Gideon responded with that automatic, military respect.

Pippen watched for a moment as Ariadne manipulated Gideon's hands, his mind filing away what she was doing so he could help Gideon later. He was pretty sure he got it. After Gideon had gone to bed, he'd looked up beginning knitting videos online and he felt like he understood the basic underpinnings of the two crafts. He was really interested in why Ariadne had felt like he could crochet when knitting seemed to be equally his thing, but he'd wait until Gideon was on a roll to ask her.

The peace of the yarn store seeped into his bones for a few moments as Ariadne helped Gideon and he worked on his own thing, and he glanced out the window to see fat flakes of snow pelting the windows. "Will they be okay?" he asked, nodding at the snow. "Driving down from Boulder?"

She let out a breath and nodded. "Craw's a good driver," she said. "And they left three hours ago, so they'll be coming down this side of the valley now. They missed the worst of the storm."

Gideon spoke, his voice low and rumbly. "Your friend—you're sure your friend is all right?"

She sighed. "He's got to have his leg set—they found a hairline fracture of his tibia in X-Rays last night—they missed it at first because his back needed to be stitched up and they were worried about the cracked ribs and internal bleeding. And because Jeremy doesn't complain about anything, but that's another story. Anyway, yeah. He'll still be ready to come home in four days and he'll still need nursing. Until then, we'll take all the help we can get with the stock and with the mill and such. Aiden's little brothers took care of their critters down at their place, but we'll probably have Pippen here take care of them tomorrow—"

"He can't drive in snow," Gideon said, just as Pippen said, "I don't know how to drive in snow."

Ariadne stared at both of them. "That was awfully... synchronous."

Pippen grimaced. "I... there's some stuff I'm not good at," he said. "Gideon's sort of... well, my dad pays him to be my driver and my bodyguard and stuff."

Her dark, bold eyebrows arched up to her hairline. "You're his...." She made the universal finger pointing thing. "Bodyguard?"

Gideon grimaced. "For lack of a better word," he said, meeting Pippen's eyes. Pippen remembered that moment in his room the night before and hugged it to his chest. Gideon remembered it too.

"Okay, so I get that argument you keep having over whose fault it is," she murmured. Then, "Why? Why was it so necessary that you come out here and yell at some sheep and alpacas not doing a fucking thing to mess up your day?"

Pippen took a deep breath and remembered that part of being a man was owning up. "My... my dad's sort of a piece of work," he muttered. "We... we were getting some of that out of our system, before we...." He shrugged.

"Before I killed him," Gideon said, voice flat, no play in it at all.

Ariadne stared at him in surprise, and then, before Pippen could be afraid of what she'd think of the two of them, in understanding. "Oh," she said softly. "Okay. So next time that happens, you go and take your frustration out on sticks and string. Both of you," she ordered, looking from one to the other. "That's our saving grace here. Craw's got a mouth like a sailor and a temper to match when he's working. We get pissed at him,

119

knit on our breaks, and remember that he's a decent guy trying to feed a lot of people on a shoestring, and it gets better."

"Fair," Gideon said, with a quick, worried glance at Pippen.

A glance Ariadne caught. "No yelling?" she asked courteously.

"Not with Pip," Gideon said, jumping in immediately.

"Gid, I'm not an infant," Pippen protest. He got it. Intellectually he understood how yelling over machinery could be a job necessity, particularly if you were trying to give directions. He wasn't an idiot—he'd seen street workers and movies that had factories in them.

But that was intellectually. *Emotionally....* He swallowed, remembering that big, gruff, red-bearded man with the shotgun. He'd been *so* angry, and for a moment, Pippen had feared for his life. And then, realizing *why* the man was so angry, he'd *wished* the man had killed him. Anything, *anything,* but face the realization that he could have killed a person—a *child*—by being stupid and angry—God, he'd been lucky.

But....

Ari's hand on his shoulder, gentle and strong, stopped the trembling in his hands as he tried to make his next stitch. "No yelling," she said simply. "I get it."

"I'm sorry," he whispered.

"We've got something else for you to do," she said. "Gideon, you stay here and keep... uhm... working. Pippen, come with me. It's time to feed the stock."

DAY JOBS

STANLEY REALLY hated seeing Jeremy in the hospital again—but he was sure happy to be able to have him to talk to.

"So," he said, the sweater he was working on for Johnny just flying off the needles, "we've got time this year, and money, but my boss and her family are staying back east for Christmas." Oh, he loved his boss's darling daughter, Candace—she'd been in tears as she'd confessed over the phone to him that she was staying because she'd found an unworthy boy to keep her in New York, and her mothers were, of course, flying to meet her. "And I'm going to really miss them," he confessed, hating that he was whining. He couldn't help it, though. Margaret and her true love and Margaret's children—they were the family that had gotten him through nearly twenty years in Boulder, Colorado, as the floor manager for all of Margaret's businesses. This was his first year without them, and it hurt.

But Jeremy really *was* the world's sweetest guy because he didn't tell Stanley to go piss off, or even pretend to nap. He just sat there and listened, working gratefully with the sock yarn and needles that Stanley had brought him, producing thick and sturdy cabled socks without hardly looking. If Stanley didn't know Jeremy and Aiden spent the winter locked up with DVDs and their knitting and not much else to keep them company, he'd be mad jealous over Jeremy's knitting skills, but as it was, he was, again, just grateful for the company.

"You know," Jeremy said as Stanley paused for breath, "Aiden and me, we didn't get a chance to decorate the house. I'm gonna be laid up until after New Years with this bullshit—" He wiggled his toes and gave a hard breath around the healing ribs. "—and I'm thinking maybe, if you or Johnny want to, you can come decorate *our* place. That would be a load off my mind."

Stanley paused, both his fingers and his trilling mind, and rolled that one over in his mind. "That would be... like an outing," he said, loving the idea. He and Johnny really wished they lived closer to Craw's little slice of heaven—except they both loved the city and hated getting shit on their Italian leather shoes. But they did love the people, and for all their gruffness—and bluntness—Craw's family in Granby was always the first on the phone with offers of help, or even just, "Hey, how are ya, it's been a minute, you all okay?"

"We could make a day of it," Stanley said happily. "You're going back Friday, right?"

"Yessir," Jeremy said.

"Well, that's our day off. The weather's supposed to hold good for a couple of days—maybe we could bring you home and decorate the house while you're sleeping off the ride."

"We got some fresh off the mountain Christmas trees in town," Jeremy told him. "You might want to get one for yourselves. And there's a fairly spectacular Christmas fair over the weekend. Craw's got a booth, but you all might be able to pick out the ornaments."

Stanley's fingers stilled on the sweater and he looked into space, imagining the drive—which he wasn't fond of—and Aiden and Jeremy's little house, which he *was* fond of. The cats would be fine with some extra kibble and some water, and for a day, they could be tourists in a charming little village that, Stanley knew for a fact, had their own tree in the center of town, lit by school children and decorated too, on the Saturday after Thanksgiving.

It was charming—rustic, charming, and they'd be doing Craw's family a solid by taking Jeremy home.

"Sounds perfect," Stanley sighed, his fingers moving again on the wool. He paused. "But Jeremy, won't you be camped out on the couch? I mean, that's a rough place to have company in, when you can't get away from us."

Jeremy grunted. "I'll still be on all the good drugs," he admitted. "You might want to just let me sleep if my eyes close. You okay with that?"

Yeah, Stanley thought happily. "Let me ask Johnny—you ask Aiden when he calls. This might work after all."

JEREMY WAS comforted when it *did* work. Stanley had brought him knitting and decent food during his hospital stay, and he would be forever grateful. But the best thing Stanley did for him was take him home—and make sure Aiden and Craw didn't have to take time out of their mill work to get him there.

Ariadne had kept him briefed on how the "help" had been doing. Jeremy had commiserated thirdhand as poor Gideon got put through the paces Jeremy himself had needed to master when he'd been working in the mill. Ari said he was doing fine—competent and smart, probably from his time in the military, but also distracted, mostly by worry for his companion.

"I thought you said the boy was doing the animals and other things?" Jeremy told her, confused.

"Yeah—and he's not stupid. I think…." Ariadne let out a frustrated sigh. She and Jeremy had always been real good at shorthand, ever since they'd shared adjoining beds in this selfsame hospital, but Jeremy got the feeling what she wanted to say was hard to put into words. "Gideon told us not to yell at him. For that reason alone we didn't put him in the mill, 'cause sometimes Craw yells because he has to."

"That was a smart move, right there," Jeremy agreed. "You all told Aiden not to get short with him, right?"

"Well, Aiden mostly doesn't have a thing to do with either of 'em," Ariadne admitted. "I think he scares them both with his silence. He's still mad, Jer. They hurt you, and they both know it, and… well, it makes things uncomfortable. But something about the way Gideon protects Pip—it's… it makes me think that that horrible thing, that demon, that drove them both to scream at the stock and cause a ruckus—it's a big demon. It's a scary one. I know they both wanted to be here on Saturday, but Pip's old man—the rich guy who owns the big house—has some sort of function that they both have to be at. It's like… like they'd rather come *here,* and work off a debt that it hurts them to look at, than go *there,* and deal with the scary man who made Pippen so afraid."

Jeremy sucked in his breath and regretted it because of the cracked ribs. He understood those people, the scary men who yelled.

"Sounds like Mario Carelli to me," he said, trying not to let his fear get the best of him.

Ariadne sucked in her own breath, free and clear with no pain. "Jeremy, that's a powerful name," she said, talking about the man who'd almost beaten him to death five years ago. "This guy, he's rich and—"

"Just 'cause he's rich doesn't mean he's not mean," Jeremy said. "Just means he's better at not doing mean stuff that gets him busted. We used to stay away from the rich mean guys, Ari. We'd rook the middle class, but we wouldn't go after the super-rich bastards 'cause they wouldn't have us arrested, they'd have us *killed.* You make sure Craw's mortgage is in good, trustworthy hands, you hear me now? Any debt he's got, make sure it can't be sold off somewhere Pip's father can get it. 'Cause if he *can* get it, he can call that marker in right now, and we're all out on our ass and there goes all Craw worked for, you hear me?"

"Jeremy...," Ariadne said softly. "That's extreme—"

But Jeremy had seen those guys in action, those rich, powerful men who weren't mobsters but worse. Mobsters came after you with guns—rich guys came after your *dreams,* and they smiled in your face and said the right words and there went your home. Jeremy and his old man, they'd fled towns from the rich guys taking the houses of the people that Jeremy and Oscar had merely taken a few dollars from.

"Just do me a favor," Jeremy said, "and make sure his mortgage is safe. Have Ben look into it. See who's buying. Look at the guy in the big house. If he's mad at us for dealin' with his kid, he can make shit go south. And it sounds like his kid is tryin' to be decent. Bad guys don't like that, you understand?" All the knowledge he'd had as a con man, that he thought he'd given up a long time ago, floated up now to help him protect his family.

"Okay," Ariadne said softly. "I'll ask Pippen too. He... he's a sweet kid, Jeremy. His father—I think Gideon isn't just worried that his dad will yell at him, if you know what I mean."

And Jeremy got it. He'd seen boys like that—boys who had to scream at the sky because screaming at the person who bruised their hearts, or their bodies, was right out of the realm of possibility.

"I look forward to meeting them both," he said with dignity. But then, he also looked forward to sleeping in his own bed—or at least his own couch—and having Aiden there in the evenings to talk to. And God, did he want his damned dog. She was such simple companionship, but she sure did settle his heart when he was home.

He hung up looking forward to being in pain in his own house (hey, when you were in the hospital, sometimes it was the best option) and thoroughly unsettled.

BEN MCCUTCHEON didn't talk much about his life in the city, but most of that was because he loved his life in Granby so much more. Most people didn't know this about Rance Crawford, but when he decided to talk about books or music or politics, he was not only razor sharp but also sardonic and funny, and—given his occupation as business owner, mill operator, stock wrangler, and fiber artist—he was also surprisingly aware of the ebb and flow of almost every current to affect the wind and water of his little corner of the world.

Ben could talk—or not talk—to Rance all day. Even listening to him bitch was entertaining—as, Ben figured, Rance frequently meant it to be.

But that was most of the reason Ben didn't talk about city life. The small part of why he didn't talk about city life was because he was ashamed. He'd worked as a software engineer, cleaning code from computer games—a Bug Man, as he'd called it—and he'd liked the work just fine. Still did a lot of it as a consultant, and it had helped Rance keep his land. But he'd done the work and had felt so... so *smug* about it. Yeah, he'd worked hard through school as an electrician, but he didn't have to *do* that anymore. For that time in the city, he'd felt that arrogance about living a life that didn't get his hands dirty. He didn't have to work food service or retail, and he felt like that made him better somehow.

It wasn't until he'd moved into his Aunt Gertie's home, had discovered all the work that went into living someplace that was his, in a sometimes inhospitable place, that he'd realized having skills like that was a worthwhile thing. He'd mowed his lawn and tended his tiny bit of stock—chickens, some bunnies, a sheep—and fixed up his Aunt's little house with efficiency and pride, and he'd watched as Craw and Ari and Jeremy and Aiden maintained Craw's mill with that same sort of efficiency and pride. All of them—all—had shown themselves tougher, more complex, simply *more* than he'd seen in those first months. Jeremy's beating, Ariadne's rough pregnancy, Aiden's responsibilities, the baby's medical difficulties, not to mention fires, floods, and damned near bankruptcy had forged the entire group of them into a tight, tough, *kind* little family unit, and Ben was embarrassed at how much of that he had to learn at Craw's knee.

But proud that he *had* learned it, when all was said and done.

And one of the things he'd learned was to trust the people he knew. When Ben had arrived in Granby five years before, he'd trusted everybody, the world, even. And Craw had shown him that even the grumpiest bastards could have a heart of gold. But the things that had happened to his family since had—while not darkening the sunshine that Rance seemed to love in him—simply made that sunshine more private, given to those deserving.

When the giant black town car pulled up in front of Craw-Daddy's 'Paca Farm and Shop, Ben wasn't sure what made him suspicious—but he was.

The shop and the house didn't used to be attached. But Craw, seeing the need for a bigger stockroom, had figured it would be easier to attach the two buildings and insulate the space between them. There was also a couch and a table back there, so his staff could take their breaks there, if the store was busy or something was going on in the house, and generally, it had been a good investment.

It also gave everybody who tended the shop a way to call for help or backup without looking like they were calling for help

127

or backup. A body could walk into the house and out through the shop door without attracting any attention at all, and as Ben watched the car pull up, he texted Ariadne, who was doing inventory for their next big mail order, and asked her to come listen at the door. He recognized the town car—it lived across the road at the big, mostly vacant ski chalet, and since Gideon and Pippen had started working at the mill in their efforts at atonement, Ben figured this could be something that needed a witness.

Ariadne and Craw hadn't been the only ones who had seen Pippen flinch or Gideon get all ruffly and protective. That big black car looked damned ominous.

So Ben plastered his best, most public sunshiny smile on his face as the bell rang to the store and a fiftyish, distinguished-looking man strolled in, wearing a black wool coat and store bought gray cashmere scarf and hat. Behind him was a driver, a paunchy, sixtyish man with a bitterly lined face in an honest to God chauffer's suit and hat, looking grim and blank and not particularly friendly.

Neither of them looked to be the knitterly sorts.

"Can I help you?" Ben asked, making sure to arch his eyebrows up so he looked pleasantly baffled and surprised.

"We're looking for my son," said the younger man—the rich one with the cashmere scarf. His face was relatively unlined, a nice, bland rectangle of a face. Some people might have said it was handsome. Pippen, for all his callowness, still had more character in his roundish face than his father did in his square-jawed one.

"And that would be?" Ben asked, keeping his own look bland. Craw had a garage—he kept a battered truck, an SUV for Ben, Ariadne's minivan when she was staying for a while, and, over the last few days, the smallish SUV that Gideon had driven him and Pippen in. He'd asked, full of humility and hat in hand, if they could hide his vehicle. Nobody in the store had asked why, but Ben had an inkling. By God, he did.

"Peregrine Madison," said the older man, his rheumy blue eyes flitting restlessly around the neat little store, with its rainbow of yarn skeins dripping from boards on the walls, on the shelves—every surface, really. "What is this place?"

"Peregrine who?" Ben asked. He didn't want to grace this man with an answer. Anybody who disdained Craw's yarn was not welcome there.

"Madison," the man answered, his upper lip curling up. "We live right across the road from you."

Ben blinked mildly at him. "Oh," he said airily. "Are you here this year? This is my sixth year, you know—I think you've only ever been here once before. Pleased to meet you." He held out his hand. "Ben McCutcheon. My husband owns this land."

He'd dropped the reference on purpose, just to watch Talbot Madison—yes, he knew the man's name—flinch.

He was not disappointed.

"Husband?" the man asked, that curled lip in evidence as he eyed Ben's extended hand with distaste. Ben dropped his hand but kept his smile.

"Yessir. I guess maybe we should buy ourselves a rainbow flag, but, you know, the yarn in the shop is pretty rainbow, so maybe not."

"Oh. Yarn." Madison scanned the store again but didn't seem any more impressed, which was too bad, Ben thought, because Craw had one of the best local yarn stores in the state.

"Yessir—yarn. Which you obviously don't want. About your son—how old is he? Should we get out a search party? Is he on his bicycle with friends? Does he have a cell phone?" These were, of course, ridiculous questions, but Ben was not admitting that he knew the boy. He got the distinct impression that Gideon would do anything to protect Pippen from his father, and so far, those two kids (as Ben thought of them, in spite of the fact that he wasn't much older) seemed to be making good on their promise of amends.

"He's twenty," Madison said with distaste. "And he's merely dodging a responsibility. I tracked his cell phone to this place. Why would it be here?"

"I have no idea," Ben lied baldly. "What sort of responsibility is he dodging? Did he forget to do his chores?"

Madison gave Ben a sort of narrow-eyed look that said Ben was, quite probably, an idiot. Well, Ben didn't think much better of Talbot Madison. "He was supposed to come with me to pick up a friend's daughter from the airport. The young lady is to be his date for the holidays, and I'm not particularly impressed with his inability to man up to that."

It was the "man up" that hit Ben hardest. He'd heard it all from his mother's relatives—but then, besides Gertie, they hadn't thought much of his gentle mother, either. Pippen was, quite obviously, gay—and Gideon was just as obviously, desperately in love with him. Suddenly Ben knew why the two of them would need to drive over a downed fence to scream at sheep—it was almost a healthy alternative to beating this guy over the head with a briefcase until he changed his entire personality.

"So, you're telling me your son is old enough to vote, almost old enough to drink, and old enough to drive, and you're here in our place of business because you are trying to tell him how to date." There was no question there. Ben nodded. "Well, can't say as I blame him for making himself scarce—but I think this sounds like a domestic situation that has not a fucking thing to do with anybody on this property, don't you?"

Until the curse word fell from his lips, Ben hadn't known he'd use it. Those were usually Craw's domain, but this man, this snide, disdainful man, had hit Ben McCutcheon's last fucking nerve.

Suddenly Talbot Madison's complete attention was focused on Ben, and Ben stared back, refusing to give ground. "This… this yarn store," he said carefully, "this belongs to you?"

"And my husband," Ben replied, taking a tiny bit of satisfaction from watching the man flinch from the word.

"You own the animals on the property?"

"Yes."

"Is there anything else here?"

"His mill and our home," Ben replied, and he could feel the menace coming from this man in rolling waves. Oh God. Jeremy's words to Ariadne had been right on target, he thought, keeping his panic to himself.

"Interesting. I take it you *like* living here?"

Oh yeah. It was a threat. "We do," Ben replied evenly. "I take it you can't wait to get back to New York?"

The man's eyes widened, and Ben realized he'd better have a damned good reason for knowing where Talbot Madison resided.

Then he realized he did.

"You're a financier who made a killing on Wall Street," Ben said dryly. "I'm hardly clairvoyant. And in spite of what you obviously think of us here, we're not stupid either. We like to know who our neighbors are." And now that he knew, he was going to do a whole lot of research to know how this obviously rich, obviously powerful man could hurt him and his family.

"And yet you don't know my son," Madison said slowly.

"Hasn't introduced himself," Ben replied with a shrug. At that moment he heard a long-legged, heavy stride on the stoop of the shop, and he prepared himself to look frantically at Aiden as he blew in with the cold.

"Aiden," he said, "this is—"

Aiden gave the two men a hard nod. "Craw says he needs you in the back. I'll take over the shop for a sec. Ariadne's class is gonna be here soon, and you need to get lunch."

Ben nodded, getting it. Ariadne's class was actually scheduled for tomorrow, and Aiden was in there because he didn't get physically intimidated. Which meant Aiden knew exactly who these people were and wanted his own shot at them.

"Can do," Ben said. He eyed Talbot and his chauffer. "Gentlemen," he said with a nod. "Too bad I couldn't interest you in some yarn." And with that, he used the door through the darkened stockroom to go back into the house.

He saw Gideon on his way through, hiding between a shelf and the entrance, close enough to listen but not close enough to be seen. Gideon's face was etched in stone, worry and unhappiness radiating from every line, but he held his finger to his lips as Ben passed. Ben nodded, and Gideon's look of relief was so profoundly grateful, Ben almost wanted to hold the boy.

God, these kids. He should be angry with them—he knew that. But not even Aiden was giving the two of them up, and that was saying something. When Ben was sure he couldn't be seen anymore from the doorway, he dodged behind a shelf and peered through, the better to see what Aiden would do when confronted with that much concentrated malice.

"You're not buying yarn?" Aiden said from the front of the shop.

"No, sir."

"Are you buying fleece?" Aiden asked.

"No," Talbot replied.

"Roving?" Aiden asked, his questions hard and sharp, like bullets.

"No, but—"

"Needles, hooks, looms, or spinning wheels?"

"No!" Talbot almost growled. "I don't want—"

132

"Stock? Are you here to sell us stock?"

"No, I'm here looking for my son—"

"Does your son want to buy any of these things?" Aiden asked.

"I have no idea," Talbot huffed. "How should I know?"

"I don't know, sir," Aiden shot back. "You're the one in the middle of a yarn shop about to get mobbed by little old ladies who want to capitalize on our rare fibers sale before Christmas!" And with that, he gestured toward a bucket of skeins, each in a different color or colorway, all of them with luxury fibers such as rabbit, chinchilla, cashmere, or qiviut spun in with the wool.

"Little old ladies?" Talbot asked, obviously caught off guard.

"And some young ones," Aiden replied, as though it was an obvious conclusion. "As far as I know, me, Craw, Ben and Jeremy are the only men who knit in Granby. Unless your son—"

"*My son does not knit!*" Talbot roared.

"*Then why are you looking for him in a yarn store?*" Aiden roared back. "You're the one standing at my counter, sir—don't get pissy with me!"

Talbot Madison glared at Aiden, his face red, his breath coming in pants, and it occurred to Ben that this man was not in great health. His skin was sallow, his nose was red—he looked like the typical walking heart attack, and for a moment, Ben feared the man would have that heart attack in their store.

Sadly not. He turned on his heel without another word and strode back out, his chauffer eating his dust—and apparently getting an earful as they went.

Ben waited until the town car peeled out of the driveway, the spray of gravel doing more damage to the paint job than the road, before he crept up to the front of the store again.

Gideon had already peeped out, and the young man looked like he wanted to faint as well, although he'd been a hard and sturdy worker in the mill.

"Oh God," Gideon breathed. "Mr. McCutcheon—"

"Ben," Ben corrected for the umpteenth time.

"Ben," Gideon repeated without thinking, "that was a really nice thing you did, and I'm grateful, but God, that was not smart."

"I know it," Aiden muttered. "I do. But as pissed as I am at you and Pip, I wouldn't turn a snake over to that guy—the snake would die of hypothermia."

Gideon let out a rough chuckle. "I appreciate it." He chuckled again. "And… uhm, when I tell Pip about that conversation, he's going to laugh for the first time in a month."

Ben chuckled too. "Aiden, you were brilliant," he conceded. "'Then why are you looking for him in a yarn store?'" He chuckled some more, helplessly, and almost hysterical. Oh God. That man could buy and sell this mill, this house, and this property, four, five, six times over, without batting an eyelash.

"Where's Pip?" Aiden asked, taking some of the giggle out of the conversation.

"He went with Ari," Ben said. "To prep the house. Jeremy's supposed to be here in a couple of hours, and she wanted to put in some of the stuff—you know, the toilet stuff and shower stuff and the steps to the bed—that'll help him get around."

Aiden grunted. "God. He's gonna make our lives miserable, you know," he said, but he had a smile on his face anyway, because he obviously missed Jeremy when he was gone.

"Unlivable," Ben agreed. "We won't be able to keep him out of the store."

Aiden eyed Gideon levelly. "Your boy gonna be able to take care of my man?"

They had decided that Pippen, who was pretty good with stock and hauling boxes but not good at all with any of the machinery, would be a good bet as Jeremy's companion until Jeremy could be trusted to get around on his own.

"Yessir," Gideon answered smartly. Ben judged the two men to be about the same age, but something about Gideon's military background—and Aiden's unquestioning self-possession— made Aiden the commanding officer.

Aiden nodded and let out a sigh before looking at Ben. "What can he do to us?"

Ben grimaced. "Before COVID? Not a damned thing. Craw's dad owned the place outright and Craw hasn't been late on taxes or fees a day on his life. Pays early when he can. But with the crash...." He gave Aiden a frustrated look. "We had to take out a loan on the place—especially after Rory and Ariadne moved in. It was the local bank, so I can get them to tell me if somebody comes sniffing, but...." He bit his lip. Tommy Marshall, their guy at the local bank, was a sweet guy in his sixties—but he wasn't Talbot Madison's match.

"Tommy Marshall?" Aiden asked, probably because his parents had needed to take out their own loan after the Estes fire had burned down their place. At Ben's nod he murmured, "Tommy's tougher than he looks. Call him up and ask him for a heads-up if he gets any nibbles. A big firm tried to buy up all the Estes Park loans after the fires, and Tommy put 'em off until he could find someone who wouldn't evict half the town. If he knows that situation's brewing, he'll at least tip us off."

"Will do," Ben said. Then, "So, uh, you gonna go meet Jeremy when he's here?"

Aiden gave him a shy, tired smile. "Well, yeah. My mom's dropping off casseroles for days, and Stanley and Johnny promised to bring takeout, since they're staying for the weekend." His smile took on a sad little twist. "That'll boost his spirits, you know. Jeremy's. He's always so tickled when he's got company. His entire body'll feel like it's on fire, but he'll be working to stay awake for company."

"Why?" Gideon asked, startling them both into staring at him. Gideon managed to look embarrassed. "I… I mean, even when I lived at home, I sort of hated company. Living at the Madison residences hasn't changed my mind any."

Aiden's eyebrows gave a very grown-up little quirk. "Depends on the quality of the company," he said dryly, and then, because he was the boy Ben and Craw loved, he gave an honest answer. "Jeremy's childhood was… unconventional. He was pretty much raised on the grift, you know? Having friends—friends he's not trying to screw over—stay with him because they care about him? To Jeremy, that's livin'." Aiden swallowed, and Ben saw his eyes grow shiny. When he spoke next, it was without bitterness or recrimination—it was a very gentle warning. "Jeremy's why we believe in second chances. He's why we didn't turn our backs on you and Pippen. And you almost took him out of the world. Make your own second chance count, right?"

"Right," Gideon said, his own voice throbbing.

For a moment, the yarn shop was silent, then Aiden took a breath. "I'm gonna go scarf some lunch so we can get that final batch of sock yarn dyed before they call." He smiled through eyes that were still a little red-rimmed. "My boy's comin' home."

"Yeah, he is," Ben said softly. "Yeah, he is."

"YOU SAID you'd text!" Ariadne told Stanley as she and Pippen scattered salt down the walkway in a panic.

"I'm sorry!" Stanley called from the fence, where Johnny had parked their SUV. "Jeremy was going to, but as soon as the road flattened out, he fell asleep and we didn't notice."

"I don't blame him," Pippen said earnestly, so glad for the snow boots that someone at Craw's mill had loaned him that he was almost in tears. God, he'd be hurting right now if he had to depend on the pricey, useless things he'd bought at a boutique last year. "As soon as I don't have to keep the car on the road with my mind powers, I'm out like a light too."

Stanley, a small man with white-blond hair, merry blue eyes, and a plump little mouth, laughed appreciatively. Pippen decided he liked him—and his brooding, dark-haired, Italianate mob-land-style boyfriend who was standing by the driver's side. The boyfriend, Johnny—who was wearing a long black wool coat and a fedora—looked like someone Pippen's father might know, but one of the nicer men, who'd smiled at Pippen as a kid.

"You let us know when the walkway is safe," the boyfriend said. "He's still not a big man—I can carry him and you people can carry all the crap he has to worry about to walk."

"Hey," Ariadne said, taking a shovel to the residual slush on the walkway as Pippen finished with the salt. "That reminds me—has anyone thought to text Aiden? He's going to have to finish up whatever he's doing to get down here, and I think his mother is waiting in the wings with a casserole or twelve."

"Well, she's going to just have to wait," Stanley said with a little flounce. "We brought steaks, and they're still steaming up the back of the car."

"Craw's favorite place?" Ari asked as Pippen tested the walkway. "You think Jeremy's up for that?"

"We'll cut it into little bites," Johnny said. "I… I think he'll like anything, honestly. Jeremy, he'll just want Aiden to say hello."

Ari nodded, and Pippen gave the walkway one more hard push with his boot, relieved when the tread stuck.

"I think we're safe," he said. "I'll go get the door."

He and Ariadne had just been finishing up prepping the house, and God—if Pippen hadn't felt horrible guilt and responsibility before, just seeing what they needed to install so the guy could go use the toilet helped him feel it *now*. Besides that, the house—snug and cozy, with two bedrooms and a bathroom in the upstairs and a kitchen, living room, mudroom, and bathroom in the downstairs—was so... so *sweet*. Aiden— who terrified Pippen when they were working, because he was big and gruff and angry—mustn't forget angry—*lived here*. He lived in this place with handmade lace valances, and well-worn, rectangular, masculine doilies on the recliner. He lived in the place with the felted rug in the entryway and the rustic picture of the wolf and the rabbit on the wall. The furniture was tough, worn, and comfortable, and there were area rugs in all the right places to keep your feet warm. There were rabbits and chinchillas in a small *heated* hutch behind the house, and Ariadne had brought the ginormous dog named, of all things, *Bluebell* with her to fix the place up because the dog was apparently *Jeremy's* and Pippen had sent Jeremy to the hospital and the dog had been depressed without him.

Oh God. Pippen was going to hell. There were not enough good things he could do for these people to make himself feel better for the bad thing that had almost happened. He'd fed the sheep and alpacas and a couple of cashmere goats in the barn and watched Ariadne's charming daughter in the shop and even cleaned Craw and Ben's kitchen after lunch and waited on customers over the last six days, but nothing had prepared Pippen for visiting Jeremy and Aiden's home and seeing the heart of the man he'd injured.

And then seeing what would be needed to accommodate Jeremy's injuries. He needed a ramp up the porch into the living room and a framework over the toilet and little chair inserts for the recliner so he didn't mess up his back anymore and pads on the couch in case the cuts on his back opened and *Pippen had done that.*

And after five days feeding the creatures in the barn, he wasn't feeling so hot about spooking the stock, either.

So as he was running food to the refrigerator and Jeremy's knapsack to the laundry room and Bluebell's kibble and water to her food spot in the mudroom, he was really hoping he'd be treated like crap. Like a servant. Like someone who was doing their penance in blood and humiliation.

He was so not expecting the two bright blue eyes of the little man with the white-blond hair to interrupt his bustling for an introduction.

"Hi—I'm Stanley," he said, sticking his hand out. "You must be Pippen, right?"

Pippen nodded, wishing he'd disappeared. "I... uh... I did this. I... I'm the reason Jeremy's hurt." Perhaps Stanley didn't know.

"Yes, but you didn't mean to," Stanley said, like that was all the forgiveness Pippen needed. "And look at you, helping out at the store and here—you'll have to meet Jeremy. I understand you'll be his company after Johnny and I leave."

They were in the mudroom where Bluebell was presently horking down dog food like she'd never seen kibble before, and Pippen had to peer over Stanley's shoulder to see the man himself, laid on his side on the couch, covered in one of the almost ridiculously lush throws from the back of the couch and fast asleep.

"What does he like to do?" Pippen asked, thinking if entertaining Jeremy was one of his duties then he should do a stand-up job of it.

Stanley laughed a little. "Knit or crochet," he said. "Talk. Read. Watch old movies. Play card games. Simple things."

"I… I just learned to crochet," Pippen told him. "I… uhm, don't know what I'm making. Ariadne says it's a beginner project, so, uhm, it shouldn't suck too much."

"Jeremy can help you," Stanley said encouragingly. "And you're at the right place, right? I bet Jeremy and Aiden have more premium yarn under their bed than most folks have worked with in a lifetime."

Pippen felt heat coming to his cheeks. "I, uh… Aiden saw me working and told Ari she'd be better off buying craft yarn. What does, uhm, that mean?"

Stanley winced. "Well, it probably means you need a little practice," he said. Then, as though confiding something, "And he might still be a little mad about Jeremy. Jeremy's been hurt before—it always rips Aiden's heart out."

Pippen nodded. "I'm so sorry," he whispered, feeling stupid. He could say it all he wanted but he couldn't make it better.

"Well, once Jeremy forgives you," Stanley said, patting Pippen's arm with a nervous little gesture, "you'll feel better about it."

"Can he—how can he—" Because that was something Pippen hadn't imagined.

Stanley shook his head like the forgiveness was a foregone conclusion. "Oh, honey," he said, in such a way that would have made Pippen's father go miles to avoid him, but Pippen really loved. "You managed to wound the best man in the world, and on one hand, the crushing guilt is the downside of that. But on the upside, he'll make you feel like even *that* isn't an unforgivable sin."

Pippen had to laugh, because it sounded unlikely. But this sweet little man with the twinkling blue eyes had made him feel better, and that made him more efficient.

"I'm going to dish up the food," he said, needing a moment to think about what Stanley had told him. "But, uhm, thanks, sir."

"Stanley," he said, like, "Duh!" "I'm just a friend, Pippen. You'll be okay—I promise. When we're young, we do stupid things—and we either learn from them or we don't survive. You seem to be learning—you'll be okay."

And with that, Stanley trilled his way into the living room to see if Jeremy was awake yet. If he wasn't, Pippen wagered he would be soon, which meant Pippen should get to work. He really wanted Jeremy to have a good first day home.

Pippen expected all that good will to stop when Aiden stomped in, but something… unexpected happened when Aiden arrived.

First, he went around back to the mudroom to get his boots off, and Pippen heard him talking to the dog, his voice gruff but soft too. He said terrible things to the dog—but the tone of his voice made the dog know that "Idiot food vacuum" was really a compliment and Aiden would feed this dog forever if she'd let him scratch her rump.

Next, he ventured through the kitchen, wearing leather moccasins for house shoes, and one of two battered, hand-knit sweaters that had been folded on a rack over the washing machines over his jeans. Pippen realized he must have left his battered denim jacket and sweatshirt, the ones with the frayed cuffs and the dye stains, in the mudroom, and it hit him. The Aiden he saw everyday was Aiden at work, frustrated with the loss of his work partner, worried about his husband, and working full tilt for the Christmas rush all at the same time.

That was the Aiden who yelled.

This was the Aiden who sat in the recliner or on the couch and read everything from magazines about stock breeding to art and fiber journals in the evening.

This was the Aiden who was worried about his husband, and who had a huge soft spot for his dog.

"How is he?" the man asked as he peered across the open counter in the kitchen into the living room, where Johnny and Stanley played a quiet game of chess. Ariadne had left ten minutes earlier to go pick up her daughter and then work the store. She'd promised to return that evening, so Jeremy could visit with Persephone, and Pippen's heart twisted a little as he remembered the last time Jeremy had seen the girl—while saving her life.

"He was asleep when he got here," Pippen told him. "He woke up, ate a little bit of lunch, and fell asleep again. He, uh, was asking for you." He'd smiled at Pippen as Pip had brought him lunch and some warm tea. Pippen, finally getting a look at the man, had seen a once-pretty man in his early thirties, with brown hair and brown eyes and a nose that had been pretty badly broken, and the faded scarring on his face that indicated he'd had some surgery done there, once upon a time. He'd been hurt before—it was the only thing Pippen knew about him. That and the fact that he could smile kindly when he was obviously tired and in pain.

Aiden glanced at Pip and nodded. "Yeah. We didn't know they'd arrived—"

"It wasn't your fault," Pippen said hurriedly. "Apparently he was supposed to text when they got about twenty minutes away, and he fell asleep right before then."

Aiden's chuckle surprised him. "Yeah—he always could sleep on a trip. I used to have to wear earplugs to keep from killing him when we went out for deliveries because he wouldn't shut up, but once he found out I was doing that, it was like he took it as permission not to talk. Hasn't been afraid to cop a nap since."

Pippen smiled, surprised, but before he could say anything, Aiden sobered and turned to him outright.

"Before I go wake him up, you should know your father paid us a visit today."

Pippen wasn't sure what he looked like then, but his face had gone cold and the room seemed to spin around him.

"Easy there," Aiden said, surprisingly kind. He took Pippen's elbow and guided him to the battered wooden table. "Yeah, I kind of got the feeling the guy wasn't warm."

"What'd you—" Pippen gasped. "Did you tell—"

"We didn't tell him a goddamned thing," Aiden said, nose wrinkled in disgust. "Craw had Gideon put the SUV in the garage—your dad—"

"Just call him Madison," Pippen muttered, gagging slightly. The appellation "your dad" always made him feel dirty, and false. Dads were kind. Dads were decent. Dads cared about their kids.

Talbot Madison didn't give a *damn* about Pippen.

"How about 'that asshole'?" Aiden asked. "'Cause that's really all I wanted to call him since I saw him."

Pippen found a smile curling in the corners of his mouth. "Yeah," he whispered. "That's fine."

"Well that asshole demanded to know where you were, and when Ben didn't know and I didn't know, he left, but he… well, he didn't say the thing, but we *felt* the thing—"

Pippen's vision started to go dark, and suddenly Aiden, who hadn't said a kind word to him since Pippen had almost killed his husband, was rubbing his back and talking softly to him.

"How you doin', boy?" he asked after Pippen got his breath. To Pippen's surprise, Stanley had come into the room and brewed him a cup of tea as he'd been trying to get his bearings.

"Sorry," he said in a small voice, wishing desperately for Gideon but realizing Gideon was probably still at the mill, doing the lion's share of fixing things while Pippen was failing at housework.

"Don't be sorry 'bout this, boy," Aiden murmured, and Pippen caught the look between him and Stanley. "I'm getting the feeling this thing ain't nobody's fault but that asshole's. He was threatening us, wasn't he?"

Pippen nodded, trying to find his voice. "My father... he buys and sells people. Places. He ruins people. His driver?"

"Mealy-mouthed fella, didn't say a word?" Aiden clarified.

"Yeah. He... he found a better job, once. When I was a kid. One that would let him be with his family more, spend time with his wife. My dad called his new employer—a good guy by all accounts—and told him he'd sell the mortgage on the guy's house if he didn't fire James. The only place James could get a job after that was with my dad, and he had to take a pay cut and longer hours." Pippen shook his head. "His wife left him after that. James... his heart sort of died, you know? He used to... I dunno. Smile."

"Oh dear," Stanley said. "Johnny, did you hear that?"

Johnny nodded. "Don't worry 'bout it, cupcake. Me and Ben—we both got different contacts. We'll reach out. He won't come at us unexpected-like, right?"

Pippen took a deep breath, and then another, and looked at the men surrounding him and tried to understand. "Why... why didn't you just... you should have just told him where I was," he said faintly.

Aiden shook his head. "God, kid—you got enough problems. Naw. You're being stand-up. That asshole doesn't need to know where you are. Don't worry. Nobody here'll tell him."

There was another exchange of looks above his head, and Pippen was suddenly tearful. "I'm sorry," he gasped, the fear flooding out of him in a painful rush. God. Of all the things he'd expected when trying to make amends, finding people who had his back was not one of them.

"Boy?"

The voice was groggy and faint, coming from the other room. "Boy, that you?"

Pippen glanced up from his own misery to see Aiden's handsome, closed face open like sunshine. "That's me, Jer. Calming down our new helper, that's all."

"Sweet kid," Jeremy mumbled, and Pippen wondered how he could remember when all Pip had done was brought the man his dinner and some tea.

"Yeah, he's all right." With that, Aiden gave him a strained wink and then, with a glance that said he was making sure Pippen was being watched after, he stood and hurried into the next room, where Jeremy was.

Pippen watched him go unashamedly, and the smile on Jeremy's face as Aiden approached was nothing short of a miracle. Yes, he was still pale and wan, his features still tight with pain, but right there, Pippen could see the once-pretty man who had fallen in love with the beautiful wolf who had so terrified Pippen.

And like that, Pippen understood the picture that hung in the living room, the wolf and the rabbit. That was *them*. This wasn't just a home—this was like living in a fairy tale.

"They're really very sweet," Stanley said softly from Pippen's elbow.

Pippen nodded. "Yeah," he said gruffly, and then, because Stanley had been kind to him, he said, "I… I don't know what to do about my father."

"We'll figure something," Stanley said cheerfully. "Here— take a sip of your tea and then let's go check on Jeremy's 'critters'. It's getting late, and he always double-checks to make sure they've got water and such."

Pippen did, appreciating chamomile and rosehip tea like he never had before. As he stood up, he heard Jeremy's faint voice from the couch.

"Boy, let me talk to the kid—I've got a favor to ask him."

"Sure, Jer." Aiden stood with a sigh. "I'm gonna go help Craw finish up anyway so I can come home early. He's gonna stop by later, check on you, and my mom's gonna bring casseroles."

"Boy…," Jeremy protested. "I'm not fit company for your mother!"

Aiden placed a gentle kiss on Jeremy's forehead. "Which is why you're gonna pretend to be asleep and let Stanley, Johnny, and the kid entertain her." He moved the kiss to Jeremy's lips, tenderly, before pulling back. "God, Jer, I'm glad you're home. Now get some sleep and let these nice people take care of you. Love you."

"Love you back."

Jeremy's face was so sunshiny, gazing up into Aiden's, that Pippen could have cried. That was some faith right there. No wonder Aiden was so fierce. To have someone believe in you like that? It wouldn't matter what sort of mountains you'd climb, to live up to that faith.

Aiden left then, going back through the mudroom and changing clothes quickly, and Pip approached the couch uncertainly. "You, uhm, needed me to do something?" he asked.

Jeremy's smile was a little embarrassed. "So, uhm, I hid everybody's Christmas presents out in the critter hutch," he said, with a sideways glance at Johnny and Stanley. "*Everybody's,* including Aiden's, and not all of them are finished. I'm gonna be awful bored in the next couple of weeks. Is there any way you could bring that box in and help me hide the finished ones?"

Pippen stared at him. "Uhm... where is it? I've been in there and—"

"Top shelf, over the back door, to the left, in the big plastic containers," Stanley said pertly, and Jeremy stared at him.

"How in the hell do you know—"

"Oh, Jeremy—I had to look. Two years running you made somebody the exact thing I was making them, and you're about a thousand times better than I am. I've been checking your secret stash to see what you had planned since the pandemic."

Jeremy was still staring. "But Stanley, then you know what I'm making *you.*"

Stanley preened. "And then I knew what to buy to match it."

Pippen couldn't help it. He snorted laughter and then covered his mouth. "That's... uhm, Stanley, that's terrible."

Stanley rolled his eyes and wriggled his tush as he sat on the recliner. "Oh, pumpkin—that's self-defense when you're a struggling knitter among maestros. I mean, Craw's knitting is simple, but he spins his own yarn. Aiden *dyes* it, so it's always perfect. Ariadne does the most exquisite lace, but for all-around perfect workmanship and this sort of effortless technique? Jeremy's your guy. So yes." He *humph*ed. "I cheat. It's the only way to win the knitting the gifts game around here."

Pippen looked at Johnny, who was staring at Stanley with an indulgence that warmed Pippen to his toes. "What do you, uh, do for gifts?"

Johnny lifted one shoulder. "Gift certificates," he said frankly. "Ariadne? She can knit whatever she wants for herself—

except a spa day in Boulder. Their little girl? It takes a lot of love from Uncle Johnny to keep that kid in pink sneakers and Barbie dolls, believe me."

Pippen laughed.

"He also likes to buy us warm boots," Jeremy said, although he sounded tired already. "Which is, like, proof that he's the world's best guy." He yawned, and Stanley patted his arm gently.

"You sleep. We'll go fetch your stuff from the hutch. Tomorrow, you and Pip can get to know each other, and we can leave you in good hands over the week."

"Okay," Jeremy murmured. "Thank you, Stanley. You and Johnny are sort of the greatest." He yawned again and fell asleep, almost mid-sentence, and Pippen stood to go collect his jacket and do the chores. Johnny stayed in the house, the better to watch over Jeremy and man the phones, while Stanley accompanied him to the rabbit hutch.

"So Johnny buys him boots?" Pippen asked, because it was such an odd sort of gift. It wasn't that he didn't get it— he'd just been thinking about how much he loved the ones Craw had lent him, but he didn't realize somebody could just give them as a gift.

"All of them," Stanley said, sounding a little distracted. "But that's so he can buy them for Jeremy."

And that sounded *really* odd.

"Why does your boyfriend buy Jeremy shoes?" Pippen asked, his curiosity overriding subtlety and, well, everything else.

Stanley chuckled and paused on the little walkway between the house and the hutch. For a moment he looked around, taking in the gray shadows of twilight in the little bowl valley and the fat, falling flakes of a gentle flurry of snow.

"Johnny and Jeremy knew each other," Stanley said, closing his eyes as he turned his face to the sky. "In their lives before coming to Granby. For Johnny, having good boots—that was the sign of a good man. A well-put-together man. They—I guess you could say, they both had long, hard, different paths to get to the same place. Johnny helped Jeremy back in the day. Jeremy put his life on the line to save me, a few years later. Johnny… well, he was so grateful. And then he found out that when Craw found Jeremy, asked him to come work here, Jeremy had been so down on his luck, the soles of his shoes had worn out. So the boots… they're sort of code, I guess. Between the two of them. Jeremy doesn't ever have to worry about not having good boots."

He paused and looked at Pippen, snowflakes captured in his eyelashes and in the thin strands of hair at his widow's peak. "You never know," he said after a thoughtful moment—one totally at odds with the tush-wiggling flirt who had so comforted Pippen back in the house. "There's no roadmap for whose life you'll save, or who will save yours. My boss's daughter, Candace, has been my darling for nearly fifteen years. Three years ago, she got stuck in an elevator during a panic attack. A woman in the elevator calmed her down. Held her hand. Told her stupid stories about her grown children. Candace got out of the elevator and called a therapist to help her handle her anxiety, and while she might never see that woman again, if I could, I'd knit her a giant shawl, or a scarf, or a thousand different things, because she helped my darling out when Candace needed her most. When the people in your life are the ones who saved you, I think… I think you should thank them as often as possible, don't you?"

Pippen nodded, speechless, and together they ventured out to the rabbit hutch.

After feeding the creatures—who were all so very gentle—and brushing them, and making a note that tomorrow they should take their waste to the pile on the far side of the property, near the rock wall, Pippen and Stanley found the two big sealed plastic bins and brought them in.

Stanley, true to his word and, Pippen thought fondly, his nature, checked inside the bins and gasped.

First he brought out parts of an amazing sweater with the outline of a silver wolf crocheted into a midnight blue background.

"Well," Stanley said in wonder, "*this* is why we have to see what he's making for us, do you understand?"

"For Aiden, do you think?" Pippen asked.

"Most definitely. And Jeremy only started crocheting this year. I'm jealous. I'm *madly* jealous. He's going to have to teach me by Christmas or I'll never forgive him."

Pippen gave a shy smile. "Can I sit in? I'm… I'm not that good yet."

"Absolutely," Stanley said, folding the sweater and placing it carefully back in the box. "Now, what else do we have… what… oooh. Look at this yarn. This purple, fuchsia, and red—do you see it?"

It was hard not to. "Ariadne?" Pippen hazarded, and Stanley gave a snort.

"As. If. No—Ariadne gets shawls. Jeremy's the only one who makes them for her, and she has a collection that will break your heart."

Pippen had seen the woman wear them—delicate lace shawls, hardy shawls made in thick bulky yarn, everyday shawls made in subtle patterns—and always very practical. "They're beautiful," he said.

"And what colors are they in?" Stanley asked, as though instructing.

"Usually blues and greens and reds—oh." Pippen got it then. "Those are the colors she wears a lot, so—"

"Those are the colors Jeremy knits for her. *These* colors," Stanley said proudly, "Are definitely mine."

Pippen took in the smaller man's black slacks, turtleneck, and sweater, all of them cut slim and nattily, but topped with a bright red scarf with a warm, subtle cable in it and a purple hat with the same cable. "Did he make that set?" he asked.

Stanley shrugged. "I made the hat. The first scarf I ever made got... well, badly washed, and it was itchy. Jeremy made me this one out of yarn that wouldn't fall apart with a little soap and water. But yes. You see? Whatever he's planning to make— that yarn's for *me.*"

Pippen laughed—but also marveled a little at how much it seemed to mean to the man. He thought of the thing he was working on. He'd asked Ariadne what he was making and she told him, "A square."

"A what?"

"A square," she'd said. "A square can be a rectangle—you just have to keep going. Keeping that in mind, a long square can be a scarf or a hat. A big square can be a blanket. Four medium sized squares can be a sweater. What you're making right now is a square. If you make it longer, it can be a scarf for someone. If you stop a little sooner and do some sewing, it's a hat. Get your square right, and we'll decide what it wants to be."

He'd decided on a hat for himself, using the Wedding colorway, and it was almost done. The yarn he'd picked for his next project was a bright, sturdy blue, with a sort of black overlay, and he'd thought of Gideon, because the darkness and the practicality were part of Gideon, but the brightness of the blue underneath was also Gideon. "I'm working on a hat," he said rashly, thinking he wanted Gideon to wear something he'd made. "Or a scarf. It depends. I need to ask Ariadne."

Stanley smiled gently at him. "Is she having you make a square?"

"Yeah."

"Well, as soon as you know what it wants to be, tell her, and she'll tell you what comes next."

Pippen smiled back. "I think... my body, erm, guard, Gideon. He needs a hat."

"Well, a hat it shall be. I think Jeremy or I could help you. Don't you worry, young man. We'll make it happen."

Pippen nodded and helped Stanley get the boxes out of the hutch and into the house. Suddenly finishing the hat—and making sure these nice people who believed in the holy power of yarn were safe from his father—were the most important things he could do with his life.

Stitched into the Fabric

GIDEON ENDED up giving Craw a ride to Aiden and Jeremy's the night Jeremy came home, because there'd been a mass exodus to the little house on the bottom of the property and somehow that's how it turned out.

Gideon didn't mind, really.

Rance Crawford could yell, it was true, but so had Gideon's superior officers in the Marines. As it turned out, Craw was a good boss, all things considered. He explained what he was doing and why, he made sure Gideon had lunch—which Gideon himself didn't do a lot—and only yelled when Gideon was about to do something that would get him hurt.

Gideon had expected the ten minutes in the car to get to Jeremy's to pass in strained silence, and he was pleasantly surprised.

"The house is small," Craw said as he pulled out of the driveway of the farmhouse and mill. "I just find a chair in the corner and try to say as little as possible."

Gideon smiled to himself because it seemed he and Craw and Aiden were alike that way. "Understood."

"You'll need to say hi to Jeremy, though. He'll want to meet you."

Gideon grimaced. "I can't imagine why."

153

"Because you're part of us now," Craw replied, sounding surprised it even came up. "He needs to know who his people are. It's… it's a big deal to Jeremy."

Gideon let out a breath. "Craw, we… we pretty much ruined the guy's life. I—I don't know what we're going to do about Pip's father. I—"

"Pfft." Craw waved his hand. "Come in. Pet their stupid dog. Tell Jeremy you're sorry and that the work is going okay. Say something nice about the baby. It'll be fine."

Gideon couldn't help but smile. "Persephone *is* cute."

"And now you're speakin' our language," Craw said.

Until that moment—right there—Gideon hadn't realized that his shoulders had been strung tight on a tripwire, muscles screaming, tendons taut and clenching—since the fucking airplane had left New York. Knowing that he was going to be the only force between Pip and his father, knowing that this trip was some sort of meet-and-greet for potential mates for Pip—-gah! Just knowing how much Pip's father liked to dick with people— all of it had set his muscles screaming, and he'd been carrying a load on his back for *weeks.*

That tripwire snapped with Craw's words, and his shoulders sagged, and his eyes burned with the release of tension. He felt himself struggling for breath, his hands too tight on the wheel, and a big, masculine hand settled on the back of his neck.

"Okay, kid. We're going to turn in this driveway here. This is Jeremy and Aiden's. You're going to take deep breaths, calm breaths, until we get past the house to the flat spot around the side by the outbuilding they use as a garage. You can't freak out on me now, kid—not driving in the snow. C'mon. C'mon. That's it. Calm 'er down. It's fine. Calm it down. There we go."

Gideon did what he said, the muscles in his arms relaxing just enough to respond to the wheel, his chest loosening enough to let in air. Finally he got to a place where he could park, and he turned off the ignition and melted into the seat.

"Oh God," he mumbled. "Sorry. Didn't mean for that to happen."

"How long?" Craw asked, moving his hand. Gideon had appreciated the touch—it had been kind and firm and parental. Not a come-on. Of course, Craw had Ben to come home to every night—he wouldn't risk that, and the safety of it helped Gideon relax a little more.

"How long what?" he mumbled, tilting his head back and staring sightlessly out the window into the asphalt gray twilight.

"How long you been protecting Pippen from his father?"

Gideon let out a broken laugh, not even trying to deny it. "Three years," he said. "God—that's half the time I was in the service, but it feels like longer."

"His dad know about the two of you?"

That made Gideon sit up a little straighter, turning to look at Craw. The man's bearded face was inscrutable as always, but Gideon thought he saw a glint of compassion in his eyes.

"There's not a two of us," he admitted. "Really."

"Yet," Craw prodded gently.

"Yet," Gideon admitted. "He was still a kid when I took over as his driver. I... it's his second year of college. I think he's just figured out he's gay."

"With other people," Craw deduced, and Gideon wasn't mistaken—there was pity in his voice.

"He's so young—"

"Aiden was his age when he killed a man," Craw told him baldly.

Gideon sucked in a breath. "I'm sorry?"

"Guy was gonna kill Jeremy—damned near did. Aiden didn't even slow down to take the shot. Police questioned him for hours. Aiden kept saying, 'He was going to kill Jeremy, now let me go so I can see him.' To this day, I think it was Aiden's conviction that kept him out of jail. There was nothing that was more important than keeping Jeremy alive."

Gideon swallowed, not even shocked. He'd known about Aiden's self-possession. It had kept Gideon in line for most of a week, and Gideon didn't cow easily.

"Why are you telling me—"

"I get you're city people. We marry young here. We don't do the casual thing. But maybe... maybe let Pippen know where you stand, so he can make his choices and you can make yours."

Gideon thought he'd done that, after that first day here in Granby, when he and Pip had talked. Pip had smiled more easily at him, and their silences—usually knitting in Pip's room, when they were sure the old man was asleep or in a meeting—had felt different. Warmer.

They'd needed to be so careful in the mansion, because if Talbot Madison found out, Gideon would be lucky to escape with his life, and that wasn't an exaggeration.

"His dad...." Gideon shook his head.

"Would kill you. For real. With blood." Rance didn't sound scared or doubtful, and Gideon blessed the older man for getting it.

"Even if I lived, he could find ways to destroy my parents. Bankrupt my family. It could get so bad—"

Rance nodded. "I hear you. Hard, when he's got all the power. But let Pippen know anyway." He gave a flicker of a smile. "You'll never know what kind of backbone the boy has until you give him a chance."

Gideon nodded and gave a hard shiver, because the night cold of the Colorado dark was seeping into the car. Craw opened the door and stepped out, and Gideon followed him to the back porch, which had just, thank God, been salted down because it was starting to freeze already.

Without knocking, Craw opened the back porch door into a mud room, where he and Gideon took off their coats and laid them on the dryer and kicked off their boots, leaving them under the sink with a few other pairs. Then they ventured into the warm kitchen, which smelled like casserole and steak, which was an odd combination but Gideon didn't care. He was suddenly starving.

"Craw!" Ariadne cried, her thin face lighting up with happiness. Next to her, tall and blond and stoic, was a good-looking man enough like Persephone to be her father, Ariadne's husband. Glancing at Craw, Gideon saw the usually scowling countenance he always wore lightening up, relaxing.

This place, these people—they made him happy.

Gideon resolved for the millionth time not to let this family suffer for their good deeds.

Craw gave his friend a one-armed hug and then indicated the laden table and counters. "Food for years, here. What happened?"

"My mother," Aiden said from the other side of the counter. "Stanley and Johnny brought lunch, which was kind, and your meal is in the oven to keep it warm. But Mom was so excited Jeremy was coming home, she… well, she brought everything. That woman's been cooking for five days—I had no idea."

Craw looked over to the couch, where an exhausted-looking Jeremy was holding Persephone on his lap and doing the nod and smile thing for Aiden's mother, who was probably briefing him on the doings of every one of her five children, including Aiden's little brother, Ford, a hellraiser if Craw had ever seen one.

"You need to rescue him from that," Craw murmured, and Aiden grimaced.

"I would, but he's going to need two of us to get him up the stairs to bed. The doctor told him no stairs for a week, but...." Aiden shook his head. "I'm not going to sleep upstairs if he's down here on the couch, you know?"

"I know," Craw said. "You, me, and Johnny can take care of it until he can get by with only one of us. But in the meantime—"

Persephone wriggled and Jeremy let out a hiss and set her on the ground. "Sorry, Persy—I—"

"Uncle Jeremy's got to go sleep now," Pippen said, approaching from the other side. "C'mere, Persephone—I'll take you to Mom."

"Kith!" the little girl lisped, and as Gideon watched, Pippen lifted her up so she could plant a gentle kiss on Jeremy's cheek.

"Thankth, Pip," she said and Pippen grinned at her before setting her down.

Pippen watched her run into the kitchen, straight into Craw's arms, and then he lifted his eyes, his gaze colliding with Gideon's so forcefully, Gideon lost his breath.

Pippen's face was open and relaxed, confident and happy, in ways Gideon wasn't sure he'd ever seen. These people, Gideon thought dimly. This little family—it was what had been missing from Pippen's life.

But then, Pippen wasn't looking at anybody else in the room the way he was looking at Gideon.

Gideon found himself lost in the wide-open skies of Pippen's fathomless blue eyes. The smile tugging at his full mouth was cautious, still, but for Gideon, it was also joyous. Gideon's heartbeat sped up, but time slowed down as, for a moment, the two of them were alone, spinning like a disco ball, in this quiet, rustic room.

A hand on his shoulder pulled Gideon out of it, and he turned as Ariadne put a plate in his hands. "Here—Pippen hasn't eaten either. I gave you enough to share."

Gideon nodded and moved toward the living room, surprised and not a little dismayed when he realized the only place to sit had just been cleared by Aiden's mother, and was next to the man they'd injured. Jeremy.

"Sit down, boy," Jeremy yawned. "I don't bite. Pip, sit next to him—Ariadne gave him two forks, which probably means we ran out of plates. This is the biggest party since Ben's birthday, I think." His smile was a little dreamy and a little tense, like he was fighting pain. "It's funny—I think everyone ends up here because we work up at Craw's so much. And 'cause Rory and Ariadne's house is super small if you eliminate the studio for Rory to paint."

Pippen nodded but didn't sit next to Gideon right away. "Jeremy," he said gently, "it's time for your pain meds. And then I think Aiden wants to take you upstairs to bed."

Jeremy let out a sound close to a whimper. "Gotta tell ya, Pip, I wouldn't argue with that. I'm not loving this whole recovery thing."

Pippen left to go fetch Jeremy's pain meds, leaving Gideon there next to him, assessing a prettyish man in his early thirties who looked like he could sleep for a month.

"Recovery sucks," Gideon murmured, taking one of the forks and starting in on the casserole. His mother back in Jersey liked making this sort of thing, and the taste of comfort food melted on his tongue. "I got wounded in the service—six weeks in the medical tent will make anything sound fun."

Jeremy laughed a little. "Yeah, I'm not the best patient. I gotta keep reminding myself, last time I was in for three months. This time, it was less than a week—I'm the luckiest man in the world."

Gideon grimaced. "You gotta know how sorry Pip and I are. About hurting you, about freaking out the stock—"

Jeremy grimaced and held up a hand. "Craw and Aiden say you're working to keep us afloat. I gotta thank the two of you. Extra hands, especially when they're a man down—it's not a small thing you're doing. I know Pippen thinks he's not doing much, but Ariadne sure does appreciate the help looking after the kid and the store. You know, she used to help Craw and Aiden with the machinery, but we just don't want Persy to think that's a good idea at *all*. So far the noise has scared her off, and we hope that lasts a while."

"It's hard work," Gideon admitted. "And yeah, that machinery isn't for the faint of heart, you know?"

"I know it," Jeremy chuckled. He held out a hand that showed some gnarly, faded scars. "Lost concentration for a second, back when I first started. You watch out for pretty much anything in there—it all bites."

Gideon nodded and took another mouthful of casserole. "I'll keep that in mind, sir."

"But remember," Jeremy said, "if you get hurt again, *now* you know how to knit!"

Gideon grimaced. "I'm… I'm not picking it up like Pippen is. He just sort of took the hook and ran with it. I mean, I get knitting better than I get what *he's* doing, but…." He shook his head. "Makes me feel stupid."

Jeremy nodded soberly. "It's an honest thing. You're taking raw materials and making something serviceable. That's as real as it gets. If you can keep your life that real, you're doing—" He paused to yawn. "—okay."

At that moment, Pippen returned with two pills and a cup of water. Jeremy downed the pills with ease and handed Pippen the cup.

"Guys, it's been nice to meet ya, and I'll probably see you tomorrow. Pip—you bring your yarn work tomorrow, we can work on it together."

"I will," Pippen said.

"Good." He swallowed and raised his voice a little. "Boy?" he asked, and there was a note in his voice, a needing note, plaintive and in pain and vulnerable.

"Right here, Jer," Aiden said from his side. "Here. Craw's got your other side, and we'll make a sling and take you up the stairs. Me and Johnny'll get you in the morning, okay?"

"Thanks, boy," Jeremy murmured, leaning his head against Aiden's shoulder as Aiden lifted him upright off the couch.

Craw arrived, and the three of them made it to the stairs as Pippen sank gratefully down onto the couch next to Gideon and took his own fork. There was some quiet then, and some heartfelt calls of "Good night!" but the roomful of people did not simply scatter as they left.

Well, Gideon expected most of them were family.

"Thanks," Pippen said through a full mouth, leaning against Gideon's side and eating from the plate.

Gideon looked at him bemusedly, marking that Pippen's usual careful distance had melted away in the warmth of the room, and he was nearly in Gideon's lap. "You seem comfortable," he said, draping an arm around Pippen's shoulders and shuddering, like you did when you were cold and letting warmth in.

"They're all so nice here," Pippen confided, taking a bite of casserole. As he chewed he scooped another bite up on his fork and held it out for Gideon, who took it.

Gideon chewed and swallowed and melted into this feeling, of safety, of Pippen, of being comfortable. "My parents are like this," he confided. He'd been home only briefly since he'd gotten out of the military, but he texted or e-mailed on a regular basis. Pippen would probably be surprised at how many pictures Gideon's mother had of him.

"You never visit," Pippen murmured. "You must miss them."

Gideon let out a sigh. "I… Pip, your dad—"

Pippen made a hurt sound and started to pull away, and Gideon squeezed him tight.

"Don't go," he whispered. "I've wanted you… just like this, for so long."

And then Pippen said a very wise thing. "We had to feel safe."

"Yeah," Gideon said softly. "And I wouldn't feel safe near your father. Not for me—I'll take on whatever he has to dish out. But for you. He can make your life hell. I hid my family, you understand? Before I even knew you. I put down my old CO as a contact. I just… I had a feeling. You're the only one who knows where they live, because I trust you."

Pippen burrowed closer, which was both wonderful and terrifying. This time, Gideon was the one who picked up the fork and fed them both a bite of casserole.

"Thank you," Pippen whispered after he'd swallowed. "I… I'm such a wreck, Gideon. Such a… a nothing. You trusted me—that's such an honor."

Unexpectedly Gideon's eyes burned. "You're such a good kid, Pip. Your heart is so good. Don't say you're nothing. Please."

"Kid?" There was a hint of coyness in his voice, and Gideon had to smile.

"Young man," he murmured, and fed them both again.

They were quiet then, probably because they were both hungry. Pippen leaned forward so Gideon could reclaim his hand and they finished off the plate. Pippen stood and took it to the sink and then helped Ariadne with dishes.

Some of the people had cleared out by the time they were done—Aiden's mother and a couple of siblings, Ariadne's husband and the little girl—leaving Craw, Ben, Ariadne, Aiden, and a couple Gideon hadn't met yet all lingering in the living room. The couple was sitting at a chess board, a fortyish guy with Old World slick looks and manners and a slightly younger man with the mischievous blue eyes and corner-crinkles of a wicked elf.

Gideon yawned and then stood and glanced around, realizing there was an air of repressed conversation. His heart stuttered, and he thought, "Oh no. This is where they tell us not to come by anymore. This is when we're not allowed to help out, and Pip and I are on our own again."

"So," Craw said after a moment. "We need to address a couple things. First off—Gideon, that old bastard knows what your vehicle looks like. Can he track it?"

Gideon blinked. "Uhm, it's through a rental agency in his name, so probably."

Aiden spoke up. "Jere's got a car—you can borrow that when you're here or at the mill. If you two can walk to the bottom of the driveway tomorrow, I'll pick you up."

Gideon realized he was breathing through his mouth in surprise. "Uhm—"

"Good," Craw said. "Pippen, you did a great job cleaning up and helping Jeremy today and he seems to like you. You okay with working here?"

"It feels like a cheat," Pippen said hesitantly. "I... I had a real nice time tonight."

Ariadne and Ben both cackled. "It only feels like a cheat because he was tired tonight," Ariadne offered by way of explanation. "Wait until he's trying to navigate the steps on his crutches and refuses to take his pain pills."

"And he cheats at cards," Ben told him with a rather sweet earnestness. "He says he doesn't, but I think he doesn't even think about it."

"Naw," said the big Italian guy. "Jeremy don't cheat—he's just that smart. Now me…." The guy gave a wicked chuckle and the blond, elfin man next to him piped up.

"I'm starting to spot his cheats," he said proudly. "It's only taken me five years."

Gideon chuckled. "Okay, then. So Pip, play cards with Jeremy but expect to lose."

Pippen gave a sunshiny grin. "I can do that!"

There was some quiet laughter, and Ben said the thing Gideon had been about to ask. "And neither of you," he said firmly, "should worry about Pip's father's visit to us, okay? You are both adults, you both made a bad decision, took ownership of it, and came to make things right. You've done nothing wrong. We're going to keep you away from that guy, but in the meantime, when you're working for us, don't worry about him." He gave an understanding look to both of them. "We get the feeling you'll be worrying plenty when you're stuck under his roof."

Gideon swallowed, and so did Pippen.

"Thank you," Pippen said in a small voice. "You've all been… very kind. Kinder than we probably deserve—we… we're grateful you're letting us be here. Help you. Try to make up for being stupid. Thank you."

"Thanks for *just* having a stupid moment," Aiden said. "And not being stupid in general. We appreciate the help you're giving us. You both seem like decent people. Makes us glad we didn't shoot you on day one."

Craw grunted. "Yeah. Mostly. Gideon, for fuck's sake, leave the drum spinners alone. They're just doing their job."

Gideon grimaced, remembering the mess he'd made with the spinners the day before. "Sorry, Craw," he said meekly, but at the same time, he felt warmed. The idea that he didn't have to be perfect—that sometimes people screwed up, but they could be forgiven, even if real world consequences had to be met—was such a relief. Suddenly he wanted to hold Pippen to his chest and confess everything, the interest that had built to longing, the longing that had built to need, *everything* that had built from that first interview, when Pippen had gazed past Gideon's ear and said, "All right, Dad. He's fine." The moment would have been heartwrenching, except as Talbot Madison had lowered his head to sign the contract, Pippen's eyes had met Gideon's, and Gideon had seen… softness. Hope. Connection.

Gideon had winked, and Pippen's mouth had twisted into a ghost of a smile until Talbot looked up. They'd both put their game faces on in less than a heartbeat, and Talbot didn't indicate by so much as a blink that words had been exchanged, *volumes* had been exchanged, with the simple pass of glances in a silent room.

They needed to look each other in the eyes again, hands touching, maybe bodies too, and see what the other had to say.

"I'll stay away from the spinner," Gideon promised now, and there was a faint, tired chuckle in the room, and then they all made their way to the mudroom to put on their boots and coats before they left.

Gideon and Pippen paused as Aiden shut the door behind them. The others hurried to Ben's older model green Subaru and started it up, waiting briefly for the windows to defrost. Gideon took a step toward the giant, ostentatious black rental SUV and paused, turning to see why Pippen wasn't following him.

"Look," Pippen murmured to his unasked question. "Look up."

Gideon did, and caught his breath. Starlight wove an intricate web above them, stopping abruptly at the edges of the valley. Mountains loomed ominously at their front, toward Boulder, and the closed pass over Highway 34 threatened at their back, past the small tourist town of Grand.

But above them was a glittering, glorious diamond tapestry, every star showing ownership of being a faraway sun. It was so clear—*so* clear—Gideon could see the subtle colorations, the red stars, the yellow, the blue, and the Milky Way roared with light, an iridescent river.

"Ooh," Gideon murmured, his heart beating faster with the moment, the beauty—and with Pippen's hand in his.

Gideon squeezed the hand, covered in hand-knitted gloves. Who had made them for him? Gideon wondered, feeling a shaft of jealousy that it hadn't been him.

That suddenly he understood everybody's obsession with craft, with yarn, with beauty.

Human beings couldn't weave stars or knit moonlight. They couldn't take loops of sunshine and give them to their loved ones. Yarn was all they had.

"I want you to have everything," Gideon whispered under that honest sky. "Your education. Comfort. Love. Everything. I am afraid of what will be taken away if I kiss you right now."

"That's funny," Pippen replied, and Gideon sensed him turning inward, closing the gap between their bodies, turning his face slightly upward. "All I'm afraid of is that you never get around to kissing me."

Gideon's smile came unbidden, and he lowered his head, lost for a moment in the stars in Pippen's eyes. Then their mouths touched, their breath mingled, and he was simply lost.

Pippen gasped, parting his lips, letting Gideon in, and Gideon teased with his tongue, asking to be let in. Pippen opened his mouth just enough, and Gideon took permission, took over the kiss, made it deep, and hot, and long.

The stars swept through him, exploding behind his eyes, and he was no longer lost. He'd found all he'd ever wanted in a simple kiss under the night sky.

Midnight Doors and Morning Windows

THE GREAT dining room overlooked the Madison parcel of property, which meant Pippen and Gideon's headlights could be seen as they traveled up the drive to the recently rebuilt chalet-style mansion.

"Uh oh," Gideon murmured as they spotted the extra rental in the carport. "It appears your father has company."

Pippen pulled out his phone and frowned. "He hasn't texted me—it might be a business acquaintance." Talbot Madison *had* no friends.

Gideon gave him a skeptical glook. "I don't know, Pip—your dad's been pushing the arranged marriage thing pretty hard."

Pippin smirked—he couldn't help it. "Yeah, too bad *that's* not gonna work."

But Gideon didn't smile. "Pippen, don't... don't take this lightly. Do you think you'd be the only gay son married off to make an heir and a spare?"

Pippen shuddered and let out a breath. "I... I can't," he said apologetically. "Not now. Not...." His smirked changed, grew—he could feel it. His face *ached* with the transport from scared boy to actual adult. "It would be a horrible life," he said softly. "To never hold hands in public with the person I really loved. To go home to someone who didn't know who I was. To have... have acquaintances but no friends, because friends would have to

168

know me. I… I'd die," he said, his voice choking unexpectedly. "You saw the sky tonight—you were with me, under it. Can you imagine, after seeing all that…" Love. Acceptance. Kindness. "…sky, I'd go back to living in a box under my bed?"

"No," Gideon murmured, taking his hand. "But if you did, I'd guard that box under your bed with my life."

And now Pippen's eyes burned. He didn't want to talk about the boys he'd brought back to his apartment. The dates, the makeout sessions he'd had while Gideon had been in the room next door.

"I'd rather stand next to you under the sky, thank you," Pippen said, his voice shaky but his resolve still sound. "Let's go in, piss off my father, and pretend to go to bed."

"Pretend?" Gideon asked, turning to stare at him.

"Did *you* want to finish that kiss?" Pippen demanded.

He felt Gideon's blush from across the center console.

"Me too," Pippen answered. "I…." And it was his turn to blush, but it was only fair. "I… uhm, have never gone all the way, uhm, finishing a kiss."

Gideon's quick look at him cemented the fact that Pippen had been a first-class heel, even if it had been for a good reason. "No?"

"No," Pippen answered simply. "I… I had to know, Gid. I had to know I wasn't just crushing on… Gideon. My friend, my protector. I had to know I was… you know. Crushing on Gideon. A man."

Gideon sucked in a breath. "I *would* have offered my services as a test rodent," he muttered.

Pippen shook his head. What was it Jeremy kept saying? "That wouldn't have been honest, Gid. What if… what if I just thought you were really cool? I could have…." He swallowed. This felt presumptuous to say.

"Broken my heart," Gideon rasped, and he relaxed a little.

169

"I didn't want to hurt you at all," Pippen murmured, taking his gloved finger and rubbing Gideon's high cheekbone. "I tried to figure out the way that would hurt the least, but my other choice would have been to… to run away to kiss boys, and my dad would have made your life hell."

Gideon gave a sideways smile. "I am really tired of your father's stone-cold shadow, Pip. What do you want to do about that?"

"I have some ideas," Pippen murmured, taking Gideon's chin between his thumb and forefinger and holding him there, so Pippen could lean forward and kiss *him* this time. Oooh… just as heady as under the stars, but warmer, cozier. Amazing. He pulled back reluctantly. "But first let's go be nice to whoever is sitting at my father's dinner table."

"What are we going to tell them about you not being able to hang out?"

"I've got an idea about that," Pippen said. He gave his best, most haphazard grin. "Trust me!"

"Sure," Gideon said as they both unbelted, grabbed their yarn bags, and headed for the door inside the carport. "Why not?"

Well, lots of reasons why not. Pippen was a mess who hadn't yet proven he could support himself or live his life not under his father's thumb. Pippen had been the one to charge for the animals just minding their own business and scream at them, enjoying the power over something, even if it was just a dumb sheep or alpaca. Pippen was the victim, ever and again.

But Gideon had kissed him that night, under a sparkling shawl of stars, and suddenly Pippen could do anything, as long as Gideon was next to him.

And he'd do anything to make *sure* Gideon was next to him as well.

They found Talbot in the living room, with another stern, humorless father figure and a quiet, thin, mousy young woman who looked just as miserable as Pippen felt most of the time. Pippen gave her an especially sweet smile as he and Gideon approached, and she returned it, looking surprised.

"Hello, Father," Pippen said formally—as Talbot required. "Sorry we missed dinner. I didn't see your text that we were having company."

Talbot smiled thinly. "A surprise. This is my colleague, Charles Walton, and his daughter, Hillary. I understand Hillary is your age." The unspoken part, the part about Pip being expected to squire the poor girl around this small tourist mecca and the ski resorts, loomed large over their heads, but Pippen had a plan.

"So nice to meet you, Hillary. How long are you going to be here in Colorado?"

"A month," she said, meeting his eyes. He could read the "Help me!" in their depths.

"Well, sadly," he said, "I have plans for tomorrow—"

"What?" his father snapped. "What are you doing tomorrow?"

"There's a Christmas fair in the center of town this weekend," Pippen replied, because he and Gideon had promised to help with it on Sunday. "I'm going shopping for my friends from college—I have some booths I need to hit very early, and I don't know how long we'll be." He smiled prettily. "I'd hate to drag you along with my own agenda—that's not fair at all." Then he said, "But I'd be happy to meet you there on Sunday and we could shop together?"

Hillary nodded, looking relieved. She had bags of exhaustion under her eyes, and Pippen thought if she'd been anything like him right after finals, she was really looking forward to the rest.

"That sounds awesome," she said, the gratitude in her voice making him hopeful. "I could really use the sleep tomorrow. Sunday would be so much better."

"That's great." He smiled at Gideon. "Sound like a plan?"

Gideon nodded soberly, like he always did when Pippen was making plans in front of his father, but Pippen could see the questions in his eyes. That was okay—Pippen had answers to those too.

"Pippen," Talbot said, as though the pleasant exchange between two young people hadn't occurred. "You need to turn your phone on. I tried to text you today, but I couldn't reach you."

What he meant, Pippen thought, was he couldn't *track* Pippen, and that was because Gideon had given him one of his own waterfall phones and had disabled all the usable apps in the one his father thought he used. That one, he kept off.

"I'll try to remember," Pippen lied, and he smiled at his father evenly, so Talbot would *know* it was a lie.

"Do that." Talbot regarded them icily, and Pippen was suddenly tired. Not exhausted, just tired of this *game* he played with his father every time they spoke.

"I won't," Pippen said cheerily. "If I want you to know where I am, I'll tell you. Like I just did." He smiled at Hillary and winked. "I'll see you Sunday morning at breakfast, around nine? That way we can make it into town by ten. They're having a hot chocolate contest—I sort of want to taste the entries."

Hillary laughed, her eyes sparkling a little, and Pippen dared to hope that they could be friends, or maybe allies. It wasn't necessary for what he wanted to do, but it would definitely be helpful.

He excused himself and Gideon then, and together they walked up the stairs to the second floor, where most of the bedrooms were. Talbot, of course, had the suite on the third floor, the suite that made him king of all he surveyed.

"I need a shower," Gideon told him, apropos of nothing but Pippen's hopes, Pip thought.

172

"Me too," Pippen agreed. He winked. "So, uhm, want to, uhm, practice knitting over snacks in about three hours?"

His father would be asleep at ten, like clockwork, and that would give them an hour of silence in the vast chalet.

"Knitting?" Gideon asked, the corners of his eyes crinkling.

"Or crochet," Pippen said with an innocent shrug.

Gideon's smile made him look young, when not much else did. "Or crochet," he agreed soberly. They didn't kiss then because there were too many potential eyes in that hallway, but Pip had no doubts at all what Gideon would be expecting after Talbot Madison went to bed.

PIPPEN TURNED his phone on long enough to charge—and to get all the texts his father had sent him over the day, most of them blisteringly angry.

He ignored those.

He showered, he practiced his yarn work, he napped for nearly two hours, and then he awoke in his flannel pajamas and grabbed his yarn bag, slipped into his moccasins, and made his way through the house.

There were running lights in the hallway and on the stairs—the place was never really dark—and as he ventured into the kitchen to put together two sandwiches with some chips and apples and sodas for their snacks, he could hear the television on in the downstairs guest bedrooms, as well as one in the servant's quarters.

Good. Television was good. The walls were sturdy, and television was a great distractor.

Snacks made and packed in a bag inside his plain canvas yarn tote, he made his way back up the stairs to Gideon's door.

He couldn't knock. A knock in the hallway would be heard.

173

He took a chance and slid through the door, making sure it was locked behind him.

Gideon had apparently done what Pippen had and taken a nap. He was sprawled, facedown, on his mattress, one arm covering the empty pillows next to his head, one leg stretching over to the corner. Well, he'd have to make room for Pippen—both of them would be making adjustments.

He set his yarn bag down on the small reading couch in Gideon's room and put the lunch box of snacks on his desk. As he turned and moved toward the bed, he saw that Gideon had turned his head and was watching him, dark eyes wide in his sharply cut features.

"You have bunnies on your pajamas," he said with a smile.

Pippen stopped, suddenly uncertain. It was hard to plan a grand seduction when you'd never really been fully naked in front of someone with the intention of carnal activity.

"Is that bad?" he asked, biting his lip.

Gideon shook his head. "No. I just… I know a lot about you."

"Yeah?" Pippen said, moving toward the bed—still in his pajamas. "Like what?"

"I know how you take your coffee," Gideon said, rolling to his side and propping his head on his hand. He was, Pippen saw with a gulp, shirtless, and his bronze skin gleamed softly in the lamplight. "I know how you look when you're mad or hurt and trying to hide it. I know you chew the end of your pinkie finger when you're thinking hard."

Pippen moved closer, putting one knee on the bed, and Gideon pulled back the covers to let him in. "Anything else?" he asked, sliding down so they were face-to-face.

Gideon reached out to grab his hand and lace their fingers. "I know you are surprisingly strong," he whispered. "And braver than you think."

Pippen hid his face in the pillow—but he didn't unlace their hands. "And...," he teased.

"And I know you wear your bunny pajamas when you are scared, or worried, or nervous, or sad," Gideon murmured, his lips near Pippen's ear. "Which one is it, Pip? I don't want you to be scared or worried or sad."

Pippen's mouth curled up at the corners, and he gave Gideon a shy glance sideways. "What about nervous?"

Gideon kissed the corner of Pip's mouth. "We'll work on that one."

Pip turned his head all the way and allowed Gideon to take his mouth. Like magic the nervousness bled away, and so did the worry. This was Gideon, who had protected him from the very beginning, who had been kind and funny and gentle to a poor little rich kid who needed to get his shit together.

Of course Pippen loved him as a man—but of course Pip had simply loved him, from the very beginning, no matter who they were destined to be together.

As their hands roamed over each other's bodies and Pippen's clothes disappeared, an article at a time, Pippen couldn't help but feel that this—*this*—was how they were destined to be together.

Gideon took the lead, of course—Pippen had always gotten the feeling of experience from Gideon, right down to his advice. It had always been gender neutral—*Male, female, it doesn't matter, Pippen—don't stick your dick in crazy*, or *It doesn't matter if you plan to be with them or not—be kind.* Gideon's advice had been in his ear that evening as he'd spoken to Hillary. *If you treat people respectfully, you'll find more allies than you can imagine.* The one time Gideon had broken down with his advice had been when they'd spooked the animals at the pond, and even then, Gideon had come through. *We need to own up to it, Pip. We hurt people. Good people. We need to do what we can to make it right.*

And tonight, Gideon's lips on Pippen's bare collarbone, along his neck, sucking on his *—Ah!—*nipple, Pippen heard Gideon's voice in his head again.

You can put your Tab A into any slot, Pippen, but unless it's someone you care about, it's not going to be anything but sex.

Gideon meant *everything*. His bare skin under Pippen's mouth was heaven, and his mouth on Pippen was everything Pippen had ever dreamed.

This wasn't just sex. It wasn't awkward or fumbling—Gideon knew what he was doing and Pippen knew what he wanted. Wanting Gideon was the smartest thing he'd ever done.

When Gideon made his way, kiss by stroke by tender touch, to Pippen's cock, Pippen thought he was ready for what would come next, but he'd had no idea. The mechanics were the same—unless humans developed alien physiology, a blow job would always be a mouth on an erect penis—but the intent....

Gideon intended to pleasure Pippen, and he did.

Pippen silenced his soft cries in his hand. The walls were thick, but he didn't want anybody in this house to have any part of this, not even their noises. This moment belonged to them.

Climax was a silent explosion, and Gideon's throat worked as he swallowed come. Pippen shuddered, suddenly wanting to be on the other end of that, wanting to know Gideon's body like he knew Pippen's now, but his hands were shaking, his voice was shaking—everything was a trembly, blurry mess as Gideon boosted himself up to the pillow next to Pippen and grinned.

Pippen grinned stupidly back, and in the ambient light from the vaulted window, he could see the wet gleam of ejaculate around Gideon's mouth. He wanted it, the taste, the earthiness, the proof that they'd *just done that.*

He took Gideon's mouth with his own, and they rolled, Gideon on bottom this time, and Pippen set about learning everything he could about the man in his arms. He listened, he tasted, and every time Gideon suppressed a moan or a gasp, every time he shivered or trembled, Pippen knew more and more in his bones that they were each other's, for as long as they could hold on.

Gideon's fingers tightened in Pippen's hair right before he came in Pippen's mouth.

"C'mere," he whispered. "That's not where I want to come."

There was more then, slickened fingers at Pippen's entrance, a twinge of pain, of stretching, as Pippen closed his eyes and relaxed, giving himself to Gideon in this sex act as he'd put his trust in the man for everything else. When Gideon positioned himself, thrusting gently, Pippen opened his eyes, taking in the careful way Gideon moved to not hurt Pippen, taking in the way his eyes roamed Pippen's face, searching for pain or discomfort or regret.

Pippen cupped his neck then and whispered, "Hey, it's okay. I want this. I want you and only you. Please, Gideon—we can do this."

Gideon nodded, his head drooping, his eyes closed. "Just dreamed of this," he confessed.

"Me too," Pippen murmured. "Make it true."

And then Gideon slid inside him, and there was a little pain, and a lot of intensity, but mostly there was Gideon, where Pippen needed him. In his core, in his heart and his soul, moving, moving, moving, until they both closed their eyes and whimpered into each other's mouths as their world exploded into stars.

Gideon collapsed into his arms then, and there were sweaty, blissful, confused moments of stroked shoulders and incoherent praise, babbled promises. When Gideon finally rolled to the side, Pippen turned to face him and clasped Gideon's hands to his chest.

"Okay?" Gideon asked, making sure.

"I love you," Pippen murmured, not sure if he'd said this yet. "You should know that."

Gideon closed his eyes, his sharp cheekbones throwing stark shadows against the planes of his face. "I love you too," he said.

"I want to do this somewhere not my father's house. Somewhere we're free. A tiny apartment, while I work retail and you work security or law enforcement or whatever you want. Anywhere it's us, it'll feel like the world."

Gideon's eyes opened then. "Do you mean it?" he asked, sounding vulnerable. "Can we leave tonight?"

And suddenly Pippen felt the burden of responsibility. Oh God—how terrifying, that he needed to pull them into the real world.

But then, if he couldn't do this now, he didn't deserve Gideon in his bed.

"We can't," he said, and then, before the disappointment could bloom in Gideon's eyes, he hurried on. "Not until Jeremy can work again. Not until…." He swallowed.

"Until we know they're safe," Gideon filled in, and the dreaded disappointment never materialized. Instead, his eyes gleamed with something like pride.

"Yeah," Pippen said.

"You're right," Gideon told him. "We need to know we didn't leave any damage here." He swallowed. "Your dad sounded pretty mad. Do you think he'll go after them?"

Pippen nodded grimly. "I know it," he said. He cupped Gideon's cheek then and fanned his cheekbone with his thumb. "But don't worry. I've...." He let a little smile slip through. "I've got a plan."

Gideon's bit his lip, looking hopeful. "A plan?"

"Yeah." Pippen looked away, trying not to sound too pleased with himself. "You know what happens on the twenty-first of December, don't you?"

Gideon's breath caught. "You turn twenty-one," he said, surprised. Then, as if it dawned on him, "You come into your trust." While Pippen was dependent on his father for everything now, his mother's estate had left a modest trust for him that he could claim at twenty-one. It wasn't support-him-in-style money. It *could* be support-him-while-he-got-his-education money. What it was *not* was run-away-from-his-rich-father-and-stay-untouchable-without-sacrifice money. But Pippen was starting to see that it didn't have to be.

Pippen nodded and then met Gideon's eyes. "I... I have some plans for how to spend it. It... it will mean we really will be broke for a while, but...." He swallowed. "Our friends might not have to pay for our mistakes," he said, seeing his dreams of college disappearing for a moment—but not for good. He could wait. He could build a life with Gideon, poor if they had to be. For a week now, he'd been living an honest life—he couldn't look at Gideon, touch him like this, if that wasn't how they meant to go on.

"Anywhere with you, Peregrine," Gideon said. He pulled their twined fingers up to his lips and kissed them softly, then smiled. "So, uhm, I know you can't stay here *all* night, but...."

Pippen grinned. "Snack now, or snack later?"

Gideon's laugh was positively filthy, and it made Pippen tingle to his *toes*. "Depends on what you mean by 'snack.'"

Then they had to muffle their giggles like little kids, staying up past bedtime… and then, there was nothing childlike about their noises at all.

PIPPEN FINALLY left Gideon's room in the wee dark hours after midnight, so they could both get some sleep before they had to go meet Aiden. He moved quietly, his yarn bag over his shoulder and what was left of their after-midnight feast in the bag in his hand, but he didn't expect anybody to be up.

He almost had a heart attack when he saw Hillary coming toward him from the direction of the stairs, moving stealthily, her eyes scanning left and right, making sure she didn't get caught.

She was so busy looking behind her that she almost ran into him as he stood near the door to his room, his heart hammering in his throat as he thought, "This is it!"

As she drew near, though, a beam of moonlight from the great windows of the front and dining room caught her, and he could see her hair was mussed and her lips were swollen, and if she'd had a night anything like his, she probably had razor burn in places that would chafe in the morning.

She gasped when she saw him, and he felt a wicked smile taking over his face.

"Fancy meeting you here," he whispered, and she stared at him with horrified eyes.

"I'm… I'm…."

He waved his hand, trying to put her out of her misery. "Don't worry," he said softly. "You seem very nice, and I'd be happy to escort you to the fair on Sunday, but, uhm, I don't think we were ever going to be an item."

His tone must have worked, because she lowered her hand enough to give him a smirk and rolled eyes. "My boyfriend might object," she said dryly.

"So might mine," he replied, and watched as her eyebrows danced with amusement.

"I knew it!"

"Well, if you won't tell, I won't," he said, and made his voice a little sharp. "That's important, Hillary. Please respect that."

She nodded and swallowed, like it had occurred to her exactly what happened to people in their world if they didn't marry right. "I hear you," she said, looking sober, and he had hope that she really did.

"Fair," he said, then he reached into his pocket and pulled out his cell phone, the one his father had been texting. "Look—this is my phone. My dad traces it all the time, but as far as I know, he hasn't cloned it. I'll call you from my burner number tomorrow. We really *should* meet on Sunday, but how about you carry this with you while you're here. You can say you're with me, my dad thinks I'm doing what he wants, and both our parents can plan a wedding we have no intention of attending. You game?"

Her look of relief was profound, and she nodded, taking the phone. "I was planning to spend my time skiing, if that's okay with you?"

"Perfectly fine," Pippen told her. "Text me from your phone tomorrow, and we can keep in touch and keep our stories straight. But, uhm…." He gave her a smile. "Did you still want to go to the fair? I mean, I really *was* going to be there on Sunday. I'm helping to run one of the booths, but I could show you around if you like."

She nodded slowly, and then with conviction. "Absolutely," she said. "I'm…." She let out a breath. "I'm happy to meet you, Pippen."

"Right back at you, Hillary." He gave her a quick grin. "Now me and Gid are going to be out of here by eight a.m., so I've got to run. We're not taking the SUV, so if you can catch Gideon before we leave, we can give you the keys and you'll have some freedom. Just, you know, don't wreck it, or the jig's up."

She gave a shiver. "Freedom. I may just fly away, but buddy, I promise I won't wreck my wings."

He grinned. "Aces. But you've got to find us super early, remember! We've got places to go."

"Can I ask where?" she asked, but he shook his head.

"No—just in case. Our fathers are sharks," he said soberly. "It's sort of our job to protect all the sweet little mammals from the sharks, right?"

And on her face he could see her own reckoning with the fact that they were playing for keeps.

"Roger that," she said softly. "I'll find you in the morning."

"Awesome. Night!"

And with that, he let himself into his room, dropped his stuff at his desk, set his phone from Gideon in the charger, set the alarm, and collapsed into bed. He was still afraid—of his father, of what his father could do to the people he was starting to care about, not to mention Gideon, whom he loved. But he was also as free as he could ever remember being.

He dreamed of soaring over the bowl valley, Gideon another bird at his wingtip, as together they disappeared over the horizon and into the sunlit glory of the world.

JEREMY LAY, eyes closed, in the predawn cold, but his body, attuned to the rhythms of feeding stock and getting to work, couldn't settle down.

And Aiden was awake, watching him, his boy's green eyes wide and anxious as Jeremy tried to assess his physical condition while he yearned for the darkness of sleep.

"You are watching me too loud," he said after a moment.

Aiden chuckled gruffly. "I'm so glad you're home," he said.

"Me too." Jeremy smiled at him, Aiden's face lit by the last light of the moon as it sank behind the edge of the valley. Aiden looked more wolf than ever, at these times, and Jeremy almost expected him to change, like one of those creatures in the stories, until he smiled back.

Aiden loved him. With that smile, he had no doubt.

And then, to Jeremy's eternal delight, he began to sing "The Book of Love."

Jeremy's breath caught, and he let his boy's voice wash over him, warm and throaty and whiskey rough. When he got to the part about singing, Jeremy joined him, knowing his own voice was thin and thready. But Aiden's eyes lit up as they sang softly about love in the predawn darkness.

When they were done, Aiden kissed him, and neither of them cared about morning breath, they just cared that their person was there *this* morning, and they could touch each other in warmth and tenderness.

Aiden pulled back reluctantly. "I've got to shower—and I figured you'd want one too."

Jeremy nodded, feeling the rankness from the hospital all over his skin, in spite of the sponge baths he'd gotten. "The cast is removable," he said, gesturing to his leg. "But it's wrapped pretty tightly underneath, so we should cover that and keep it dry."

"I hear ya, Jer. You stay right there, and I'll go get you some pain meds and a trash bag. You got any bandages on your back?"

"One," Jeremy murmured. "Stanley bought me a new winter coat because I guess my old one was pretty tore up. We owe him."

"We do," Aiden said, nodding. "But mostly 'cause he brought you home. I'll be back."

He put on a sweatshirt over his bare chest and moccasins on his bare feet before he ghosted lightly down the stairs, but when he came back he had the promised pain meds and trash bags.

It took a little doing, but Ariadne had set up the shower stool like he'd needed the last time he'd been hurt, and soon he was sitting naked on it while Aiden stood in front of him, sheltering him from most of the pressure coming out of the pipe, and soaping himself head to toe.

"You gonna share with me?" Jeremy asked, lowering his head so he could get it wet. Oh, he wanted nothing more than clean hair right now. In a moment he felt the full pressure of the shower saturating his scalp and Aiden's warm fingers massaging the soap in. Jeremy let out a groan that was sheer hedonism, particularly when Aiden detached the showerhead and used it close up with a warm, soapy washrag on all of Jeremy's pits and creases.

Of course, the angle Aiden was leaning in put his lean-hipped nakedness right close to Jeremy's hands and face, and Jeremy couldn't resist touching his boy.

"You're being forward," Aiden murmured, but he sounded indulgent.

"You're tempting me," Jeremy told him, glad the spray was elsewhere so he could lift his face to Aiden's and give an impudent grin. "You can't hold me responsible for answering to temptation, can you?"

Aiden chuckled and replaced the showerhead before bending again and taking Jeremy's mouth, but this time with purpose and need.

Jeremy returned the kiss, his hands wandering, and when he found Aiden's cock, it was more than a little erect.

Five years they'd been pleasuring each other. Jeremy knew how to make it *fully* erect, and how to use his hands and his mouth to pleasure his husband.

Aiden's moan of completion resonated deep in the pit of Jeremy's soul, and he swallowed Aiden down and then let the shower spray take what was left on his face. Aiden bent and took his mouth again and then stood and pulled Jeremy's head against his middle, gently.

"God, Jeremy. You scared the shit out of me. Let's try not to do that again, okay?"

"Yeah, boy," Jeremy answered, out of fight about this. "We'll do our best." They both knew that either one of them would have done it for Persephone or Ariadne or any one of their family. But they had each other to live for—they didn't want to leave this planet early, either.

Aiden turned off the water then and dried them both off and got them dressed. The sky was growing gold above the edge of the valley, so it was probably getting to the point where Aiden had to leave.

"I'm gonna pick up them kids and drop Pippen off here before I take Gideon to the mill to work with me," Aiden said as he was brushing Jeremy's short hair so it would dry. "You liked Pip, right?"

"Yeah. I know he's gonna be with me today while Ariadne and Stanley and Johnny work the booth, and tomorrow, it's you and me while Pippen and Gideon go to work the booth with Stanley and Johnny." Craw tried hard to give them all at least Sunday's off, even when the work was off the charts busy.

"Well, hopefully he's good company," Aiden said seriously. "Doc said this thing's on ya until the week after New Year's." He gestured to the replaced walking cast with his chin. "He's going to be here, taking care of the stock, watching you, cooking meals—maybe even watching Persephone if the occasion calls for it. So it's nice you seemed to be getting along."

Jeremy had liked the young man with the large, innocent blue eyes and little bee-stung mouth. "Sweet kid," he said indulgently. "I think he's tryin' to learn how to be honest." To Jeremy, who had spent so much of his life on the grift, that was the highest compliment of all.

"Well, I can't think of a better teacher," Aiden said, helping him up. "How you doing? How's your pain? Do you think we need Johnny to help you down the stairs?"

"Naw," Jeremy murmured, leaning against Aiden. "You and me, we can get it done."

Aiden's arm around his shoulders was strong and safe, and the kiss Aiden dropped in his hair was even better. "Yeah, we can. Now let's get you downstairs so you can sleep some more, and I'll go get that Pippen kid so he can make you breakfast."

Jeremy closed his eyes and savored Aiden's warmth. "Aiden, do you think those two kids'll get together? Be happy? I sure would love to see that."

Aiden grunted. "Well, Jer—you especially should know it's never as easy as it should be, right?"

"Yeah," Jeremy agreed. "But it can still happen."

"Yeah, it can. You ready for the stairs? Here we go."

Recovery and Christmas

"Oh, I love the Sweeps box," said a younger woman—late twenties—tugging on her husband's hand. "You never know what you're going to get and the colors are so different!"

"But Monica," her husband complained good naturedly, "this store is *in town*. Some of these other booths are only here once a year!"

"But this is the good stuff! And they often have festival pricing!"

Ben smiled slightly and set his own knitting down to go wait on the woman, but Gideon beat him to it. Ben and Gideon, strictly speaking, were *not* supposed to be there. The schedule Craw had made up said Pippen and Ariadne were supposed to be there while Craw went to talk to some of the vendors who created things like artisan shawl pins and blown glass knitting needles, but Ariadne had come down with the slightest of sniffles (her words, but Craw apparently was super protective) so Ben was there, and Pippen didn't *go* anywhere without Gideon, and that went doubly true after... erm.

After.

It was good that Gideon came today, though, because Pippen had needed to make that date to squire Hillary around. Gideon's eyes tracked them as they visited booths—Pippen was making small purchases, his eyes alight as he looked at the artisan offerings. Incandescent pottery, stained glass, carved

187

items, fresh herbs, baked goods, quilted items—all of it top-notch and waiting in the tiny portable booths, each one warmed with a propane heater in the chill of the Colorado Christmas season. When Gideon had first heard that the staff was getting ready to participate in such an event, he'd had an uncharitable thought that it would be this booth and the booth of the local mental health clinic, but he'd been more than pleasantly surprised.

There was beauty everywhere, he thought now, watching as Pippen laughed at something Hillary said.

"She's a very pretty girl," Ben said carefully from his elbow after the couple had left. The day before—and the morning rush for all the people who'd decided to come back the next day—had finally cleared off, and Gideon had expected some talk. He'd welcomed it, even, because the people at Craw's mill were funny and knowledgeable. Even Craw, who liked to pretend he only knew about ten words.

Gideon snickered, which was juvenile of him, he knew, but he also knew he had nothing to worried about. "Too bad he's fantastically, fabulously gay."

Ben snorted. "You noticed that, did you?"

Gideon sent him a sideways look and just smiled.

"Ah," Ben murmured. "We were hoping as much. Not much to do out here—worrying about other people's love lives is a hobby."

Gideon smiled and bit his lip. That was nice. It was always nice when somebody was rooting for you. "We, uhm, can't be out. Not yet."

"Pippen's father?" It wasn't a question, not really. "He seems the type. What can he do to you?"

Gideon grimaced. "Not much when he flies back to New York and we're not on the next plane." Because that's how they'd book their flights—on purpose.

"Oh!" Ben said, surprised. "When's that?"

"First week in January," Gideon said. He paused. "But we can't stay here. He'll be back. We need to be long gone."

Ben nodded and looked about. "It's a shame," he said, sounding sincere. "We don't have much, but we could have given you a start."

Gideon smiled and met his eyes. "You already gave my boy courage. It's more than I could have asked for."

Ben smiled back, thoughtfully. "Maybe he already had the courage," he said softly. "Maybe you told him it was worth it to be brave."

Gideon shrugged and looked out to the fair again. Pippen was holding a tiny, porcelain-featured doll on his hand, with a beanbag satin body. It was probably a harlequin, and Hillary looked enchanted. Pippen raised his eyebrows and nodded his head toward the doll and Gideon nodded back, making a mental note to go buy it after they'd left.

"Does the, uhm, young lady know?" Ben asked delicately.

"Yeah," Gideon said, still not believing their luck. "This is a very public date."

Ben looked around comically and Gideon laughed and shook his head. "No—she's got Pip's cell phone. Pip's dad has a tracker, her dad has a tracker—she's going to go visit her boyfriend on the slopes and Pip and I will carry on here." He shrugged. "But it's only for a short time. We can deal."

"Mm…," Ben murmured. "See, I'd like to say that I had it easier, but I had to make Craw *talk*."

Gideon threw his head back and laughed in the shade of the Rocky Mountains, his body still alive from the lovemaking the night before. Perhaps he and Pip would cool it this night—the last two nights had been amazing, but shouldn't they be more afraid of being caught?

Perhaps not.

He was starting to wonder if he could sleep at all without Pip's body in his bed.

HILLARY ENJOYED their morning at the fair—and Pippen enjoyed taking her around. He knew Gideon would buy her the little harlequin doll as a Christmas gift because she'd seemed genuinely enchanted with it, and while he did that, Pip took Hillary to the hot chocolate booth and brought back four different kinds for Gideon and Ben to taste.

"Who are these people again?" Hillary asked curiously as they balanced large paper cups of dark chocolate, cinnamon chocolate, apple cider chocolate, and hot chili chocolate in drink carriers back to the knitting booth.

"Just folks we've met while we were here," Pippen said vaguely. "They needed a little help, and it was a chance to see the fair. I've never been to something like this—it was fun!"

"My parents go antiquing on Cape Cod all the time," Hillary said. "This is a little like that—but all in one place. All the artists here—it's really something."

"I'm always happy to see beauty in the world," Pippen said, his eyes catching Gideon as he bent his head to help an impossibly old woman, wrapped in a parka as big as she was, as she filled the bag at her wrist with yarn. Jeremy had told him that some people at the fair didn't travel much in the winter. Where this woman wouldn't have an opportunity to go to Craw's store until the snows lifted, there was a senior bus that brought folks to the town square to see the Christmas trees that had been decorated for the town contest as well as all the vendor booths. Colorado had a wealth of artisans—everybody from glass blowers to metal workers and beyond were here. Pippen imagined he could spend half his trust in small things that just made him or Gideon smile—but he had better things to spend it on at the moment.

"He *is* very pretty," Hillary said perceptively as they drew near the booth.

"I can't comment on that," Pippen murmured. "Besides, they're both pretty."

"Yeah but…."

Craw—big, burly, red-headed and terrifying—had entered the booth, and his gentle hand on Ben's hip as he traveled around him said all sorts of things that Pippen might not have.

Including the fact that Pippen wasn't there for Ben.

"I can't talk about it," Pippen said again, his voice kind but firm. "Hillary, there's more here at stake than you know, okay? When this month is over, you can fly back home to your parents and whatever fallout you have to face is yours. My dad has threatened people here already—innocent people. The fallout here could be huge—so please."

Hillary nodded, her mouth pinching at the corners. "I'm sorry to tease you," she murmured. "I… I wish we could. I wish I could bring Scott to your place at night for movies and pizza and we could compare classes and visit each other in the summer. I keep forgetting, you know?"

Pippen smiled at her a little. "Look—when this is clear, maybe I'll try contacting you, okay? Maybe we can do that sometime."

She gave him a relieved smile. "I'd really like that, Pip." They paused outside the booth, waiting for Gideon to finish with his customer. "Now, who's not getting hot chocolate?"

Pippen sighed. "Me and Gid'll split the hot pepper chocolate," he said with a sigh. He'd forgotten about Craw, who hadn't been at the booth most of the day.

Craw heard them and stared at him. "Oh please," he said. "If that isn't coffee, I don't want a fuckin' thing to do with it."

Ben sputtered into his hand before reaching out to take the cinnamon one from the drink holder. "He's not kidding," he said seriously. "I, on the other hand, would *love* some."

"Besides," Gid said, holding his head sideways to see what was written on the side of the cups. "You want the dark chocolate one, right?"

"Yeah," Pippen said, wrinkling his nose. "But you like the really hot stuff, so I thought you'd want to give it a try."

"Which leaves me with the cinnamon apple!" Hillary said happily. "Yay!" She took hers and proceeded to open the cup and lick the whipped cream from the top before looking up at all the men staring at her.

She stuck her tongue out at them before getting the dab off her nose with her thumb. "You're just jealous because I don't care," she said, and Pippen laughed before looking at Gideon.

Gideon rolled his eyes, as in, "Okay, yeah, she's not awful," and Pippen grinned at him. Gideon had been horrified to learn of Pippen's confidence in Ree, but Pippen had hope.

God knows, he'd need an ally in his father's world after this winter. Ree might not have any real power, but a good word, *anywhere,* could do it.

Hillary laughed with the men before asking to look at the yarn, and after a glance at Ben, Pippen came inside the booth and pointed out the things he knew.

"You don't want to work with alpaca first off," he said seriously. "It's got a halo, and that makes it sticky, so when you have mistakes you either can't see them or you can't fix them. As a newbie, you may want to go with the plain wool, superwash— although it makes it a little slippery—and if you don't want to spend a whole lot when you're going to make mistakes, there's the big chain stores that sell acrylic wool blends."

Hillary gave him an admiring glance. "Look at you! You sound like an expert already!"

Pippen shrugged. "I finished a project—and started another, actually. I don't think that makes me an expert." He'd finished his "long square" the day before at Jeremy's, after following the man's instructions to work on it until it was long enough to wrap around his head. What had followed had been a relatively simple explanation of how to sew and then gather, and the results had been, well, serviceable.

"It's not perfect," Pippen had said, a little depressed. The yarn he'd chosen still called to him—a just lovely gold and blue combination that made him happy. "I… I wouldn't want to give it to, say, Gideon."

"Put it on, boy," Jeremy told him. "Does it fit?"

It had—it had even covered his ears, and there'd been a little extra to fold at the forehead for a brim. "Yeah," he said, surprised.

"Does it keep your ears warm?" Jeremy asked, and Pippen grinned.

"Yes!" It had done that too.

"Then it works. You could wear it out of here—although I suggest you block it first. We've got a blocking form in the shed next to the house. You go out to get that—it's easy to spot, it's a big round wooden head-shaped thing—and bring it inside, and I'll walk you through it."

That had been fun. The entire *day* had been fun, including going up to Jeremy and Aiden's spare room and pulling out the three or four boxes of stash he had up there to the downstairs so they could go through them. He'd had Pippen plan a *couple* of projects—another hat, some hand warmers, a scarf with two colors—and pick out yarn for *all* of them, as well as a couple of skeins of impossibly fine yarn that Jeremy had plans for. Then, after Pippen had returned the boxes to where they lived in the guest room closet, he'd had Pippen retrieve a swift and a winder—two pieces of equipment whose entire job was to take a *hank* of yarn and change it into a *ball* of yarn. The half-hour had been spent talking to Jeremy as he'd learned how to put the hank on the swift and then wind it into a ball, using the kitchen table as an anchor. Looking at the battered table, Pip could see scuff marks where Aiden and Jeremy had done this, many, many times, and he felt comforted, somehow.

Without planning to, he'd entered a community of people with a history, and while the thing currently drying on the wooden form wasn't *perfect,* as Jeremy had pointed out, it would keep his ears warm, and he'd *made* it, and it was *real.*

So now, standing just close enough to Gideon to smell the chili-laced chocolate that he was drinking, Pippen felt a little bit of pride about knowing something—even the rudiments—of being a part of this world.

"What project did you start?" Hillary asked, looking over her shoulder.

Pippen darted his eyes toward Gideon, who caught the look and smiled. "A surprise," Gideon said, probably remembering when Pippen had tried to hide it from him the night before. The colors had been dark blue and forest green—masculine colors. *Gideon's* colors. It hadn't been a hard guess *who* it was for, had it?

"Ah," Hillary said, and then went back to looking at the supplies. "So," she said, after Ben was busy winding her bright maroon and green yarn, "what should it be? Crochet or knitting?"

Pippen glanced at Gideon, who shrugged. Gideon's knitting had gotten better—Pippen rather thought Gideon was making his own hat. Pippen hoped so; he was making the scarf to match the hat Gideon was working on.

"Gideon's knitting, I'm crocheting," he said. "We, uh, can't work on it when my dad's there."

Hillary's eyes got large, but she simply nodded. "Well, then—your room, tonight, after dinner, the three of us. You promise?"

Gideon and Pippen exchanged glances. "Sure," Pippen said. "But which one are you going to choose?"

In the end, she'd chosen the crochet hook, but since Gideon now had *two* sets of needles, Pip figured they could teach her whichever one worked best. He remembered Ariadne's advice—sometimes one worked, sometimes the other. He had no idea which one it would be, but suddenly the idea of having his own little circle made him happy. He loved his education, but besides the odd date, he really hadn't found a group of friends in school. The rich kids didn't want to work like he did, and the students who were serious were a little afraid of the rich kids. Pippen didn't blame them, but it had been lonely.

It was like his time here, this entire exercise making amends, had been a gift—a gift of making gifts, which was an amazing circle.

Finally, Hillary picked her yarn and then kissed Pippen on the cheek. "I've got an afternoon date," she said impishly. "Are you sure you don't need your vehicle?"

"No," Gideon said. "We've got a ride, right, Craw?"

"Yeah," Craw said gruffly. "We'll get you home." Or at least to the base of the driveway, before the cameras started, which was where Aiden had picked them up the day before and Craw had picked them up that morning. While they were at the mill or Jeremy's house, they had access to Jeremy's little car. They hadn't used it yet, but knowing they had it was a big deal.

It was, in fact, a little bit like Hillary having access to their rental.

Freedom.

195

"Will you be there for dinner?" she asked, and to Pip's surprise, Craw shook his head.

"They won't."

Ree raised her eyebrows but nodded. "All right, then. Nine o'clock, Pip—your room. See you there."

With that, she left, her new yarn bag swinging over her arm, her smile perky.

"What are we doing for dinner?" Gideon asked, finishing off the rest of his chocolate.

"Jeremy's house again," Craw said. "Ariadne and Rory's turn this time. Stanley and Johnny are leaving tomorrow morning—family."

Pippen's mouth parted, and he felt Gideon's hand creep into his. Neither of them said anything, not as Pippen came into the booth to help for the rest of the day, or as they all helped to pack up, but the meaning of it hit them square in the chest.

Family.

"THE PLACE is quiet without Stanley and Johnny," Pippen remarked the next day as he and Jeremy sat and worked on their projects. Pippen had gotten a bit of the striped scarf done the night before—he was pleased with how much better it looked than the hat, which he was wearing today. Inside. He was wearing it inside, because after its time on the blocking dummy, it fit his head perfectly and he was insufferably pleased with himself.

"They're good people," Jeremy said. "But I hope you didn't let Johnny take you too badly at poker."

Pippen laughed a little. Johnny had actually given him poker *lessons,* and Pippen felt like he was being graced by an artist. One who would never play legitimately, perhaps, but an artist. "I learned a lot from him," he said candidly. "Where did he learn to play like that?"

Jeremy was working on something that was a wee bit trickier than his regular fare—at least that's why Pippen thought he let the next thing pop out of his mouth. "Oh, them mob guys—you name any game meant to waste time and they know them all. Pinochle, cribbage, hand and foot. Didn't know a single guy without a deck of cards in his pocket and something to play with for stakes, even if it was just candy."

Pippen blinked. "Mob guys?" he asked, feeling stunned. "Is Johnny, uhm, connected?" Because of all the places he expected to find criminals, this little corner of the universe was not it.

"Naw—Johnny got out of the game same time I did. That's almost ten years—he was in WITSEC and everything. Then the guy he was gonna turn evidence on got killed and he didn't have to worry, so he could come out of WITSEC and be with Stanley. It was fine."

Pippen was en*chanted*. "Uhm, WITSEC? Wait—*you* were in the game? Jeremy, were *you* with the mob?"

Jeremy stared at him, as though he had no idea whatsoever how Pippen could have gotten *that* idea. "No! The mob wouldn't take a no-count grifter like I was—they're usually bigger money than that."

Pippen's eyes were going to dry out. "Uhm… okay. Jeremy, could you start at the beginning, maybe?"

Jeremy's attention was suddenly *fiercely* on his own hands. "It's a boring story, Pip. Whole town knows it—you don't want to hear it from me."

Oh, but he did! Pippen's fingers moved slowly as his mind raced. "Okay—boring story. Just—how do you *know* Stanley and Johnny?"

Jeremy brightened. "Well, Stanley works for one of the biggest yarn stores in Boulder—Craw used to deliver personally, but then we started just sending stock, and we all got to know Stanley pretty well."

197

Okay—that tracked. "So, how did Stanley meet Johnny?"

"Well, that's funny," Jeremy said, the brightening process continuing. "See, Ariadne's pregnancy was a real bear, and when she had to go into bed rest in Boulder, we started getting a delivery truck to come here. Johnny was the delivery driver—he met Stanley that way." He paused. "That was when he was in WITSEC," he added.

Okay, then. Pippen nodded. "You knew him before then?" He remembered Stanley telling him that.

"Yeah," Jeremy said with a sigh. He looked down at his hands and then looked up again. "See—Pippen, everybody in town knows this about me, 'cause it came out about that time. But you don't. I don't want you to regret what you and Gideon are doing for me because you're helping Craw and Ben and Aiden and Ariadne and all, and they're good people. They've never done nothin' bad in their lives to be sorry for. So I... I don't want you to feel bad about helping them, but you might feel bad about helping *me* is all. I shouldn't've said what I said about Johnny."

"But you didn't mean it bad," Pippen said softly. "You just meant that's something he had practice at. So Johnny's a good guy."

"Yeah," Jeremy said, still not looking at him.

"So are you saying you're not?"

Jeremy shifted uncomfortably and then winced, because his entire back and his ribs were still hurting and bruised. "You know how... how you don't want to be the guy your daddy wants you to be?"

Pippen blinked in surprise and nodded. "Yes."

"I didn't want to be the guy *my* daddy wanted me to be neither. But I didn't know any other way. So in the time it took me to figure out that cheating people wasn't a good way to be, I hurt those people by scamming them. That's where *I* met Johnny. Then I got in a fix—the kind of fix where they find your body in an unmarked grave—and Johnny covered for me and got me out of town. And I decided to go straight." He smirked suddenly. "Honest," he amended, and Pippen smiled. "It took two years in prison for me to figure out how. When I got out, Craw gave me the job here—and that was eight years ago. I… I been honest since, but it's not easy to tell someone who don't already know."

He let out a breath, deflating somehow, and Pippen realized he was tired. Gently, he reached out and took Jeremy's work from his hands. It was looking like a sweater, all in one piece, something simple and well made with good yarn, and Pippen didn't see a pattern that he was working from—it was all in his head. Jeremy really *was* a skilled yarn worker, and his help had made Pippen one too.

"It's okay," he said softly. "I'm not going to hold who you were years ago against you now. Stanley said you knew about giving second chances, and now I know why, that's all. It's okay you told me, Jeremy. It means I can give someone else a second chance when the time comes. That's all."

Jeremy nodded, but he'd hit his limit for the day. Pippen tucked his project in the basket by the couch and helped him move his legs onto the cushions and his head onto the pillow so he could nap.

When he was asleep, Pippen did the lunch dishes and petted the dog—mostly because he liked Bluebell and she deserved some good love—and then, out of curiosity, he got out his phone and accessed the internet.

Jeremy had said, "everybody knows about that here," and, "until the bad guy died," which meant that something—*something* might have hit the papers.

It didn't take him long to find it.

He read article after article, glancing periodically over to the man sleeping on the couch, and tried to keep the tears from burning their way into being.

It didn't work, and he had to wipe his face on his shoulder more than once.

Oh, Jeremy. *No wonder Aiden was so protective. No wonder Johnny and Stanley would do anything for you.* If anybody knew about how much someone had to sacrifice to earn a second chance, it would be the man sleeping off his injury on the couch.

He'd managed to pull himself together by the time Aiden got home with Gideon in tow. Pippen had warmed dinner, and Aiden brought Jeremy a plate so they could talk quietly on the couch while Gideon and Pippen ate together at the table.

"You look sad," Gideon said, keeping his voice low so he couldn't be overheard.

Pippen shook his head. "Later," he said, meaning *later,* when they were alone together, in bed, sharing each other in ways that had not grown any less glorious since that first night.

After dinner dishes were done, Aiden drove them partway up Pippen's driveway—where the cameras started, both Pippen and Gideon checked—and dropped them off, promising to get them at the end of the driveway the next morning. Yeah, it was godawful cold, getting picked up in the crack of dawn in the snow, but Pippen was starting to not mind. He was spending his days caring for a nice man, being a part of a nice family. It was, perhaps, the best thing he'd ever done.

They trudged up the driveway together, giving a sigh of relief when Hillary drove up behind them and gave them a ride to the carport so they could all get out at the same time. She was chatty and excited—apparently she and her beau had gone shopping in Boulder that day, and the SUV was full of bags of a thousand different things.

"Do I need to know what they are?" Pippen asked. "Will there be a quiz later?"

She laughed. "No—don't worry. Daddy's used to me spending money." Her smile faded. "I think *he* thinks it's all I know how to do."

Pippen nodded. He wanted to spill his plan for spending *real* money, and for doing it in a way that was maybe the least selfish thing he'd ever done, but as much as he liked Hillary, he still wasn't ready to share the secret of Craw's mill and the shop and the little house on the corner property, and the many ways his father could ruin it all.

"Prove him wrong," is what he did say. "You know you can do more. Prove him wrong."

She paused, mid-breath. "How?"

"Be something *you* want to be," Gideon said. "Take the classes, get the job—be the person *you* planned for. Not the one he did."

Pippen smiled slightly. Gideon knew his plans—they were Gideon's plans too.

"What are you going to be, Pip?" Hillary asked, suddenly earnest.

Pippen thought of Jeremy, sleeping peacefully in his own home, ashamed because he'd been brought up to cheat and who had paid a high price to change his life and say that's not who he was anymore.

"Honest," he said. Yeah, he could do lots of things—software, security, the law. Maybe the law—that could use some help and some change. But mostly, he thought Jeremy had the right of it. "Whatever it is I become when it's all said and done, I want it to be honest."

Pip's dad made them sit and eat. He and Gideon pushed food around on their plates, already full up on the dinner served at Aiden and Jeremy's table. They made polite conversation and rubber-stamped Hillary's account of their day. She talked about shops in Boulder and how much she loved the city and how much she was looking forward to going to Denver over the next two days. Pippen made a mental note to ask if he and Gideon could use Jeremy and Aiden's guest bedroom and mostly checked out.

It wasn't until he and Gideon had excused themselves and were fleeing to their rooms for a shower that Pippen's father stopped them both cold.

"Mr. Haze," Talbot said, "I can't help but notice tonight, your clothes are looking particularly ragged for someone who claims to have spent the day shopping."

Pippen had to keep himself from gasping. He glanced over at Gideon, who was looking at himself skeptically. His typical "uniform" was jeans and a sweater—Pippen knew he wore coveralls when working in the mill and his sweater probably got folded up and stashed in the store or the house. Gideon's boots had gotten a workout over the last month, most definitely, and apparently, today, there'd been a grease spill that had seeped through the coveralls.

And today must have been carding and sorting day because Gideon had random bits of white fiber in his short-cut, curly hair.

"A car in front of us had a flat tire," Hillary said, earning herself a glare of disapproval from Talbot. "Gideon helped replace it. The roads are nasty out, Mr. Madison—I hadn't realized he'd gotten so messy!"

"And the—"

"Stuffed animal store," Pippen said, because he'd seen a giant stuffed bear in the packages in the back of the SUV. "Jesus, Dad—sorry we don't live up to your standards. Now if you'll excuse us, Gideon would probably love a shower."

And with that, he and Gideon made their exit while he silently blessed Hillary, who was still finishing off her dinner in the dining room.

"That was close," Gideon murmured after they'd made it into his room. "I'm going to start having to bring a change of clothes for after work." They'd dropped off their canvas project bags and their coats before going down for dinner, and Pippen flopped on his love seat in exaggerated relief.

"Thank God for Hillary," Pippen murmured. "God, I thought he had us dead to rights."

"Still," Gideon murmured, sitting on his own bed and looking depressed. "We might want to cool it tonight—"

Pippen shook his head. "No," he said gruffly.

"Pip—"

Pippen felt his shock and sadness overwhelm him again. Before he could stop it, the entire story from five years ago that he'd looked up on his phone spilled out between them, while Gideon listened in growing horror.

"Three months?" he asked. "I've heard them say that—that he was in the hospital for three months. Oh God. Oh *God*." He shuddered and moved next to Pippen, obviously needing the comfort. "Oh, Pip," he said, as Pippen leaned his head on Gideon's shoulder. "Pippen, we've got to… we've got to get out of these people's lives."

"But not yet," Pippen said. "We can't yet—Gideon, they need you working. They need someone to take care of Jeremy. We… we can't leave yet."

"But we *are* going to leave," Gideon asked anxiously, and Pippen's newfound knowledge hit him hard in the chest.

"Gideon, I won't ever lie to you," he said softly. "If there's one thing I've learned in this last month, it's that if I want to be the kind of person who deserves you, I need to live like Jeremy. I need to live honest."

"Pip," Gideon said, "You were never a con man—"

"You think what I do at my father's dinner table isn't a con?" Pippen asked steadily. "Do you think this game we're playing, where we keep our activities away from him, isn't a cheat? It's a good cheat—it's for a good cause—but if I'd been honest with my father from the very start, if I'd stood up to him just once—"

"You would have spent three months in the hospital," Gideon retorted, his voice breaking. "I know you would have, Pip. I saw the bruises in those first months."

Pippen whimpered. "You stopped them," he said, not wanting to cry more today.

"But how long did you have to be alone?" Gideon's voice broke, and Pippen held him, rocking him, shedding his own tears for Jeremy who had almost died breaking away from the life he'd been born into, and for Aiden who'd gotten there in time to save him—but not in time to not see him suffer.

Their storm of tears passed, finally, and Gideon's mouth found his, briny and urgent. Pippen kissed him back and they found themselves naked, making frantic, passionate love and muffling their noises in their arms, in their shoulders, and, in Pippen's case, in the pillow in front of him as Gideon thrust into him from behind.

When they were finally, irrevocably done, their breaths coming in harsh pants in the steamy room, Gideon finally spoke. "God, Pippen—I hope this plan of yours works."

"Me too," he murmured, looking at Gideon's tear-stained face in the moonlight. "Gideon, what do you think I should be when I grow up?"

A smile played with Gideon's lips then, and he traced Pippen's cheekbones with his fingertips. "Who says you're not grown up now?"

"You know what I mean. When I get to go back to college, after you and me have a life together. I need a goal. A thing to become."

"A nurse?" Gideon offered. "A caregiver? A therapist?"

Those occupations filled Pippen's chest, and he suddenly realized how limited his own plans had been. His father had seen him as a suit—and that's how Pippen had seen himself too. But Gideon had watched him care for Jeremy, and now Gideon could see other plans.

"I love who you think I can become," he said in wonder.

"I love who you are right now," Gideon said soberly.

They didn't make love again. Instead, they talked quietly about the plan—and then *their* plan—until it was time for Pippen to shower and go to his room. He wore Gideon's sweats, hanging from his hips as he let himself into his room, and in his heart he dared somebody to see him and stop him.

JEREMY HAD hit the tired, restless part of being home—he could feel it in his bones. Stanley and Johnny had brought in a Christmas tree over the weekend, which had given Jeremy the satisfaction of helping Pippen decorate the house, so that was nice, but Jeremy had been home for two weeks at this point and he missed *everything* about his life, from working with the machinery to the shop to feeding the stock—even eating lunch in Craw's kitchen, because Ben would be there and he missed *everybody*.

The last time he'd been laid up, he'd almost killed himself going back to work too early, but this time... this time, in addition to the leg, which still ached interminably if he was on it too long, he had Pip to take care of.

Yeah, sure, he knew it was supposed to be the other way around, but as they sat and plied needles and hook (Pip was on

205

his *fifth* project now, a very basic sweater, and Jeremy wondered if Pip thought he was kidding anybody about who these projects were for because besides a scarf for his friend Ree, they were all so obviously in Gideon's colors) Jeremy had a feeling that Pip was so in need of some quiet caretaking—and some purpose—that he might take Jeremy's usual restlessness as a rejection.

So Jeremy sat back and let the young man fuss over him, and kept him busy and talking and learning and… content.

Jeremy had grown up under a controlling father, one who had seen his own son as a means to an end rather than a person to love. He knew what it was like, to break away from a set of beliefs and norms that had been bred into his very bones. He could listen to Pip, steer him away from his father's thinking, his father's words coming out of his own mouth, and give the boy room to find his own thoughts and words.

When he'd confessed to Jeremy that he wanted to go to nursing school, Jeremy had felt his eyes get hot. With this kid, that wasn't pie in the sky dreaming. Pippen would be good at that—Jeremy was sure.

But still, Jeremy was on the verge of testing the family's resolve not to let him tend his own stock (and really, how hard was it to go out to the little rabbit hutch and brush the critters? How hard?) when they were knitting on the couch one cold, mid-December morning. Pip got a buzz in his pocket and checked his phone—and turned whiter than snow.

"Pip, what's wrong?" Jeremy asked immediately. "Is it Gideon?"

Pippen shook his head. "It's Hillary—she said she ran into my father on the slopes. She… she's got my car, see? We know he tracks Gideon's rental, so we gave it to her so he'd think we were together."

Jeremy opened his mouth, because it was both smart and frightening that he and Gideon would have to take such measures to so much as visit friends or find an occupation that Pip's father didn't approve of.

"Did she say anything?" Jeremy asked.

Pip read, "'I'm sorry, Pip—he caught me off guard. I said you guys were in town and he guessed the knitting shop. He's on his way over, and he's pissed.'"

Jeremy took a deep breath and said, "Okay, so put on your hat and gloves and grab a sandwich, then go out into the critter hutch and bring your knitting."

"What?" Pippen said, his fingers flying on his phone, probably to text Gideon.

Jeremy pulled out his own phone and texted Ariadne and Ben, because they wouldn't be in the mill doing stuff that wouldn't let them hear their phones, and then looked up at Pippen in irritation.

"Boy, put on your hat, your gloves, grab your knitting bag and a book, and go out into the rabbit hutch before your father gets here."

Pippen gaped at him.

"Are you not hearing me?" Jeremy asked, feeling like Aiden probably had in their first year of acquaintance, as Aiden had tried to explain being honest to Jeremy. "Boy, go hide in the outbuilding where your father wouldn't be caught dead!"

"But what about you?" Pippen asked, looking shocked.

Jeremy scowled at him. "If this little ol' hayseed can't deal with some guy in thousand-dollar shoes, I ain't never grifted one before. But leave the dog, okay? Just in case your dad turns out to be a secret ninja or something."

Hearing the slam of the mudroom door a few minutes later as Pippen—now in boots and his warm coat and mittens and such—took off down the walkway actually sent a wave of relief coursing down Jeremy's back. He was not afraid of this rich man—not with the dog by his side—but he was afraid for

Pippen and Gideon and all the good they seemed to be doing in their own lives by helping him and his family with theirs.

The knock came after about ten minutes—just when Jeremy was about to text Pippen and tell him to come in, actually, which meant Jeremy's con man instincts were a bit rusty. Bluebell launched herself at the door, barking madly, and Jeremy let her, wrestling with his crutches and his phone until he made his way to the door.

It only took a short word to Bluebell to get her to stand down, because she was good dog, oh yes she was, and then Jeremy was face-to-face with the boogeyman.

He was met with zero surprises, from the man's pricey wool coat to his felted East Coast Fedora, down to his expensive, shiny boots. Even his chauffer, standing uncomfortably on the walkway behind him, in full uniform, was what Jeremy expected. Most bankers, he'd learned, were really highly paid grifters, and appearance was everything.

And right now, in sweats and a tatty sweater, his own appearance was exactly what he'd told Pippen it would be.

"Can I help you?" he asked guilelessly. "I'm sorry, we're not buying anything—maybe some of the houses closer to town?"

"Where's my son?" Talbot Madison asked, and Jeremy didn't have to hide his eyebrows going up.

"Sir, if you lost a child in Colorado in December, you need to call the sheriff so he can get a search and rescue team out right away!"

"He's fully grown, dammit," Madison barked. "And I know he's here—either in this house or the one behind it, with the damned animals."

Jeremy stared at him. "That's an awful big jump in logic, sir, from your grown son isn't at home to he's at the house of a man you've never met before. How in the *hell* did you get from A to B? I am *boggled.*"

"He and his man keep coming home with… with *wool* on them." Madison said the word like it was dirty, and Jeremy smirked. "What are *you* laughing about?"

"Well, sir, that fancy coat on your back is *made* of the stuff. You'll have to be more specific than that."

"Look, I won't press charges—"

"For what?" Jeremy asked, not having to feign the outrage. "Here I was, laid up and doing my Christmas knitting, and you come banging on my door asking for some random kid I might or might not know. Who in the hell are *you* and why would I know your son?"

"I'm Talbot Madison, the man who's about to own half this town, including the note on this quaint little firetrap, and I have no idea why you people seem to know him!"

"You don't own the note on this house," Jeremy said flatly, hating that he'd been right about that. "My landlord owns this house outright. He inherited it from his Great Aunt Gertie, and she was a sweet lady, and this house is snug and warm in the middle of Colorado in winter, so it's possible you don't know what you think you know. Now why are you looking for your kid here, at a private residence, and why shouldn't I sic my dog on you, or call my husband here with a shotgun? I am injured and I am in pain and I don't got no truck with stupid rich guys in shiny shoes blaming me for people I don't got no business knowing."

"Your husband?" the man asked, and Jeremy rolled his eyes.

"Yes. My husband with the shotgun. *Why do you think your kid's here?*"

Madison swallowed audibly, probably getting his temper down. "This property is right across from mine. Pippen and his driver have been walking down the driveway and disappearing or being dropped nearby by his girlfriend—and disappearing then too. I have to assume they've gone somewhere close since my son is too lazy to walk further than across his room to look at his computer."

Jeremy hadn't seen many people bustle around his house the way Pippen Talbot had, but telling this man that would be a waste of breath, not to mention the boy's safety.

"Why does it matter to you?" he asked instead. "You said the boy's grown—why do you care where he's going? Is he ditching out on work?"

"He's on a break from school, and he's *supposed* to be squiring his future bride around. I tracked his phone up to the ski slopes today, only to find he'd left the thing in his car and had been dropped off in town. *Where did he go?*"

"*Why don't you ask him?*" Jeremy asked back in the same high-handed tone. "And feel free to come back and tell me what he says—just remember, I'm asking my husband to leave the shotgun near the door, so you might want to be polite when you do it."

And with that, he took a step back into the house and slammed the door in Talbot Madison's outraged face.

He clomped back to the couch on his crutches and sank down into the cushions, trying to still his beating heart. When his fingers wouldn't shake on the keys, he texted Pip first.

Stay there for another twenty minutes. I heard the SUV leave but I want Aiden to drive down and make sure they're gone. You're warm enough, right?

Super cozy. But I'll be ready to pee by the time Aiden gets here.

Jeremy smiled. Boy, he liked this kid. *I'll have him hurry.*

Then he texted Aiden. *Talbot Madison was just here. I sent him on his way, but Pippen's in the rabbit hutch and we need to know it's clear before he comes back into the house.*

The phone rang in his hand.

"Jesus, Jer! The hell?"

"He tracked the boy's phone to the slopes and stopped by to pay a little visit," Jeremy said. "He doesn't know for sure the guys are coming here—he just assumes because we're close by, we're where they're heading when they get out of camera range."

Aiden swore. "Damn, but this guy's a tight fucker. Poor Pippen—I would have broken through the walls to get out of that cage."

"I am sayin'," Jeremy agreed. "And Aiden, whoever comes by to make sure the car is clear, you need to tell Craw or Ben that he claimed he was about to own half the town, including this house. Now since I know he can't own this house, he may be exaggerating, but I think we need to have Ben deal with the banking people, don't you?"

Aiden grunted. "Yeah. Uhm, he's been doing that, Jeremy—since you said something the first time. We didn't want to worry you, but...."

Jeremy's heart started racing again. "But what? Boy? The mill and the ranch?" He and Aiden both knew about the loan Craw had needed to take out after the fire. A lot of folks around Granby had needed to do that. If the wrong person held those notes, half the town could be out on their asses.

"Old Tommy at the bank's been putting up a pretty good fight," Aiden said softly. "But his boss found out this week that Tommy's been fending off offers. He might have to sell the mortgages before Christmas."

Jeremy let out a long breath. "Well, shit. What can we do? Do we know?"

"I don't know, Jer," Aiden said softly. "But we've faced worse, so we're not gonna panic, right?"

They had faced worse. And it had made them strong enough to deal with whatever they had to deal with now. "Yeah, boy. I hear ya. Look, send someone out to check to see if he's gone as soon as you can. Pippen's stuck in the rabbit hutch and the poor boy's gotta pee."

Aiden snorted. "Poor kid." Then he let out a long, shuddery breath. "And there you were, standing up to the bad guy again, putting yourself between him and his victim. You're getting good at that, Jer."

"Not that good," Jeremy said practically. "I should hit the head before Pippen gets out. I gotta do more than pee."

Aiden chuckled again, the sound strained, but he signed off. Jeremy went to use the bathroom then, because he hadn't been joking. Something about Talbot Madison's frigid ice-floe eyes had made his water drop. He'd seen those eyes before, in trained killers and drug-addled mob guys and stone-cold con men who would leave a man to die in a storm before giving back his last twenty. Jeremy knew from evil, and he didn't regret, not for a moment, keeping Pippin away from his father.

PIPPEN *DID* have to pee when he got out, and partly for the same reasons as Jeremy did.

That half-hour in the rabbit hutch had been close—not just with his father, but with his plan. He'd placed three phone calls in that time, each one needing more finesse than the last, his entire plan to protect Craw's people hinging on every word, every moment, with a little help from Pippen's financial connections due to being Talbot Madison's son and his B in economics.

That half-hour had the distinction of being the half-hour in which Pippen became the owner of a shell corporation using nothing but his allowance, and then had spent ninety percent of his trust in an investment he had no real hopes would pay for itself in the next ten years.

And then he'd contacted Tommy Marshall and had a frank conversation about his father, and what Pippen would do if

Tommy could put off selling the loan notices of the town until the twenty-first.

The man had been so relieved, he'd cried. He hadn't trusted Talbot Madison—or the middleman in charge of making the purchase. Nobody had been able to tell him what the notices were wanted for, and Madison's company had a reputation for evicting people and then using the property for development that they sold to foreign investors. The livelihood not just of Rance Crawford and his tiny business was being threatened, but of the *entire valley.* Pippen understood the stakes then, and had sworn Tommy to secrecy because if his father got wind of Pippen's plan, no amount of stonewalling on Tommy's part could make it work.

They had a week—that was all. One week of Pippen and Gideon sneaking around and Tommy Marshall hiding from his boss and Talbot Madison's bank guy. If they could manage to hold off the wolves for *one week,* well, Pippen would feel a lot better about what he could accomplish with his life, not to mention with the trust Gideon was putting in his hands.

He needed to be the kind of man Gideon could have faith in, or this amazing, wonderful, awful, painful Christmas would be for naught.

His phone calls were done, and he was literally dancing as he sat, when the door to the rabbit hutch flew open and Gideon stood there in the doorway.

Pippen launched himself into his arms and clung, shaking, unashamedly seeking out his warmth and taking his protection just because he offered it.

"I hear you gotta pee," Gideon murmured.

"What took you so long?" Pippen asked plaintively.

"I had to hide in my own critter den," Gideon murmured. "But lucky me, mine had a bathroom."

213

Pippen let out a semi-hysterical laugh and allowed Gideon to walk him back to the mudroom, making sure the door to the hutch was closed and the heater was turned down so the well-furred bunnies and chinchillas wouldn't get too hot. By the time he'd taken off his boots and gotten to use the facilities, Ariadne had cooked them all some quesadillas for dinner, complete with sour cream and chicken and salsa.

Pippen and Gideon sat and ate quietly, listening as Ariadne and Jeremy spoke in a weird, almost truncated language.

"Craw got—"

"All the dyeing done."

"But the specials?"

"Aiden now."

"Kay. Ben?"

"Shop."

"Percy?"

"With Ben."

"Not me?" He hit a plaintive note there.

"Aiden'll bring her!" Ariadne placated.

"Yeah, fine." Jeremy pouted, and Pippen and Gideon met eyes in gentle amusement. It was easy to see why he was everybody's favorite, but there was a core of child still in his heart. Children didn't always bear disappointment well.

"You done with Christmas?"

Jeremy made a face. "Had to add stuff."

And so on. Pippen stared at them in bemusement until Gideon said, "Aiden and Craw are the same way. Ben says sometimes that the only reason they keep him around is that he can speak human being."

Pippen almost snickered quesadilla across the table, and Ariadne sent them a droll look.

"We were in adjoining hospital beds for three months," she told them with a roll of her eyes. "Poor Jeremy's jaw was broken and so were most of his teeth—trust me, you'd invent your own language too."

Pippen swallowed. "Why were you—"

She shrugged. "I was pregnant and on bedrest when Jeremy got hurt. We were both so homesick, it only made sense to put us in the same room. I reckon we got each other through."

They both nodded, and Pippen thought the obvious question, the intrusive one that he didn't have the right to ask.

Ariadne read it in his eyes, though. "I can't," she said softly. "I'd do it all over again to have another kid, but my body won't do it. My kidneys'll shut down."

Jeremy patted her hand as they sat. "It's a good thing you had a perfect baby the first time around."

Ariadne's affectionate look at Jeremy made Pippen's heart swell. "Yeah, Jer. We really lucked out."

Pippen clenched Gideon's hand under the table, and they finished dinner in contemplative quiet.

GIDEON WAS ready for Talbot Madison when they entered the house.

He and Pippen had let Aiden drop them off in Jeremy's car, once again just out of sight of the cameras, and they'd trudged their way under dark skies and drifting snow up to the house.

He told Pippen about the little room in the barn, with a cot and bookshelves and a hotplate and a bathroom with a shower stall, which is where Craw had put him after Jeremy's text that Madison was on his way. "I guess Jeremy lived there, his first few months working for Craw," he finished with. "It wasn't... awful, I guess. It was small, but the animals were outside, and I guess Jeremy would eat with Craw sometimes, and watch TV in the farmhouse. Craw said something about how anything grander would have made Jeremy bolt." Gideon paused. "When

I got out of the Corps, anything bigger than our plain, eight-man barracks made me jittery. If the paper is right, and Jeremy worked at Craw's after prison, it stands to reason."

Pippen *hmm*ed. "He just… just told me to go hide and then answered the door. It's funny—I… I never really thought of what courage was before. I knew *you* were brave, because you were in the service. I knew people who stood up to my father were brave, including my mother, because he's a scary guy. But I never really thought about how… how a person could just answer a door and put themselves between something bad and another human being—that's a really brave thing to do."

Gideon hadn't said anything. He just grabbed Pippen's hand and vowed he'd be that guy.

So when Pippen opened the door and his father stood there, glowering, Gideon stepped in front of Pip and let Pippen slide into the house behind him.

"Where in the *hell* have you been?" Talbot exploded, little flecks of spittle hitting Gideon's face.

"Out," Gideon replied shortly. "Why does it matter?"

"You were *supposed* to be with Hillary!"

"Was she complaining?" Gideon asked.

Talbot flailed his hands, which ordinarily would have been quite amusing, but not right now. "It doesn't matter! My son is supposed to *marry* this girl—do you understand? They are supposed to be *courting*—it's the whole reason she and her father are visiting. Wherever he's having you take him, you are *defying my orders.*"

Gideon stared at him impassively. "My orders—and my contract—says I shall accompany your son where he goes and keep him safe," he said. He'd read the document a thousand times. "It doesn't say a word—not one word—about you having the right to tell me where to take him. There is no mention of you having access to your adult child 24/7. If you wish to change the terms of the contract, you'll need to run it by a lawyer, but you may want to wait until after Christmas."

Talbot stared at him in absolute rage. *"Where. Do. You. Go?"*

Gideon had no problem lying. "Ice skating," he said. Then he started for the stairs, Pip at his heels.

Talbot stayed at the doorway, gaping at them like a landed trout, until they disappeared.

That night, Pippen waited until very late to sneak into his room. When he was there, he told Gideon in the softest of whispers what he'd done with a cell phone while trapped in the rabbit hutch. Gideon had laughed a little, proud of his boy, pleased—so pleased—at what he'd managed to do. Even more, he was pleased at what Pippen planned to do when this was all over.

This man in his arms—he was someone worth knowing. Worth protecting. Worth helping until Gideon's last breath.

He planned to do just that.

Birthdays and Graduations

"CAKE AND ice cream at Jeremy and Aiden's house," Craw told Ariadne as she bustled into the shop, Persy on her hip. "You'll be there, right?"

Ariadne nodded. "Where's Ben?" she asked, and Craw tried not to look guilty.

"Bank," he said gruffly. Tommy had called Ben that morning, and the news hadn't been good. He didn't want to scare Ariadne—didn't want to scare *any* of them—but Tommy said there was some sort of *war* going on, involving half the properties in Granby. There had been a good guy and a bad guy—that's what Craw had gotten from the man, and their stand-ins were duking things out *that day,* in a bidding war, apparently for the future of the town.

Nobody put it that way. The residents of the town were completely in the dark—but Craw knew how these things went. First the bank notices got sold, then the new owners—usually foreign investors—called in the loans. When people couldn't pay, they were evicted and the property snapped up for a song. Then the purchaser would develop the land for people with money—real money—and Granby would cease to be a town where people owned their own businesses and become a town owned by a single resort, and employees were trained elsewhere and shipped in. His friends, his neighbors, would lose their jobs, their businesses, their homes, and the quirky things about the

218

area—the pub where they'd held the benefit for Ariadne, for instance, and the place that *wasn't* Starbucks where everybody got their coffee—those became chain places, places nobody remembered but everybody looked for because they were the same in Seattle or New York.

And his home, his mill, his house, his shop—all of it—would get disbanded, destroyed, leveled. It could become property for a big house, like the Madison mansion across the road, or it could become a development—apartments for the people getting shipped in. Hell, it could become a strip mall—he didn't know.

But it would cease to be the business he'd inherited from his father and hated, and then built up for himself and loved. It would cease to be the thing that employed his friends, his family, the thing that had kept them afloat and together during the fires and the pandemic and Jeremy's troubles and Persy's babyhood, and it would become neutral, scorched earth, concrete, or a haven for rich people, three months out of the year.

The worry churning in Craw's gut was a terrible thing—it was almost as bad as when Ariadne had been laid up before she had Persephone, or when Persephone had gone in for her fifty-dozen operations, or when Jeremy had been beaten nearly to death and Aiden had been facing down a murder charge with nothing more than his absolute conviction that he'd had no other choice.

Aiden hadn't, but if Craw could find a way to walk across the road to Madison Talbot's house and shoot him dead where he stood without losing his land and his family anyway, he'd make that choice in a heartbeat.

He couldn't make himself regret defending Gideon and Pippen, but God, he could make himself regret not driving Talbot Madison out of their town years ago when he'd first bought that plot of land.

And this worry was a thing he absolutely couldn't share with any of his people.

He couldn't. This was *his* land, and *his* responsibility, and he and Ben had done their best, but in the end, it had come down to leviathans, fighting for this little strip of earth, and Ben and Craw huddling in their home, holding each other, praying they were neither crushed nor scorched in the battle.

Finding out that today was Pippen's birthday and planning a small dinner celebration for the boy was much easier. Craw wished Jeremy hadn't needed to be hurt to meet the two young men, but he sure did like them now that they were in the orbit of his little world.

"Craw?" Ariadne said, for maybe the umpteenth time. "Craw, where are you?"

Craw tried to give her his usual scowl, but he must have failed, because her eyes widened and she strode to the counter. "Rance Crawford, I've called your name three times, asking about a gift for Pippen—what in the hell are you thinking?"

Craw swallowed. God, Ari was a pain in the ass. A best friend shouldn't ever be this discerning, because then you might be tempted to tell her the thing that would break her heart.

Or maybe she already knew.

"Craw?" she asked again, leaning against him as he leaned against the counter. "What's wrong?"

He turned his head and she sighed, her eyes growing bright. "He's coming after us?" she asked quietly.

"He's coming after the whole town," Craw answered, apparently weaker than he had been eight years ago. "Ari, he's buying up all the loans in Granby."

"Is there any way to stop him?"

Craw shrugged. "Tommy seems to think there's someone else—one of those rich guys who likes to, you know, give back or something. That there's a sort of… battle, going on. Ben went to the bank to see what he could do."

Ariadne blew out a breath and leaned her head against his shoulder. He wrapped his arm around her, so grateful for this woman, gruff and sharp-tongued and smart and so, so warm-hearted. He hadn't been looking for an Ariadne when she'd come asking for a job, but sometimes life gave you exactly what you needed whether you were looking for one or not.

"Nothing we can do about it?" she asked softly.

"Not a goddamned thing," he said.

"So," she said after a beat, "Pippen's present. You have any ideas?"

"A sweater's worth of yarn," Craw told her. "In a color Aiden put together called *Gid and Pip*."

She laughed, because knitter's jokes were the best sometimes. "Good heavens, Craw—what are we giving the poor boy for Christmas?"

"You'll have to ask Jeremy about that one," Craw said. "He says he's been working on it while he and the boy spend time. That and poker, which apparently Pip can't get enough of. But it should be wrapped and under the tree already."

"What about Gideon?" Ariadne asked. They'd all grown to like the stoic, dryly humored Gideon as he'd worked. Intense, yes—but he was a quick learner, and quick with a one-liner if he saw an opening.

"Aiden's making *his* sweater," Craw murmured. "Or I should say, has made." Gideon hadn't taken to knitting quite like Pippen had taken to that weird craft with the hook, but Craw didn't hold it against him. He figured the boy would have a passable hat by Christmas.

"Well, I'm glad they found something to do with their time," Ariadne said, laughing a little.

Craw gave her a droll look—during good times, Jeremy and Aiden had shown up looking bleary and razor-burned and happy enough to let the whole world know their love life didn't suffer any. Craw and Ari both had money down on what the two men would do with their time when they couldn't spend it in bed.

Apparently, the answer was still, "Knit."

Or, well, that weird craft with the hook that Jeremy seemed so taken with this year.

"Mommy!" Persephone called. "Benth here!"

They both looked through the store window and out to the parking area, where Ben pulled up. He barely stayed at the mat to stomp out the snow in his boots before he burst inside the shop.

"Well?" Craw asked.

"What happened?" Ariadne asked on his tail.

Ben stared at them and shrugged. "I… I have no idea. Tommy couldn't even give me the name of the company that won the bidding war." He gave another, smaller shrug. "All he could tell me was, you know, to don't lose hope."

Craw and Ariadne nodded, and Ben came over to where they huddled behind the counter. He put his hand on Craw's bristly cheek and rubbed under his eyes with his thumb.

"Take him seriously," Ben said. "Craw, don't lose hope."

Craw closed his eyes under Ben's touch and captured his hand, kissing it in a rare public display.

"For you," he said, "we'll try."

"Good. Now, what's Pippen's party looking like? Are he and Gideon staying for it, or are they going home and coming back?"

Craw shrugged. "Well, Gideon said he needed to take the afternoon off—but he didn't say why. He was going to have Aiden drop him off at the driveway, and said he'd be back at Aiden and Jeremy's a little later that evening."

Ben nodded. "Good." He shivered. "I… I don't know why, but I'm worried about the two of them. Something about the way they've acted this last week—like they were getting ready to say good-bye."

Craw nodded. He'd seen it too. "And they don't want to go," he said.

Ben smiled softly. "Well, maybe they'll come back."

"As long as they stay away from the stock," Craw said, needing to be snarly.

"Of course, Craw," Ariadne said, condescension dripping from her voice. Bless the woman, he needed that. "They'll stay away from the fuckin' stock."

"Good," Craw grumped, and then he went to the back room to do some hand-spinning, since he'd needed to close down the mill for the day. For the week, actually—who did he think he was fooling, expecting any of them to do much more than feed the stock after December 21st and before New Year's Day?

He wasn't going to think about that other thing—the loss of his home, his business, his pride.

He had his family. He had Ben. He could find a way to live if he had to—he'd stared down the barrel of this gun before, and dodged the bullet. Even if it landed this time, he knew he'd still walk away, as long as he had his heart and soul intact.

As long as he had his people.

AIDEN PULLED to a stop near his usual place, right before the motion-activated cameras could be seen on the trees.

"You want me to stay here?" he asked. "Because you may need to make two trips?"

Gid grimaced. Yeah. He and Pip had packed their stuff— they'd brought some of it to Jeremy's that morning, but Gideon needed to get the rest of it now.

"Why can't I come help you?" Aiden asked, and Gideon had hissed.

"Because I'm not sure what Talbot Madison will do to you if he catches us," he replied grimly. "I have it on good authority that things did *not* go well for him today. His chauffeur carries a gun—I'd hate to see him draw it because somebody pissed in Talbot's Wheaties."

Aiden grunted. He liked this man. They worked well together. Not as well as Aiden and Jeremy—Aiden missed Jeremy's patter, his wicked sense of humor, his unexpected conversation. But Gideon was snarky and dry and well-traveled, and Aiden's age, too, which Aiden had never thought would matter but did seem to be something to bond over. Aiden liked the young man, and his devotion to Pippen hit him hard in the gut.

He felt that way over Jeremy.

"Well, then," Aiden said, stepping on the gas and taking them up to the house. "Let's park near the front door, get in, get your stuff, and get out. Two trips when this road hasn't been shoveled—are you kidding me?"

Gideon gasped. "But, Aiden—he knows what your car looks like now! He'll know it's you."

Aiden had heard Craw and Ben talking around corners over the last few days. He knew what was up. "He knows it's us anyway," he said. "He's having some sort of bidding war with our entire town in the balance today, whether it's us or the pub or anybody else in Granby. And how did you think you were going to get out of Granby, by the way?"

"Hillary was going to come pick us up and take us to Boulder," Gideon said, sounding stunned. "How did you—"

"Oh, please. Jeremy spent his first six months with us making plans to bolt if the con of living honest went wrong. You think I don't know when someone's planning to take off? In this case, you actually need to go, and you need help. Tell Hillary to take her easily traced rental car to Grand and spend the night. You guys go out over the mountains in this piece of crap here. It's got good snow tires and posi-traction and you can use some of your boy's money to get something bigger when you get to Boulder."

Gideon let out a breath as Aiden neared the house. "I don't see his vehicle," he said weakly. "I don't know where he—"

At that moment his phone buzzed, and he pulled it out and swore. "It's Hillary," he murmured. "She says he's following her and her boyfriend through Grand—there's only so far they can go before they have to turn back at the National Park."

"Then we best make this quick," Aiden said, hitting the emergency brake and turning the vehicle off. "Front door or carport?"

"Carport," Gideon said. "We can go in through the door."

Aiden thought later that maybe he should have looked around the chalet more—it *was* big and rich, with lots of sanded wood and rustic walls—but the fear on Gideon's face as he went to his room and pulled out two big duffel bags and two full backpacks made him not jealous and not curious. His parents' house had been a crumbling ranch-style farmhouse, and now that it had been rebuilt, it had better floors and better walls but it was still pretty beat up from all the kids, some of whom were still growing there. Ben's house, with Jeremy, had fussy things in it left over from Ben and Gertie, and a lot of the nice woodwork had been white-painted over, but what mattered to Aiden, what *really* mattered, was that Jeremy lived there with him.

That's why he was helping Gideon run tonight, he realized. Because no matter what had triggered this moment, had triggered this flight, he could see plainly that Gideon and Pippen were working for their own little home, where their hearts lived.

225

The baggage was fairly heavy—but Aiden knew it was, for the moment, all these guys would own in the world, no matter what Pippen's bank account said.

He and Gideon were back in the car and had just turned on the main road from the driveway, when Hillary texted Gideon again.

"They're busted," Gideon read, grimacing. "Okay—so we should—"

"Park this car where we usually park it in our garage," Aiden said calmly, "and you should come in with Pippen so we can celebrate his birthday before you leave."

Gideon sucked in a breath. "But his father—"

"Doesn't know where I live," Aiden said. Or, well, he did know the house, but he didn't know Aiden lived there. "And I guarantee you, if he calls in to the local law enforcement to run down that plate today, he won't get a response until after Christmas."

Gideon let out a shuddering breath. "But he knows, Aiden—he's been by yours and Jeremy's house and—"

Aiden grunted. "Gideon, do you really want your boy to spend his twenty-first birthday on the run in this tiny piece-of-shit car with no cake?"

Gideon let out a shaky breath. "No."

"Text Hillary. Tell her good-bye," Aiden said. "Tell her thanks. Leave anything you want her to have with us. We'll get it to her."

Gideon let out a laugh. "Pippen put it in her room this morning."

"Then you'll be fine. Let's go have a celebration, so we can give you and your boy the sendoff you deserve."

PIPPEN TRIPLE-CHECKED the gifts he'd brought that morning to put under Jeremy and Aiden's tree. Of course, then he hadn't known how the day would go, but if he and Gideon needed to leave that night, he wanted....

He wanted the people here, who had made such a difference in his life in such a short time, to know who they were to him.

He ran around the house, vacuuming and dusting and making sure the Christmas lights on the tree were all aligned. The tree itself was decorated Bluebell height up—probably because the dog's tail was still and always a menace. Jeremy had confided that until this last year, Persy had been a consideration too, and Pippen remembered getting his hand slapped for touching the sparkly ornaments on the tree. Looking at the rather... asymmetrically decorated piece of pine Aiden had brought in three weeks ago, he thought that it was maybe the most beautiful tree he'd ever seen.

He'd been a flurry of energy since he'd arrived. He just... he couldn't with the waiting. His lawyer, the one representing him in the bidding against his father, would text him every time something happened in the dealings, and Pip would text back the next move. He'd seen his father in action for years, doing this—when Pip had been younger, Talbot had thought to make him follow in Talbot's footsteps.

The result had been the opposite, really—Pip had seen lives destroyed and hadn't wanted a fucking thing to do with it.

Now he was on the other side, and he was *nauseous* with worry. God, he couldn't fuck this up. His lawyer was good—he'd had his economic professor help him choose one the year before—but this... it was a delicate peacock dance of "how much are you willing to pay" vs. "how much do you actually have." The only thing in Pip's favor, he figured, was that *he* wasn't looking to make his money back.

That didn't mean he *wouldn't* make his money back, over time. These were people's homes—they wanted to simply continue to pay their mortgages over time and eventually own them. He assumed that would accrue in the bank account, his lawyer and accountant would juggle the money, and Pippen would have a modest amount of income to live on. A decent home, a car, maybe even the rest of his education, were in reach.

But Pip didn't care about that—not right now. He cared about keeping the people *right here around him* from being hurt.

Jeremy seemed to know something was up. He'd had the stitches taken out of his back two days before, and he could make it up and down the stairs with just the stair rail for help, although it exhausted him when he did so. Pip had heard Aiden consoling him about how he'd done most of his healing in the hospital last time, but this time he'd lucked out so he could do his healing at home. The more Pip thought about this gentle man being beaten almost to death, the more he wanted to join Aiden and Craw and Ben and Ariadne, standing arm in arm, to protect him from harm.

Pip checked his phone a thousand times this day to do just that, and then suddenly….

He stopped and stared at the latest e-mail from his lawyer, at the contract offer from the bank, and the caveats that the bank had clung to when he'd made his first bid to buy the loans.

His lawyer had written, *I can raise the interest rates later if you like.*

Don't. Ever. This town deserves this contract. If interest rates drop again, we pass the savings on to the people paying off their homes and businesses. Write that in.

Peregrine, are you certain?

Yes. Absolutely.

It will take you years to make a significant profit from this property at this rate.

Then I will just have to get another job.

There was a series of ellipses then, as though Ambrose Crowder, his attorney, was trying hard not to say anything he'd regret.

What he did write back finally was a surprise.

My father had to sell his farm because his lender went the other way. It's what paid for my law degree. Thank you for reminding me I can be more than a shark.

In a moment, another contract arrived, and Pippen paused and read it, hoping he wasn't missing anything.

Praying.

"Boy?" Jeremy said softly, and Pippen looked up to see Jeremy had made them both lunch. Here he was, standing in the kitchen, and Jeremy had made them sandwiches, even plating them with chips.

"Sorry, Jeremy," Pippen said softly, and then Ambrose texted him again.

It's all set to sign. I promise you, Pip—we did these people right. Your competitor won't be able to compete with these terms because he's not buying this place to serve it, he's buying it to destroy.

Thank you, Pip texted, and then looked at the contract again.

He could sign it from his phone, but he would have to put his name on it. The minute his father saw his name on this contract, saw that his son had bested him in *finance* of all things, saw that Pippen had activated the trust left to him by his mother and invested all but the barest amount of it, that would be it. Pippen would be disowned, thrown out of the house, and….

And in danger for his life.

Pippen took a shuddering breath, remembering those moments before Gideon, the times Talbot Madison had unleashed his fury on Pippen because he'd been there, in the way, imperfect and unwanted and… *him.*

Gideon had been protecting him for three years, and Pippen had no doubt his father would fire Gideon and beat Pippen within an inch of his life if Pippen let him.

Pippen wasn't going to let Gideon face charges because Pippen was too stupid to get out of the way. But he wasn't stupid enough to let Gideon go, either. They'd made plans for this. If Pippen won—and his breath caught at this notion, because it appeared he had—then he and Gideon would have to go. Far, far away.

Pippen was prepared. He had a fraction of his trust left—but it wasn't nothing. It was enough to purchase them a car, maybe some new ID's, rent a house or an apartment somewhere different. Somewhere his father wouldn't expect to find them. Somewhere else. They'd have to get jobs and work for a living, but they'd been doing that for nearly the last month, and while Pippen didn't expect he'd find himself with a family again, like he did here, he didn't mind cooking or cleaning or tending the stock. He hadn't minded working in the shop or watching Persephone when her mother was busy. Imagine his surprise to find he had real life skills and that living in his rich bubble with his father had been the real life to fear.

But it was still frightening. And God. He glanced around the humble little kitchen where he'd eaten with people who were kind and funny, and who worked ten hour days and still laughed. He saw Jeremy, seated at the table, looking at him with compassion and concern and zero judgment, a man he'd wronged so badly, but who had looked him kindly in the eyes and cared about him and set him free.

"Boy?" Jeremy said softly. "You do what you gotta. God willing, we'll still be here, and if, God forbid, we have to go somewhere else to make a living, you'll still be welcome there, in our kitchen, just the same."

And that decided him. "I want you here," he said through a rough throat. "But Gideon and I won't be able to stay here with you. Not at first."

Jeremy shrugged. "You'll send us postcards, right? Me and Aiden were going to take a trip to New York, you know, before I got hurt. California sometime too. We had plans to travel when we first got together—I didn't want to trap my boy in this valley, but we decided better here than anywhere else on earth, and better together than all the places put together."

Pippen wiped his eyes on his shoulder. "Every place we go," he said softly. "I'll send you a postcard from every place we go."

Jeremy grinned. "It'll be like we went ourselves. You'll keep with the knitting and crocheting and such, right?"

Pippen nodded and wiped his eyes again. "If I ever need to yell at the sky, I know what to do instead."

"That's a good skill." He nodded toward the phone in Pip's hand, a small man, flawed and good, who was apparently worth more to Pippen than his father, than his fortune, than his name.

But not more than his lover, and that was fine with Jeremy.

"Okay," Pippen said, and with a deep breath hit the sign function on the phone and moved his finger across the screen. *Peregrine Madison.*

He hit Send and sat down to the sandwich Jeremy had provided for him—grilled tomato and cheese. "Jeremy, what's your last name?" he asked, realizing he didn't know it. He knew Aiden's last name was Rhodes because his name was on all the bills, but not Jeremy's.

"Well, I changed it to Rhodes after we got married," Jeremy said, taking a bite of his sandwich.

Huh. "What was it before?" Pippen asked.

Jeremy shrugged. "Well, the last name I had before I went to prison was Stillson—that's the name that got convicted. It's why Aiden was hot on me to change it. It wasn't the name I was born with, you see—that's what happens when your daddy changes your name and your ID from your cradle days 'cause you're more of a prop than a son."

He'd mentioned being a con man's son before, and Pippen again felt that deep resonance. His father may have the shiny shoes and the ten homes, but he was no more an honest man than Jeremy's father had been.

"Stillson," he said thoughtfully, taking another bite. "I could be Pippen Stillson. My father wouldn't look for me as Stillson."

Jeremy took another bite of his sandwich and chewed thoughtfully. "Boy, you know, one of the things Aiden showed me how to do was keep special papers. How about, after lunch and before people start showing up for your birthday party—"

"My what?" Pippen asked, surprised. "Jeremy, Gideon and I have to *leave* as soon as he gets here—"

Jeremy waved him away. "You'll be leaving in one of our vehicles your daddy can't trace. Don't worry about it—I saw all your stuff, Pip. I know you're leavin'. Let us celebrate that you were brought into our lives before you go. Anyway—after lunch, you and me can start looking through those papers, and I can make a phone call to Johnny. I mean, we got you both some Christmas stuff, and Craw and Aiden been working on a birthday present I think you'll like, but this… this I think will be the perfect gift."

Pippen stared at him. "Jeremy," he said, both deeply moved and a little surprised. "How'd you know we'd be leaving?"

Jeremy cocked his head sadly. "When I was… God, I guess I wasn't much older'n you, I was hiding behind a curtain in an abandoned Las Vegas casino when a rabid mobster shot my daddy, and my life as I knew it ended, right there, in a flash of blood and brains and piss." He took a shuddering breath. "I can say that now, 'cause I spent nearly ten years starting the new life that moment gave me. There's been some detours. Prison was one, and while a lawyer might've helped me out there, I had it comin'. Then Craw took me on a hard left to this valley, to my boy, and I realized that whether it was the hard way, the mobster way, or an easier way, a way that was in my heart and soul, I was gonna have to get quit of my father if I was ever gonna have a life of my own. Not every boy has to. Aiden didn't—his dad's a great guy. But Craw, Ben—even Stanley and Johnny—they had to, in their own ways. Some people are lucky—growing up means growing out of the house and making some decisions that blow up at Thanksgiving and not much more. But some of us have to kill the bastard, even if it's just in our heads, 'cause he's living there rent-free and fucking up our lives without our permission. Just now, with your finger on your phone, you had the look of someone who killed your daddy in the way that would hurt him most. I gotta tell you, having met the fucker, I'm not sorry you did that. But it's a life-changer. It's a decision that'll grow you up quick. You don't need to stay here and let him hurt you anymore—and I wouldn't make you for the world. But you're not running away."

Jeremy's mouth quirked, and he pulled a paper napkin off the center of the table and handed it to Pippen.

"I'm not?" Pippen asked after wiping his face.

"Naw. You're striking out with your man, finding a new life somewhere you don't gotta worry about coming home and getting hit. 'Cause you don't deserve that. It's not running away if we're throwing you a party and wishing you luck, boy. It's graduation. My graduation day was in prison, when I got my GED. Aiden's was…." Jeremy swallowed. "When he killed a man that was gonna kill me. Yours is today, when you told your daddy he couldn't live in your head anymore. Happy graduation day, Pip. You and Gideon go out and have yourself an amazing life. Remember us back here, though—we'll be rooting for—"

Pip hugged him as he sat, probably too hard, and when Jeremy wrapped his arms around Pip's shoulders in return, Pip sobbed.

CRAW AND the others were there when Aiden and Gideon pulled up the driveway. Aiden hid the car in the garage, so Talbot Madison wouldn't have cause to see it if he did come bother them, and he and Gideon took a moment to check the sightlines from the driveway and the road to see when would be a good time to hide behind the house, then the rabbit hutch, then the garage.

"Remember," Aiden said soberly, "the hutch has a heater and some lap blankets. You two can stay there as long as you need to."

Gideon nodded, smiling a bit. "Pip loves it in there," he confided, and Aiden's heart warmed.

"So does Jeremy," he said. "I think... I think kindred souls, you know?"

Gideon nodded.

"Rabbits," Aiden said after a moment, "they're stronger than we think. Jeremy used to love this one old lop-eared bastard. The thing kicked the hell out of him when Jeremy first showed up, 'cause Jeremy didn't know how to love it. He learned. You gotta be patient, when you're learning to love someone. Sometimes you get hurt. But you both learn."

Gideon stared at him and blinked rapidly. "My folks," he said gruffly. "They... they might not like that I'm moving out with Pip."

"Well, you might be all the other one has," Aiden admitted, knowing that had never been him and feeling his good fortune all over again. "Just know that as soon as it's safe for you to return here, you'll be welcome."

Gideon nodded, then laughed self-consciously. "You know, all I have for Pip's birthday is the damned hat I made him." He pulled it out of his pocket, a misshapen thing with runs going down from the crown because he hadn't finished off right.

Aiden looked at it and laughed, then pulled out a hat of his own from his back pocket. His was nearly eight years old, and felted with use and effort and slightly singed on the top. He pulled it over his ears neatly, like a helmet, and wondered if Gideon had ever wondered at the thing.

In a company full of knitters, it was singularly ugly.

"When Jeremy finished this thing, it looked like a fruit basket, it was so big," Aiden confided in him. "We had to wash it, like, six times in hot water and let it dry over a form to get it to fit a human-sized head. The rest was time—and the East Troublesome fire. But I love it. When it felts too small for my melon, I'll use it to hold my keys or something. I'm never giving it away."

Gideon smiled shyly. "Okay, then," he murmured. "I guess we should go inside."

Aiden was careful throughout the celebration. He knew Ben, Craw, and Ari were all fretting over something, but he let them hold that to their chests. They'd tell him soon enough. He saw Jeremy giving Pip a big manila folder that Pip clenched to his heart, and Pippen give Jeremy an envelope, nodding in Craw's direction when Craw couldn't see.

The look on Jeremy's face then was hard to describe. It looked like pride and hope and joy and sadness all at once.

So there were mysteries and fears and all sorts of undercurrents at what should have been a perfectly normal celebration for a boy turning twenty-one, but there was also Persy, running into Gideon's arms and asking to kiss Pip on the cheek because—in her words, "He'th tho handthome!"

235

There was Ariadne with an iced sheet cake that she'd decorated with a skein of yarn in frosting that had apparently taken an hour and she was inordinately proud of.

There was Rory, giving Pip a miniature of Gideon, and Gideon a miniature of Pip, saying it had to be a set. The tiny paintings were perfect—sketches, really, with hints of watercolor, that could make any place they were set out in a home.

There was a flannel blanket stuffed with wool too short for spinning and machine quilted from Ariadne, and two scarves from Jeremy. Jeremy's scarves had a falcon in flight on one end and a trumpet with angel wings on the other, the designs worked into the yarn in cross stitch over a crocheted background, care of Rory and some graph paper.

"I made the scarves the same so you can wear your own colors or switch," Jeremy said, and Gideon had blushed.

There was the bag of skeins, each skein a mix of sky blue and indigo, forest green and acid green, brown and gold, that was the same mix of the boys themselves.

"Oh wow, Craw," Pippen said in awe. "That's… that's a lot of yarn! That's enough to make—"

"Two sweaters," Craw said gruffly. "Or a blanket. Or a thousand hats. Or to stuff in the walls if they're drafty. As long as it gets use."

Pippen had hugged the old bastard then, and to everybody's surprise, Craw had hugged him back.

And finally there was Gideon's first effort hat, that had taken him nearly a month, that Pippen held to his chest with shining eyes.

Aiden had no doubt which was his favorite gift of all.

When the gifts were done and the cake was eaten, Pippen and Gideon looked at each other, and they all knew it was time to go. The roads weren't supposed to get icy that night, but it was best to be over the summit and heading down the freeway before midnight, so as not to test that theory.

"Thank you," Pippen said softly. "All of you. I haven't had a birthday this happy since I was little, before my mom died. I... I never had a family like you. Don't forget to open the gifts we left you under the tree. We'll...." He gave Jeremy a shy smile. "We'll write postcards," he promised. "Because you're our home."

There were hugs then and lots of love, and it might well have gone on forever until they stayed anyway in that warm glow of Jeremy and Aiden's kitchen, but Pippen's phone buzzed in his pocket and he stiffened and checked it.

"It's Hillary," he said to Gideon. "She's at the chalet—she says Dad's figured out we're gone and he's looking at the security feed."

Gideon and Aiden met eyes then, and Aiden said, "Me and Craw'll walk you and your presents out to the garage. No more hugs—we all love you, but it's time to get the hell out."

Pippen and Ariadne were in charge of stuffing the gifts into cloth grocery bags, including the unopened ones that had been saved for the hope of Christmas, and Ariadne sacrificed her favorite plasticware to make sure they'd have leftover cake. Thus burdened, the four of them made their way out the mudroom door, and Ari and Ben were making a show of cleaning up the kitchen, which was where they were when the heavy knock came on the door.

BUNNIES FOR CHRISTMAS

JEREMY ANSWERED it—he figured he'd dealt with this man before, he knew who Talbot Madison was.

He was only a little surprised to see the gun, and grateful Persy had fallen asleep in the middle of the party and was on the loveseat in the office, under her favorite blanket, Rory with her because he'd been up before dawn himself. Bluebell took position at Jeremy's flank, and instead of her usual cheerful bark, this time she set up a low-level growling that Jeremy had no doubt she'd act on if she needed.

"Where's. My. Son?" Madison growled in Jeremy's face, and Jeremy wasn't going to play dumb anymore.

"Why do you want him?" he asked.

"None of your fucking business." The slick, shiny man of the world was gone, and in his place was a brute, a bare-knuckles fighter who would tear through Jeremy's home and grab what he wanted if he had to reach through Jeremy's chest to do it. "Where is he?"

Jeremy laughed. "Sir, would you believe I've met a guy like you before. He almost killed me. I mean, I was gone. Face busted up, organs leaking—I was gonna shit blood and die if he didn't shoot me. Would you like to know what happened to him?"

Madison stared at him, as if seeing him for the first time. The scarred face, the crutches, the growling dog. "What?" he asked, suddenly afraid.

"My boy shot him in the head," Jeremy told him, and Madison took a deep breath, as though Jeremy had slugged him in the chest and knocked some of the stuffing out of him. "Not that he'll do that to *you*," Jeremy finished up virtuously, remembering that he had to play for time. "But why do you want to see your son?"

"Little trash bag *fucked* my business deal today," Talbot spat. "I was going to *own* you, this whole fucking useless town, and that little asshole *bought me out*. Used his entire fucking trust to do it, but he *fucked* me, just to grab my balls and yank, and *nobody* does that to me, do you understand?"

Madison was building up a head of steam, but Jeremy's smile must have knocked the wind out of his sails again.

"Bought the town, you say," Jeremy repeated, a burst of joy flooding upward from the soles of his feet. "How'd he do that?"

"Rock bottom interest. He took *rock bottom* interest for those loans. Those loans can be paid off in ten years. He could have made *millions* and he—"

"He chose to serve the town instead," Jeremy said, his smile not going away. "And you're not proud of that kid? Outfoxing the old fox, doing something good with what the world gave him—you don't think that's a good son you've raised?"

"*He defied me!*" Talbot roared, and Jeremy shrugged.

"Well, sir, if that's all you can think about, then you and me got nothin' to say to each other. I think you missed a prime opportunity there, to get to know a really awesome human being better, but then, a kid who'd do that? He seems out of your league."

Jeremy went to close the door in the man's face then, because he figured Gideon and Pip were probably in the garage on the side of the house now, waiting until Talbot took off before they started Jeremy's car and took the poor old thing out of his life for good. They had directions to Stanley and Johnny's apartment, and the list of fake social security numbers and aliases Jeremy had used when he'd been grifting. He'd kept them in his Bible, the kind with the hollowed-out insides, and they'd only been on one paper, so when the Bible had filled up with other things, gifts from Aiden, he hadn't needed to throw it away. They were ready to go into Gideon and Pippen's wallet, make them harder to trace, so this man, this man with the gun and the temper and the feeling that there were no bounds on him, could never, ever find them.

Talbot blocked Jeremy's move with the door by shoving his shiny loafer in the way, and Jeremy accidentally slammed the door with Talbot Madison's toes there. Madison swore and tried to shove himself in by the shoulder, but an ominous click stopped him.

"Mr. Madison," Aiden said, "I believe we've met before when you came into my boss's yarn shop, looking for your son. You will kindly back away from the door and lower your weapon, because the last man who threatened my husband like this ended up in a box."

"You!" Madison spun, gun still out, but another click—and another shotgun pointed directly at his other ear—stopped him.

"And me," Craw said mildly. "Sir, my husband is currently calling the sheriff—right, Ben?"

"On it, Craw," Ben said. Then, "Jesse? Yeah, it's me, Ben McCutcheon—thank you, sir, I'm so glad your mother enjoyed the preserves, we were happy to pass those on. But we've got a neighbor here, threatening Jeremy with a gun—nossir, Aiden and Craw haven't shot him yet, but you may want to get down here, just to make sure." There was a pause, and Ben said significantly, "Well, sir, the man seems to think we're harboring

240

his grown son and thinks he has the right to search our house to get him back."

Talbot's growl started from his midsection, and Jeremy thought sadly that they really were going to have to wait until the sheriff got there before Pip and Gid could leave. Then he heard it, the sound of a vehicle making its way slowly down the driveway, probably passing Madison's SUV as it went. Jeremy cocked his head and met Ben's eyes, and Ben, who had been listening to the sheriff on the phone, said, "I'm sorry, Jesse—I had to ask Jeremy something. No, the kid isn't here. I can swear that on a stack of bibles if you need me too. But there is a child here, sleeping in our den, and the man is standing on the porch with a gun, so we'd appreciate it if you hurry."

Ben hit End Call and glanced at Jeremy, who turned around and looked Talbot in the eye.

"Well, sir, I'd say you're going to spend at least a night in the clink, but I suppose a lawyer will get you clear in the morning."

He shivered then, and Aiden said, "Jer, you should close the door. You don't got no jacket and we don't need you to get sick before your leg heals."

Jeremy nodded. Behind Aiden, behind Talbot, who was still facing the door, he watched as a car that had been signed over to Gideon turned its lights on at the end of the driveway and made a left toward the pass over the mountains.

"Thanks, boy," he said, smiling at Aiden with all his joy. "I'll do that. You be careful, there. If you have to shoot this asshole, it would be a shame to get a hole in Craw."

"You asshole," Craw said, but he winked at Jeremy so Jeremy knew he was laughing on the inside, which was where Craw usually laughed.

Jeremy closed the door carefully and sighed. "We should make some hot chocolate," he said. "They're going to be cold by the time the sheriff gets here to let them in."

Jesse hurried, because Craw and Aiden were inside less than fifteen minutes later, and Talbot Madison was on his way to jail. He'd told Craw quietly that he'd keep the man there past Christmas, and then ask the judge to release him on the sole caveat that he left the valley until the restraining order Jesse filed lapsed.

Apparently Jesse's father's farm had been part of the packet of properties Talbot Madison had tried to buy earlier that day, when he'd been thwarted.

"So that's what Pip did to piss off the old man?" Craw asked, his eyes crinkling over his chocolate—he sure did love his chocolate, no matter what he said about coffee. "Buy the properties and set the interest rates so nobody else could hijack the mortgages?"

Jeremy nodded, and then let his own glee slip out. "There was one," he said, reaching into his back pocket, "that I think he bought outright." He pulled out the envelope Pip had given him, with instructions to give it to Craw right away. "Here, Rance. I, uhm, think this is your Christmas present a little early."

Craw took the envelope from him with shaking fingers, and Ben stood at his side, squeezing Craw's shoulder while he opened it.

Craw's broken gasp rocked them all as they gathered around the table, and the paper fluttered to the ground.

Ben picked it up and scanned it, eyes blurring, and he covered his mouth with his hand.

"Craw," he said in awe, voice shaking.

"Yeah," Craw said, his own voice rocky, like it had been at Aiden and Jeremy's wedding.

"Guys," Ariadne said, practically vibrating with excitement and hope. "What is it?"

Craw handed the letter to her, and she let out a little exclamation of her own. Rory—who had just come in from the back room, where Persy slept on—said, "Hon, what is it?"

She handed him the letter and then collapsed against him, crying into his shoulder with what Jeremy could only hope was joy.

"Wait," Rory said. "This... this says Craw's farm, his shop, his mill—the notice has been paid off, and it's been... it's been gifted to Craw. In perpetuity." Rory stared at Ben and Craw. Craw had stood and they were holding each other so tightly, Jeremy knew this had been weighing on their souls for far too long.

"He bought the place," Craw muttered. "Right out from under his father. And he gave it to us." He let out a shattered laugh. "Merry Christmas, family. We get to keep the farm!"

OF COURSE there were more hugs after that, and some discussion of what Pippen had done and why. Finally everybody went home in a happy holiday daze, leaving Jeremy and Aiden alone and in bed, which was Aiden's favorite place to be with Jeremy.

"What'll we do tomorrow?" Jeremy asked drowsily, after Aiden had rubbed his body all over, kissing him gently until Jeremy had come in his mouth, surprised and exhausted.

It had only happened twice, but Aiden was so over seeing Jeremy's life threatened.

"Make cookies," Aiden rumbled. "Craw's shut down the mill, although the shop's open 'til Christmas Eve. We help him feed the stock, help Ari at the shop, and come here and bake cookies with Persy." He chuckled. "Stanley thinks he's got a corner on the cookie market, but I've been studying up."

"It'll be a good Christmas," Jeremy murmured. "Too bad Pip and Gideon can't be here."

Aiden closed his eyes and buried his nose in the back of Jeremy's neck. In his mind's eye was the image of Gideon and Pippen as he'd last seen them. Pippen had handed the packages to Gideon, who had loaded the trunk in the darkness of the garage. When it was all settled, Gideon slammed the trunk shut and then turned to Pip, asking if there was anything else.

Pippen had smiled slightly—Aiden had seen the glint of his teeth, of his eyes, in the moonlight flooding the garage—and raised his face for a kiss.

Gideon had kissed him, half in the darkness of the garage, half under the open sky, and Aiden had the impression of lovers emerging into the moonlight, ready to fly free.

Talbot's car had approached then, and Gideon and Pip had hurriedly gotten into the car and ducked down. When Madison parked—by himself, no driver in sight—and strode up the walkway to talk to Jeremy, Aiden had directed Craw to the rabbit hutch, where he kept the shotguns hidden in a locked case above the cages.

They'd each grabbed a weapon and then, one of them on either side of the house, had approached Madison, who was too busy threatening an unarmed man on crutches to see where the real threat would come.

That moment had frozen Aiden's blood, but as Jeremy watched a vehicle that was no longer his creep down the driveway, lights off, Aiden had held that other image, that of Gideon and Pip emerging from the darkness to the light, behind his eyes.

They'd be free, he thought now, hugging Jeremy to his chest. And their parting gift had been to set Craw and Ben—and Ariadne and Rory and himself and Jeremy—free as well.

Wherever they were, however they ended, whether they came back or sent postcards or just faded from Granby like the shadows from sunrise, Aiden wished the two young lovers all the freedom, all the joy, all the kindness and love that he had in his own life.

He hugged Jeremy to his chest again. He could never be too thankful for the love next to his heart.

Stanley and Johnny would have let them stay in the guest room for months, Gideon knew, but he and Pip couldn't let them do that. They accepted the help getting ID's and fake driver's licenses, though, the better to hide from Pip's father, because Pip knew his father would be looking. They let Johnny help them trade in Jeremy's battered little car for a slightly larger used SUV that Pip's father had never seen and wouldn't know how to trace. The car lot was a little seedy—Johnny assured them both that nobody would recognize Jeremy's car by the time it got sold again, and odds were good it wouldn't have the same license plate either.

They were on the road again by the twenty-third, heading for Utah and Salt Lake City. Why there? Gideon had wanted to know.

"Because my dad doesn't own any property there," Pippen had said.

"Mormons aren't so hot with the gay," Gideon told him gently.

"Well, they're also not going to let us go homeless if we can't find jobs," Pip said, smiling slightly. "Besides—there's *always* a place, you know that."

Gideon did. Every tour, every deployment, every city, he'd been able to spot the signs. It was dangerous—he hadn't always gone looking—but he knew.

They'd arrived in Salt Lake City on Christmas Eve and found a hotel in short order. Gideon had gone to get them takeout while Pip showered, and then he'd showered and they'd sat down at the rickety formica table together and ate their first Christmas Eve dinner, while Pip played Christmas songs on the hand-me-down iPhone that had served them so well in Colorado.

"Pip," Gideon said, looking embarrassed. "I got you a present. It's… it's sort of dumb, but I don't know if you want it tonight or tomorrow." They were going to open the presents from their Granby family in the morning, including two big packages that Johnny and Stanley had helped load into the SUV the evening they'd left Boulder.

"Tonight," Pippen said, smiling. "Tomorrow I just want to sleep all day and eat leftovers—"

"And make love," Gideon added, in case Pip had forgotten that could be on the menu after the last two exhausting days driving.

"Oh yeah," Pippen murmured, his eyes heating although both of them were at half-mast. Gideon still had that rumbling under his hands, like the steering wheel vibrating through his arms across the SUV's not-quite-mint suspension. "I can't wait."

"Good."

Gideon pulled out the giant stitch bible that had come into the shop the week before. He had savings, although he and Pip were going to go through a bit of both their savings before they found a place they could settle down in, but this book—this was the thing he felt like Pip would want most.

"See?" he said, pulling it out of the logo-stamped bag for Craw-Daddy's 'Paca Mill and Yarn Shop, because that was almost the best paper they could ask for. "It'll give you all sorts of tools to make new and different stuff and all sorts of stitches." He felt his cheeks heat. "I, you know—you love doing this now.

I wanted you to have something that would help you do it more and better and—"

Pippen kissed him, that soft, bee-stung mouth of his just as sweet as it had been that first night, under Pippen's roof. The freedom of their own choices, their own world, somehow, made it even more filling, like an apple pie with protein and broccoli too.

"It's perfect," Pippen said softly. "Everybody gave me so much yarn—this'll help me figure out what to do with it." He flipped through the pages dreamily. "I could spend a week planning a project—it's amazing. And it's both stitches—knitting and crocheting. I could learn them both. I could be...." He giggled. "Bi-craftual."

Gideon chuckled. "You could be—but I'm pretty sure it's the only bi you'll ever be."

"Right?" Pippen laughed. "Unlike yourself."

Gideon shrugged. "Bisexual, yes—but I'm pretty much a one-horse stud."

Pippen had to hold his hands over his mouth. "Yeah, yeah, *stud,*" he teased, reaching into the cloth bag at his feet for his own small package for Gideon. "Tell me how you like this."

Gideon opened the package, not surprised that it was a crocheted object, but *very* surprised at how advanced it was. "Gloves," he said, petting them with his finger. "Wow, Pip. You added color here," he pointed to the stitched trumpet on the backs. "These are almost too fancy to wear."

Pippen sobered and grasped both of Gideon's hands in his own. "No," he said, his voice breaking for no reason Gideon could think of. "Not too fancy to wear. It's like love—you wear it every day, and I will always make you more. You wear these every day, and I'll make you more, okay?"

Gideon's eyes burned. "I love you, Pippen. I don't know what the future holds, but Merry Christmas. I want us to have a home and happiness and joy—Merry Christmas. Hope—that's my gift, you know?"

"Merry Christmas," Pippen said, his voice rough. "My gift is faith. You and me—we can make it happen."

Gideon thought about the miracles that Pippen had wrought in Granby. They hadn't left a trail of destruction in their wake, although that possibility had been real. Instead Pippen had left rejoicing and miracles and hope, and Gideon would protect that sort of innocence and power with his life.

"I love you," Gideon murmured.

"I love you too."

They kissed then, and in his heart, Gideon could see them kissing every Christmas Eve, forever and ever. No matter where they ended up, this part of their hearts, the part with the faith and the hope and the joy and the creativity—and the yarn—had been discovered in a tiny town in Colorado that had taught them family.

Pippen and Gideon had that to take with them, until they could forge their own.

Keep reading for an excerpt from
The 12 Kittens of Christmas
by Amy Lane

Last Call

Killian Thornton wiped down the varnished wooden counter in front of him and fought the first yawn of the night. It was the Friday after Thanksgiving, and the rush had been fierce—lots of people celebrating their "friendsgivings" anywhere but in their own homes this year—and he was ready to clean up and go home.

"Don't do it," Suzanne, his night manager, ordered.

"Don't do what?" he asked, yawning.

"Don't do that, you bastard!" she responded with a yawn of her own. "Dammit, I still have to count drawers!"

Suzanne had been hired ten years ago straight out of college; she had an MA in history and no interest in teaching. She was smart, could talk customers down off a drunken soapbox and count a drawer at the same time. She also didn't hesitate to break out the baseball bat underneath the bar if things got rough, although they didn't often get rough in Catches. Catches was a chain bar—you could find one in most major cities in America, although usually they were found in big malls and shopping centers, along with BJ's and Cheesecake Factory. This particular Catches, though, was deep in Sacramento's midtown, maybe three blocks from Lavender Heights and sitting cheek by jowl between a mom-and-pop Mexican food place and a designer thrift shop—but right across from a Starbucks. There was enough unique and personalized business going on around them for the place to have grown a little character of its own, and for people to need the reassurance of a brand name while pub crawling through midtown.

"Go ahead and start," he said, moving on to polishing the brass fixtures. "Then we can go home."

Killian loved this area—lived less than two blocks away, in an old square apartment building with five units, vintage wood frames and floors that swelled and stuck in the summer, and wrought iron that had been painted over often enough to obscure the filigree patterns on the stair rails and the sconces in the upper apartment. He had a car, but he could walk anywhere: the laundromat across the street, the bodega a block down, the comic bookstore five blocks away, even the place he bought his shoes. All of it was close enough for a brisk walk under the Sacramento trees. What was left of them, of course, after the storms the year before.

Killian had been visiting a friend who'd worked at Catches, after he'd done two tours right out of high school. He'd come home rootless—his folks lived in the Midwest and had been happy to see the back of him—and lonely. The Army hadn't sucked entirely. Three squares, a salary, a daily goal. If it hadn't been for being in a war zone, it might have been great. But the war zone thing had been… frightening. He'd seen some action, and he'd hated it. Hated the casual disregard for life, hated the moral grayness, hated not knowing if he was going to be woken up by trumpeted reveille or mortar rounds. Hated seeing the civilians hurt, hated hurting the soldiers, felt like he had no business there to intervene but no choice but to help keep the civilians safe.

And then he'd just… left. Time served, sir. Go back to your business, go to school, get a job, nothing to see here, folks.

It hadn't sat right—guilt, anger, depression, the whole weight of it had rested on his shoulders. And he'd just come out to himself, if not the world. Going back home when he hated *everything*, including his own shadow, had not filled him with joy. Well, nothing back then had filled him with joy, but in particular going back to his fundamentalist family in the Midwest who wouldn't understand his feelings about the war or the military or other men—*that* had filled him with everything from horror to irritation to disgust. So he'd taken Jaime, who'd been stationed with him briefly in Kabul, up on his offer to come visit Sacramento in the spring, when Jaime said the sun was pleasant and not destructive, and there might be flowers on the hills.

He'd fallen in love with Sacramento—and briefly with Jaime, although that had been more of a starter relationship than the real thing. Before their sad but amicable breakup, Killian had gotten the job at Catches, and after it had gotten his own apartment nearby. Jaime had taken his savings and started his own bar up in Folsom, where he kept promising to ask Killian to come work, but Killian kept thinking that he'd miss the big sycamore tree in front of his apartment in the spring, or the way the breeze off the river could cool the whole place down in the summer. He'd miss the thick, honey-dripping light in the late afternoons in the fall or the boozy happiness of the pub crawlers on a warm Friday night. He wouldn't hear the women preening about their new looks as they left the nail boutique next door or be torn between the Starbucks across the street and the indie coffee place a block and a half down that he liked better. What if he never ate a dessert at Rick's again? All of these things, these moments, had rescued him when he'd come to Sacramento eight years before—they'd anchored him, filled him with quiet joy when he'd thought that was the impossible dream.

He couldn't leave them now. This city, this job, they'd served him so well.

And loneliness was such a small price to play for a little bit of peace.

But it meant that closing time at Catches had the same melancholy feeling as the Semisonic song. Nobody was ready to go home, but they couldn't stay there.

Tonight, though, things had cleared out rather quickly, with the exception of the kid in the oversized white sweatshirt and the skinny pants with the big denim jacket and trout-fishing hat sitting on the barstool behind him as he played one more spectacular round of darts.

Thunk. 25. *Thunk.* 50. *Thunk.* 100.

The kid with the slender, lithe body and the vulpine little chin with a wide gamine mouth—not usually Killian's type of face, but it was an *interesting* face, wasn't it?

Thunk. 25.

The kid who looked borderline familiar?

Thunk. 50.

"You got the drawer for me to count?" Suzanne asked, suddenly standing right next to Killian. "Don't you want to go home?"

Killian had been staring at the kid—twenty-two, twenty-three, maybe—throwing darts at the board with astounding precision.

Thunk.

"Wha—oh, yeah." Killian went to the old-fashioned register—a Catches staple—and hit the No Sale button, popping out the cash box along with the receipt he'd generated with all the night's transactions on it, as well as his first drawer count, done after the last—*thunk*—or, well, almost last customer had left.

Bullseye! Killian remembered who this kid was.

"Here's the drawer," he told Suzanne. "I'll polish some brass and wait until you count it out."

She snorted. "Puhleeze, Killian. Like your drawers are ever more than two bucks off."

Killian inclined his head modestly. He did like a clean count at the end of the night.

"Well, then," he said, "I'll wait to walk you to your car."

Suzanne was fit—as was Killian—but she also wasn't stupid. "How very gallant," she said. "I accept. I'll be back in a sec after I get this in the safe."

Killian nodded, because why use extra words when you didn't need to, right? And then turned his attention to Lewis Bernard, his upstairs neighbor's little brother.

Thunk. "Lewis?" he asked, timing the name carefully so as to not break the kid's stride.

Lewis, apparently, could multitask. "Hey, Killian." He yawned before bebopping to the dart board to pull out his latest round. "You almost done?"

"Yeah," Killian told him. "You weren't… were you waiting for me?" *That* seemed unlikely.

Lewis gave him a sheepish look that indicated the unlikely was true.

"See," he said with a sigh, "Todd wanted to, uhm, have some time with his girlfriend tonight—you know, Aileen?"

Killian nodded because he did know her—and Todd. Todd had been his neighbor for about four years—had been to movie nights and was, Killian thought fondly, a friend.

"Yeah, well, Todd never gets a night off—you know that-- and he didn't want his twinkie little brother around while they got their thing on. I guess it was true romance. Anyway—" He shrugged. "—I didn't want to go up until he texted me, and, well, I knew you lived in the building. I figured I'd walk home with you, you could let me in, and I'd hang in the stairwell until he remembered I didn't have anywhere else to go."

Killian squinted at him. "Did he just… *forget* you were here?"

Lewis made one of those faces where he squinched his lips together until his top lip touched the bottom of his almost hawklike nose. Killian wondered if he ever put a pencil in the space when he was a kid, bored at school, and then he put a dart in there and tried to make it balance, and Killian didn't wonder anymore.

"Lewis?" Killian prompted, and Lewis turned his head to the side with the dart caught lengthwise between his lip and his nose and smiled. The smile changed the curvature of his upper lip and the dart slid off, landing point first into the scuffed wooden floor with its own *thunk*.

"What?" Lewis asked, bending to pick up the dart.

"Did your brother forget you were here?"

"Mm… forget?" Lewis tilted his head, his shaggy blond hair falling into place with his every movement. "That's sort of a harsh word, don't you think? I, uhm, may have mentioned that he's already involved."

Killian squeezed his eyes shut. "Your brother forgot you need a place to sleep tonight," he said on a sigh. "No worries. You can use my couch."

Killian's place was small; all of the apartments in the building were small. The building was a large blocky rectangle with a peaked roof, and the two bottom apartments were built like crooked shotguns: The front door opened from inside the foyer, and the apartments consisted of long skinny front rooms connected to long skinny kitchens that led to a hallway with a bathroom and bedroom on one side and some storage cabinets on the other. Killian had never been in any of the upstairs apartments, but given there were three of them and a flight of stairs, he was pretty sure they were even longer and skinnier than the ones on the bottom floor, and two of them shared a bathroom.

"Really?" Lewis asked, eyes enormous. "That would be amazing. My brother's apartment is *small*."

Todd lived in the unit that *didn't* share the bathroom, thank God, but it still wasn't big enough for a guest. Particularly if....

"Does Todd even have a couch?" Killian asked, horrified.

Lewis shrugged. "He's got a nice recliner," he said, as though making up for his brother's shortcomings. "But you know the best thing he has?"

Killian stared at him, at a loss. "No idea."

"An address not in Texas," Lewis said, nodding sagely, and Killian sucked air through his teeth.

"Is that where you went to school?" he asked apologetically. Lewis's pretty, angular face sported two yellowing crescents of old bruises under his brown eyes, and he was half afraid to ask where those had come from.

"Don't get me wrong," Lewis said. "There are a lot of great things about Texas. Barbecue, nice people, country music, wide-open spaces. You know what's not great about Texas?"

"Fox News and bigots?" Killian asked, pretty sure this had been the reason Lewis had shown up to sleep in his brother's recliner.

Lewis put a finger to a still-swollen nose, looking glum. "Yeah. Got out of college, tried to get a job—had three different companies outside of Houston tell me they 'didn't hire my kind.'" He sighed. "I've got a degree in software engineering." He paused. "A *master's*."

Killian sighed. "Well, I wish you luck. You may have a better time finding a job here."

"And my parents' neighbors will quit signing petitions to evict them from the neighborhood," he muttered.

"Oh God," Killian said. "I'm sorry. High school must have been a *drag*."

Lewis nodded and touched his nose again—gingerly. "Bingo."

"Well, I can't solve any of that, and politics depress me. But you can sleep on my couch."

The way Lewis's face lit up right then, like Killian was his hero? Killian rubbed his chest, surprised at the warmth that look generated. It felt… potent. And *dangerous*. Like the opioids he'd taken sparingly when he'd fallen three years ago and broken his ankle. Like if he wasn't careful, he'd crave *more* looks like that. And *more*, and—he couldn't think about it.

It didn't do to need people like that.

"Thanks, Killian. That's kind." Lewis's voice had this sandpaper purr when he said "kind," and Killian had to fight that uncomfortable, needy sensation.

"I need to finish my closing shit," he said shortly, spinning away on his heel. "We'll leave when Suzanne's ready to go."

Award winning author AMY LANE lives in a crumbling crapmansion with a couple of teenagers, a passel of furbabies, and a bemused spouse. She has too damned much yarn, a penchant for action-adventure movies, and a need to know that somewhere in all the pain is a story of Wuv, Twu Wuv, which she continues to believe in to this day! She writes contemporary romance, paranormal romance, urban fantasy, and romantic suspense, teaches the occasional writing class, and likes to pretend her very simple life is as exciting as the lives of the people who live in her head. She'll also tell you that sacrifices, large and small, are worth the urge to write.

Website: www.greenshill.com
Blog: www.writerslane.blogspot.com
Email: amylane@greenshill.com
Facebook: www.facebook.com/amy.lane.167
Twitter: @amymaclane

COVERT ★ BOOK 1

UNDER COVER

AMY LANE

Covert: Book One

For Judson Crosby, the transfer to the elite law enforcement branch of the SCTF is a great escape from the death sentence he earned as a whistle-blowing patrol officer. Calix Garcia, the fierce new guy, makes a perfect partner, catching bad guys while minimizing collateral damage. Crosby loves working with him.

Of course, he'd also love to work him over in a totally different way.

Garcia has waited his whole career for a solid, dependable partner like Crosby. But after six months fighting crime together, he's done fighting their attraction.

Their coming together promises to be everything they need… until a threat from Crosby's past comes back to haunt not just him, but their entire team.

When Crosby goes undercover to keep them safe, Garcia is frantic with worry. One false move could get Crosby killed and Garcia exposed. But they have to fight their way clear, because hiding your lover under the cover of darkness is no way to live. Crosby and Garcia will risk everything for the chance to live their lives in the light.

www.dreamspinnerpress.com

With some faith,
love, and elbow
grease, they might
just get a miracle
for Christmas...

AMY LANE

CHRISMYTHS

After courtship, cohabitation, and learning about love and each other, Andy and Eli face the ultimate test: being separated at Christmas.

Eli's seen the propaganda—the country boy goes home from the city and realizes his heart is back among the snow, trees, and chickens. A big happy family is something Eli, with his demanding job running a shelter for LGBTQ youth, can't provide. He's been readying himself for the other shoe to drop anyway—Andy's mother is a force of nature, and she wants her little boy home.

Andy may be in Vermont, but his heart is back in Brooklyn with the man who's battling basement floods and crumbling buildings to bring Christmas to sixty kids who've had their hearts broken too many times already. Holiday myths may say that Christmas means going back home to a happy family, but Andy knows happy endings don't come without a little faith and a lot of hard work. He's got an army ready to put in the elbow grease. If he can get Eli to believe in him, they might just save Christmas after all.

www.dreamspinnerpress.com

AMY LANE

Sometimes the
best magic is just
a little luck…

THE
RISING TIDE

THE LUCK MECHANICS BOOK ONE

The Luck Mechanics: Book One

The tidal archipelago of Spinner's Drift is a refuge for misfits. Can the island's magic help a pie-in-the-sky dreamer and a wounded soul find a home in each other?

In a flash of light and a clap of thunder, Scout Quintero is banished from his home. Once he's sneaked his sister out too, he's happy, but their power-hungry father is after them, and they need a place to lie low. The thriving resort business on Spinner's Drift provides the perfect way to blend in.

They aren't the only ones who think so.

Six months ago Lucky left his life behind and went on the run from mobsters. Spinner's Drift brings solace to his battered soul, but one look at Scout and he's suddenly terrified of having one more thing to lose.

Lucky tries to keep his distance, but Scout is charming, and the island isn't that big. When they finally connect, all kinds of things come to light, including supernatural mysteries that have been buried for years. But while Scout and Lucky grow closer working on the secret, pissed-off mobsters, supernatural entities, and Scout's father are getting closer to *them*. Can they hold tight to each other and weather the rising tide together?

www.dreamspinnerpress.com

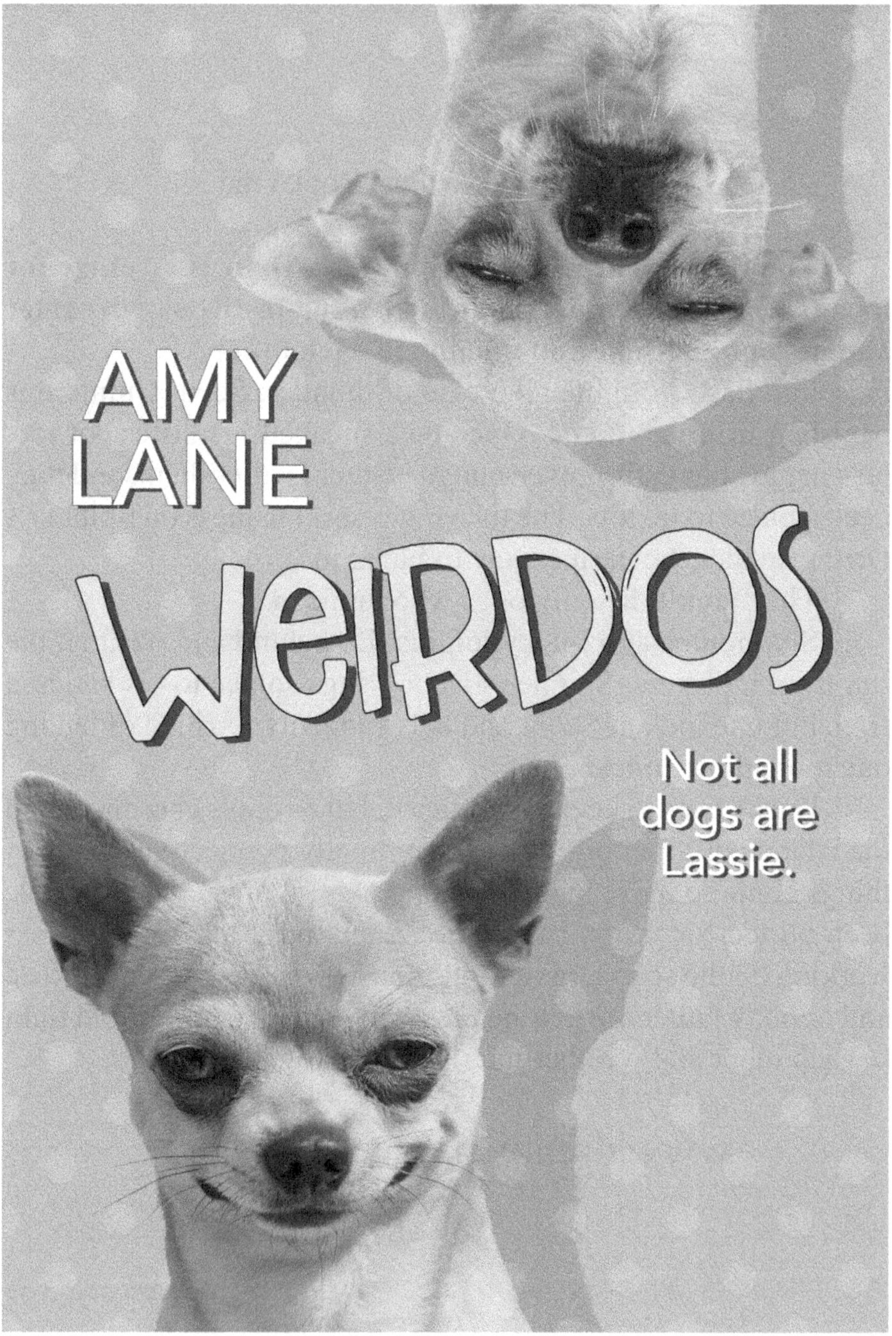
AMY LANE
WEIRDOS
Not all dogs are Lassie.

If Taz Oswald has one more gross date, he's resigning himself to a life of celibacy with his irritable Chihuahua, Carl. Carl knows how to bite a banana when he sees one! Then Selby Hirsch invites Taz to walk dogs together, and Taz is suddenly back in the game. Selby is adorkable, awkward, and a little weird—and his dog Ginger is a trip—and Taz is transfixed. Is it really possible this sweet guy with the blurty mouth and a heart as big as the Pacific Ocean wandered into Taz's life by accident? If so, how can Taz convince Selby that he wants to be Selby and Ginger's forever home?

www.ingramcontent.com/pod-product-compliance
Lightning Source LLC
Chambersburg PA
CBHW051145030726
47504CB00004B/1058